Tales from a Spacious Place

ELIZABETH FRERICHS

ISBN: 1466344806
ISBN-13: 978-1466344808

To God, who rescued me and brought me out into a spacious place—this is all Your plunder!

CONTENTS

He reached down from on high and took hold of me;
he drew me out of deep waters.
He rescued me from my powerful enemy,
from my foes, who were too strong for me.
They confronted me in the day of my disaster,
but the LORD *was my support.*
He brought me out into a spacious place;
he rescued me because he delighted in me.
~ Psalm 18:16–19

A Bitter Draught

ONE

And do not grieve the Holy Spirit of God, with whom you were sealed for the day of redemption. Get rid of all bitterness, rage and anger, brawling and slander, along with every form of malice. Be kind and compassionate to one another, forgiving each other, just as in Christ God forgave you.
~ Ephesians 4:30–32

I tapped my foot, waiting for the elevator. It's just a day. Get through it and tomorrow will be better.

The doors opened—thank God the elevator was empty! I sagged into a corner, then risked a glance at my reflection in the mirrored walls. I grimaced. Even with every hair in place and one of my favorite outfits, something about me still screamed my distress. The elevator dinged and stopped at the 10th floor.

Mrs. Dodd stepped in. She was a kind, motherly neighbor. I knew her in passing and couldn't just ignore her. I forced my pale features into a semblance of a smile.

"Morning," I said. One could hardly call it a good morning.

She smiled, her laugh lines creasing. "Good morning. How are you today?"

"Oh, fine. How about you?" I glanced back at the floor indicator, willing it to hurry.

"Good! I'm so glad the weather is supposed to be nice this weekend."

I nodded.

"Are you sure you're all right?" she asked, her brow furrowed.

I opened my eyes wider and turned to face her. "Why yes, thank you for asking. What are your plans for the weekend?"

"We're not sure. My son will be in town visiting. Perhaps we'll go sailing if the weather holds."

"That'll be nice."

I turned back to study the indicator. How much longer could this elevator take?

She took a half-step towards me, then put a hand on my arm. "I hear you're still alone these days. Would you like to join us if we go sailing?"

I stiffened. Still alone? I hate living in such a small building! I glared at her. "No, thank you."

Mrs. Dodd retired to her side of the elevator. "Is something wrong? You don't seem yourself at all today."

"I'm fine," I snapped.

Her eyes widened, and the elevator doors opened. I smiled a sickly sweet smile and made my voice as light as possible. "Thank you ever so much for your kind invitation. Perhaps another time. I must be going now or I'll be late for work. Have a perfectly wonderful day!"

Without waiting for an answer, I slammed out the front door and barreled towards the train station.

Stupid woman for messing about in my personal business! Stupid neighbors for gossiping! So what if I chose to live alone?

"De-struc-tion," "de-struc-tion," my footsteps pounded out on the pavement. I had once termed this day "The Anniversary of Destruction"; the name had stuck, even though I longed to forget.

I slowed, trying to change the pattern of my steps. Mrs. Dodd was right: the weather was lovely. The early spring sun shone in a gleaming sky. Blooming flowers had been set out along the sidewalk, and the air felt deliciously clean after last night's rainstorm. It would normally be the sort of day that made me love living in the city.

But not today. If I couldn't spend today in bed, the weather should at least be miserable. But no, it had to be a lift-your-spirits kind of day. Mrs. Dodd wouldn't be the only cheery soul out and about.

Her look of hurt flashed through my mind. Why hadn't I just held my tongue? Stupid day!

I sighed. Would I ever be happy again on this infamous date? Every year it came along and ripped the veil off my hurt and anger. The twin prongs of my own pain and his lack of punishment held me captive.

I hope he's having a horrible day. He needs something to give him a good kick in the pants. That man refuses to change, despite his desperate need to do so.

I pictured giving him said kick if I saw him today, then shuddered. I didn't think I could bear to see him today of all days. All these years and he hadn't even apologized. It certainly wasn't for lack of opportunity. The big lout hadn't had the decency to go back to where he'd come from—never mind he'd moved here for me.

I started down the stairs to the subway, praying I'd be able to find a seat. Then I could feign sleep or absorption in a book. It never failed: on the one day of the year I most wanted to avoid conversation, random strangers hounded me. If I saw someone looking like a ticking time bomb, I would have the decency to leave them alone.

All at once I realized not a soul was in sight. I checked the clock, worried I was late. 7:16 a.m. Right on time. Strange for this time of day, but definitely welcome. "They really need to check the lamps down here," I muttered. The one in front of me was putting out a heat haze. I wheeled 'round the corner, then stopped abruptly.

The concrete steps had been replaced by a steep, wooden staircase. Narrow and uneven, it was not the sort of route to take at breakneck speed. However, the lanterns that hung at regular intervals revealed it was in good repair. The walls, too, had changed. I now stood in some sort of sloping, stone tunnel. It didn't look like the subway at all.

I looked back up the way I had come. A wrought iron door barred my way. It was secured with a padlock, which seemed silly; I couldn't see anything except blackness on the other side.

I gritted my teeth. Why, of all days, does this have to happen today? I picked my way down, one hand on the rough stone wall. Icy fingers crept down my spine as I noticed that the worn places in the steps fit my own petite feet. What is this place? It seemed so familiar, but like something from a recurrent dream.

The stairs ended in a narrow, stone passageway. I grabbed one of the lanterns at the bottom and proceeded cautiously into the dark space. At least there weren't any giant cobwebs festooned about. Still, it was like being transported back into medieval times. A path had been worn into the large, rough stones that formed the floor, and the stone walls seemed almost unworked. The air was humid and still.

Before long the passageway widened and I stepped forward into a large cave. Rows of glowing bottles lined the walls, and a wine rack stretched down the middle of the cellar. The strange greenish light filled the cavern.

I set the lantern down, then pulled out one of the closer vintages and examined the label: *Hurt and anger from the driver who almost hit me—I hope you get pulled over soon.* It had been bottled only yesterday and barely even glowed. Looking at it, I remembered the event and even recognized my handwriting on the label.

As I inspected the bottles, I noted the severity of the offense grew with the age of the vintage. I doubted the one from yesterday would receive the necessary care to preserve it for long. It wasn't worth my time and energy.

I walked to the end of the rack and removed the oldest vintage. This one was labeled with only the date—today's date, years ago. The pain had been too sharp for me to even put the incident on paper, as though, by leaving the label blank, I could make the ache disappear.

I sighed, wishing for the thousandth time that things could be different. If only it hadn't happened. If only someone would do something to fix it. Despite the empty label, my pain remained as deep as the day it had occurred. If anything, it was worse, sharpened by the intervening years barren of judgment and recompense.

I'd lost count of the times I'd been told to forgive and forget. But how could I forgive if he refused to admit he was wrong? One would think God Himself would be offended by his continued lack of punishment, but evidently not. He was yet another person who hadn't lifted a finger.

I examined the vintage again. My hurt and anger had fermented into a well-aged bitterness. It had become a thing of beauty, a silver lining in the midst of my cloudy existence.

Suddenly I realized why I was here. I lifted a thin chain over my head. It had a small, recently-emptied vial hanging from it. Both the chain and the vial were silver, dull and tarnished. I uncorked the bottle and unstoppered the vial. Just as I was about to fill it, I heard a man's voice say, "I wouldn't do that."

I started and narrowly avoided dropping both the bottle and vial. I whirled about, trying to spot the intruder while juggling the vessels and their respective stoppers.

No one was there. Just my imagination. It's the day. I'm extra jumpy today.

I resumed the exacting process of pouring my precious bitterness. This time I put the stoppers on the wine rack. Then, as I was about to tip my well-aged hurt and anger into the vial, the voice again warned, "I wouldn't do that."

"Who are you? And why are you in my cellar?" I called back, trying to sound stern and brave, but only managing to sound upset.

A tall man materialized out of the wall, like a whale breeching the ocean. I thrust my bottle behind me and backed into the wine rack.

"Someone who would help you. Why do you keep coming here?" he asked, as though I were a poor lost child.

I stiffened. "To fill my vial."

"Why? Why keep it at all?"

"How else am I supposed to remember?"

He eyed my chain and grimaced. "Why do you need to remember?"

How honest did I want to be? I decided to focus on the righteousness of my anger, rather than plumb the depths of my pain—much easier to talk about. "Somebody has to! He ought to get what he deserves."

He raised an eyebrow. "So you feel malice towards him? And you want to hang onto that?"

"No! I just want him to get what he deserves."

"And drinking poison will accomplish that how?"

"It's not poison! Do you have any idea how much work it takes to ferment such a fine bitterness? Just smell the bouquet."

I handed him the cork, but it fell right through his palm onto the floor. A luminescent stain spread from where it landed. The stone floor began to hiss and smoke.

I stood aghast. "Look what you've done now! That's going to be impossible to fix!"

"You seem very concerned about your cellar. What do you think that liquid is doing to you?"

I stammered incoherently, more enraged by his invasion of my privacy than anything else.

"Let's look at your bitterness in a different light." He held out his hand, then smiled, and his eyes sparkled with laughter. "This is your opportunity to prove me wrong."

He really knew which buttons to push. I decided if nothing else, it was my duty to educate him on the importance of justice. I exhaled gustily. "All right, fine." I refastened my chain around my neck, restoppered my bottle, then wiped my sweaty palms on the front of my pants and took his hand.

At once we were transported into a meadow. Grass swayed and rustled in a gentle breeze. Birdsong filled the air. Wildflowers blazed with color. Somehow things here appeared incredibly vivid and substantial, making their counterparts in the real world seem dull and lifeless. Everything, even the air, emitted light. The man himself gave off a soft glow I hadn't noticed in the cellar. I looked around. To one side, I could see a forest not far off; to the other, grass stretched on and on. There was no indication of where my cellar might be.

"So, what do you think of your poison now?" he asked.

I struggled to hang onto the bottle, which had grown inordinately heavy. Unlike the rest of our surroundings, my precious vintage emitted darkness, as though it were overpowering and destroying the particles of light surrounding it.

I shook my head to dispel the disturbing image. "Well, my bitterness looks different here."

"It looks heavy. Is it difficult to carry?"

I nodded as my muscles shook. Talking was rapidly becoming more effort than I wanted to make.

"You can set it down if you'd like."

I looked around, trying to find a safe place.

"Here." He pulled a leather drawstring bag out of his pocket and pointed to a nearby tree. "You can hang it on that branch."

I barely managed to get my bottle into the bag and onto the branch, but once I did, I couldn't help but smile, proudly surveying my handiwork.

He shook his head, "Why did you say you carry that around? Because you want revenge?"

I scowled. "No! Because he deserves to pay for what he did."

"Ah, yes, that's right," he said, giving me an enigmatic smile.

"Why is it so heavy here?" I asked, determined to take control of the conversation.

"Because objects have their true weight here, weight based on their essential nature."

Would all my bottles weigh the same, or did the severity of this event and the supremacy of this vintage increase its weight? I brightened a little; perhaps its heaviness proved what a worthy vintage it was.

He seemed to study me for a moment. "I think there's someone you should meet. Come with me." He turned and began to walk away. "Oh, you can leave your bottle on the tree. No one will bother it."

I hurried after him, not wanting to be left behind in this strange unreality. The forest stretched on and on, and the man kept up a smart pace. It felt like we'd been walking for hours. Just when I thought I had to rest or collapse, my guide paused at the top of a large hill. I stumbled to a halt, and, bent double, tried to catch my breath. Once I straightened, all the hairs on the back of my neck stood on end.

Innumerable circles of sparkling blackness polka-dotted the valley below, as though it had been carpet-bombed. Nothing grew in the centers of those circles. Instead, patches of barren earth lay naked to the sun, like exposed wounds. Plants closest to the lifeless ground were burnt black. Further away, they gradually brightened to a dull green. Dead trees littered the scene. The few living trees appeared wilted and stunted.

"Shall we?" the man asked, inclining his head toward the valley. Without waiting for an answer, he began to descend.

I guess we shall.

After a while, a little old man with a dirty, white beard came into view. His hair and beard were stringy and his clothing ragged. He sat on a fallen log in the center of one of the circles, cradling a pack and muttering to himself. Why in the world would anyone stay here?

We moved closer, and I caught a whiff of something vile. I drew shallow breaths through my mouth as the stench grew and grew. However, the awfulness of the smell paled in comparison to the appearance of the man's skin. Hideously dark veins snaked under his flesh. All at once I realized my initial observation was backwards. The man wasn't sitting in a preexisting circle of desolation; the darkness emanated from him, just as it had from my bottle. My stomach clenched.

My guide halted in front of the man. I fought to keep the revulsion off my face, but my guide seemed more sad than disgusted. "Hello, Jonah," he said.

The old man started, then squinted up at my guide. "It's you again, eh? What do you want this time?"

"The same as always. I also brought someone to meet you."

"Who? Why?" He glared up at me.

"Oh, I thought I would introduce you since the two of you have so much in common. She has a bottle too."

Jonah perked up at this news. "Finally! Someone who's got her head on straight—none of this taking justice lightly. Mercy, pah!" He spat, a dark, gooey substance that made the unfortunate plant it landed on hiss and turn black. "Have a seat, m'dear," he said and waved his hand toward a nearby spot of ground.

I hesitated, but then exhaustion overrode my reluctance. I collapsed gratefully onto the dead grass.

"Mercy is not the absence of justice, nor does the delay of justice make it any less certain," my guide said, gentleness in his eyes. Then he drew himself up, and his face became set. The light he radiated intensified exponentially, and my eyes began to water. "Make no mistake," he said. "Vengeance is mine, and *I will* repay.[1] The day will come, and no one shall be able to stand in it."[2]

My face blanched. I shaded my eyes and tried to make out his features through the blazing light. Who was this mystery wall-walker? Gradually, the light dimmed back to a manageable glow. I studied his face, but I still couldn't place him.

"So why do either of you"—he waved a hand towards us—"need to continue drinking poison to 'remember'? And why do you think you can remember better than We[3] can?"

I squirmed away from His piercing gaze, realizing at last with whom I was speaking. I may have been a little slow on the uptake, but who expects to meet Jesus?

With eyes still watering from the light, Jonah spoke. "How do I know You'll do anything about it? You haven't exactly taken care of things yet. And I know who You are: 'A gracious and compassionate God, slow to anger and abounding in love, a God who relents from sending calamity.'[4] The moment they cry out to You, no more justice." Jonah raised a fist, his eyes bulging. "I want to see them punished! I deserve vengeance!"

I inched away from him. Now I understood why Jesus had categorized my bitterness as malice. How would He handle Jonah's outright contradiction? To my surprise, He just stood there with sorrow and love on His face. No lightning bolts or anything.

And then something clicked: Jesus obviously hated the sickness, the evil, the brokenness of sin, and yet, simultaneously, He had a relentless love for His creation. Jonah had complained of God's patience and love, yet without it, he would have already been judged. Even though Jesus longed for the destruction of evil, He wasn't eager to destroy those who clung to evil.[5]

"Why do you expect Us to do anything about it when you refuse to give it to Us?" Jesus asked softly. It was true Jonah had a death grip on his pack full of bottles.

Jonah began to shake. "I'm getting so old and tired. I need a drink. It'll give me some energy, fix me up all right and tight." He poured himself a sizeable dose out of his bottle and gulped it down. Jonah's eyes brightened, and he seemed to gain new strength. The darkness in his veins also grew, pouring out of him even more intensely. Horrified, I realized there were gaps in his skin. The darkness was consuming him. I wondered how long it would be before there was no Jonah left.

"Now see, that's the kind of potation that will give a man new life," Jonah said. "I almost feel strong enough to get up out of this valley. I think if I rest for just a bit longer, I'll be up to it yet."

Jesus sighed and shook His head. "Wouldn't it be easier if you didn't have to carry around that bitterness? It's not just your bottles that weigh you down; the heaviness is in the very cells of your body."

"Well," Jonah drawled, (I was impressed by his apparent composure—I would have been tongue-tied and shaking in my shoes.) "it might, but then where would I get my energy from? No"—he crossed his arms—"it just won't work."

"What about you?" Jesus asked, turning that soul-piercing gaze on me.

"Wh-what do You mean?"

"It permeates your cells too. Didn't you feel it when we walked?"

Full of dread, I examined my hand. A darkness, so faint it was almost indistinguishable from the blue of my veins, pulsed through me. I remembered how fatigued I had been from walking.

"Don't you listen to Him," Jonah called out. "It's better this way."

Jesus knelt down in front of Jonah. "Jonah, I can heal you. My Father sent Me to bind up the brokenhearted.[6] You can be free. No more siphoning off your time and energy to live alone in the past. Come live your life with Us."

Jonah seemed to consider Jesus' words for a moment. He leaned forward, lips parted as though to give answer. Then he shook himself and settled back onto his tree. "What's the catch?"

"You have to give your bitterness to Me. It's poisoning you and sapping your strength."

Jonah barked a laugh. "I knew there was a catch. Next You'll be telling me I have to forgive those who hurt me and cozy up to them."

"No, you only have to forgive if you want to be forgiven, but forgiveness is much more than 'cozying up' to someone."

"What *are* You talking about?"

"If you forgive others when they sin against you, you can be forgiven. But if you don't forgive others, your Father won't forgive you.[7] Unforgiveness is not a trivial matter. However, forgiveness isn't the same as restoring the relationship.[8] It takes two people to make a relationship work."

"But—but if you love someone, don't you have to do whatever it takes to fix things?" I asked.

He put a gentle hand on my arm. "Depends on what 'things' you're talking about. Sometimes it's more loving to reject an unhealthy relationship and to hold out for a right one. You may have to wait for the other person to grow closer to Us."[9] He turned back to include Jonah. "I'm not saying whether you will, or will not, end up being reconciled. Forgiveness simply involves opening yourself up to Our will in the matter."

"Humph," Jonah said. "Sounds like a lot of hairsplitting to me. Now it's time for my nap. I've got to save my energy, you know. You two get out of here." He nodded at me, a gruff half-smile on his face. "Nice meeting you, dear."

I pasted on a smile. "It was nice to meet you too."

Jonah waved farewell, then stretched out on the ground. Moments later he began to snore.

Jesus turned and walked back up the hill. I trudged after Him, thinking about Jonah and all I'd heard. At the top of the hill, I paused to look back.

"How long has he been trying to get out of there?" I asked, stunned by the sheer number of dark circles Jonah had burned into the valley.

His eyes grew distant. "Far too long."

I rounded on Him. "Then why don't You do something? If You really love him, why don't You rescue him? Or prevent whatever put him there in the first place?"

Jesus held my gaze for a moment. "What do you think I just entreated him to do? Did you want Me to carry him away from his bitterness kicking and screaming? He'd only start another bottle, get himself stuck in another valley. Change has to start on the inside. And as far as prevention goes, if it wasn't that event, it would be another." He dropped His hands onto my shoulders. "The problem is the presence of evil, not the presence or absence of Jack in your life."

I flushed. I had long since stopped using his name. He doesn't deserve the courtesy.

"To prevent pain, We'd have to rid the world of evil—and all those who are still clinging to it—or create people without the option to choose evil. Do you really want to be a puppet?"

I shuddered. "No."

"That's not what I want for you either."

TWO

We walked on in silence. Wrestling with His words left me little brain power for conversation. Plus, I felt pretty winded just trying to keep up.

In the distance, I could see the tree where my bottle hung. An ache throbbed in my middle—some indefinable hunger that bordered on painful. All thought fled. My heart began to pound; I wasn't sure I could traverse the remaining expanse.

Jesus put a hand on my arm. "Let's stop and talk here for a moment."

"What?" I asked. My bottle was so close.

"Let's stop here for a minute. Look at Me!"

Startled, I obeyed.

"That's right. Now let's just rest a moment. You're worn out. Besides, I can tell—once we get over there, you won't hear a thing I say."

As I looked at Him, I could feel my thirst recede, along with the fog in my mind. I nodded, my cheeks burning, and sank down onto a nearby hillock. He sat down opposite my bottle, forcing me to turn my back on it.

"What'd you think of Jonah?" He asked.

"He seemed so . . . disturbing."

"How so?"

I began shredding grass in front of me. "He's been stuck there for ages."

"Sin does have a tendency to do that."

"Do what?"

"Sweep you away to places you don't want to go."[10]

All at once I saw myself being carried away by my own sin, like a tiny leaf struggling through white water rapids. I blinked several times.

"What do You mean? I understand the concept, but does it actually happen in real life?"

He quirked an eyebrow at me. "Haven't you ever said or done something you regretted because you were responding out of bitterness?"

I remembered that morning when I had snapped at Mrs. Dodd. My own pain had overflowed out of my mouth and wounded her.[11] I had cursed my tongue, but perhaps the problem went deeper . . . . Jesus was right: my bitterness did take me places I didn't want to go. I resolved right then and there to pray for self-control so my bitterness wouldn't get out of hand.

"No," Jesus said. "It doesn't work that way."

"Huh? Work what way?"

"You're trying to figure out how you can hang on to your bitterness, to mitigate the consequences, but you can't control sin. Besides, self-control is fruit of My Spirit.[12] He doesn't work in areas you haven't given over to Us."[13]

I wondered if that were really possible. I knew Jesus wouldn't mislead me, but to categorize my vintage as sin . . . .

I swallowed hard. "Then what are my options?"

"You need a new perspective; truth sets you free.[14] Bitterness isn't a precious comfort." He pointed to my vial. "You are coddling poison.

"Once you understand that, you have a decision to make: Whom are you going to serve? Sin or God?[15] You can't serve two masters."[16]

I gaped at Him. "Are You saying I would have to give up the whole bottle?"

"You would have to give up the whole cellar," He replied steadily.

My mind reeled. All those years of work just gone. And he gets off scot-free!

Jesus reached over to take my hand. "Who do you think is bearing more of the pain for those wrongs? Is it the one who injured you and now unknowingly controls you? Or is it you, who carries this heavy load, and has to arrange your life around your bitterness?"

I'd never thought about it that way. I bristled at the idea of anyone controlling me. But the more I thought about it, the more I realized I wanted to reject the idea simply because I disliked it, rather than because it was false.

"Even though his sin hurt you, ultimately it was against Us.[17] It's Our right as the one true Judge to mete out justice. We will deal rightly with the sin and the sinner."[18]

I remembered His implacable hatred of evil and knew judgment was certain, but still I hesitated.

"You can't dispense true justice anyway. Only We know the full situation, so only We can judge it appropriately."

"What don't I know?"

He gave me a pointed look. "Do you know what was going on inside him?"

I started to say yes, then realized how ridiculous it sounded. "I suppose not completely, but I know some of it."

"Do you know how the situation has affected and will affect every person it's touched?"

"Well, no."

"Right. Only We know all those things. In fact, We're the safest person to leave vengeance to. We're the only One who will give proper weight to your injury: We won't minimize it or overemphasize it because We're feeling lazy or having a bad day. We won't forget to deal with it,[19] no matter how long it takes. We will repay appropriately.

"Stop worrying about other people. Worry about yourself and your own sin. Darling, what are you going to do about your bitterness?"

I was torn. Meeting Jonah had made me determined never to end up like him. But still, I thirsted. I could almost taste the cool liquid sliding down my throat and the familiar burning sensation that accompanied it.

I took my hand back. "I can't go without drinking something!"

"You're right," He said, surprising me. "Vacuums get filled, often with whatever's closest, even if it isn't your first choice. I wasn't suggesting dehydration."

"But—but what would I drink?"

He leaned forward. "Drink from the living water welling up inside you.[20] I've already installed it. Stop quenching it, and you'll never be thirsty again. Be filled with My Spirit, not your own vintage."[21]

"How do I know it'll work? I tried it once before. It was wonderful, but it just didn't stay with me."

He paused for a moment. "How often do you drink your poison?"

"Depends on how often it comes to mind. Sometimes several times a day. Sometimes I might go days or even weeks without it."

"And how often did you drink living water?"

"Well, just once. Isn't it supposed to 'satisfy you forever'? Why would I need more?"

"You can be forever satisfied.[22] You'll never have to look elsewhere, but your thirst will recur if you don't drink," He said patiently.

I narrowed my eyes at Him. Was He back-pedaling?

"Look, does your poison ever really satisfy you? Does it fill your longings or only emphasize how deep they are?"

I shrugged. "I'm never fully satisfied, but isn't that just part of the human condition? We're needy and broken."

"It is part of being human—when you're separated from Us. But if you're My Father's child, it isn't natural unless you're quenching My Spirit."

I had nothing to say to that. I still didn't want to give up my bitterness, but . . . . I cleared my throat. "All right, let's just, let's just *say* I wanted to switch. How would I go about it?"

"You'd change your direction. Turn away from your bitterness, and turn to Us. Give Us your bitterness and your illusion of control. Let Us be the one to judge. Let Us heal your wounds instead of preserving them on your own. Then your sins will be wiped away, and times of refreshing will come from Us.[23] We'll fill the void left by your bitterness and teach you new ways to handle your hurt and anger—Do you want to give it to Us?"

I stared off into the distance. Did I want my beloved poison in my life anymore? I thought about Jesus' promise to heal me; I was certain He could do it. When I thought about being swept away by my sins and becoming like Jonah, I longed to be rescued. A smile peeked out—Jesus had come to rescue me before I even knew I needed rescuing. He must really want me.[24]

But as I thought about my bitterness, I hesitated. It was familiar, and I'd come to depend on it.[25] It was the only thing that helped with the pain, especially when I saw the person who had hurt me. Bitterness and pride gave me the strength to project the illusion of happiness and health.

Yet if I was healed, I wouldn't have to pretend—I'd be healthy. I thought about Jesus and His loving-kindness towards me. He hadn't treated me as my sins deserved.[26] I didn't have to end up like Jonah. I could still change.

I turned to look Him in the eye. "I want to, but I'm not sure I can."

"Would you like help?"

"Oh yes! Can You help me?"

"Everything's possible if you believe.[27] And, if you were to ask for help, We'd give it to you."[28] His eyes twinkled. "But perhaps you *were* asking. Perhaps it was just a slip of your grammar."

I smiled back. "You know what I meant!"

"Yes," He said, sobering. "I just wanted to make sure that you did too. Shall we begin?"

"Now?"

"No time like the present," He said and took a necklace out of His pocket. It seemed vaguely familiar. "May I have your chain?"

I slowly fumbled open the catch and handed it to Him. At once I felt several pounds lighter, even though the vial was empty.

"Thank you." He handed me the new necklace. I now realized it was the same one He'd given me long ago. I had stashed it somewhere and forgotten it.

My old necklace had never seemed ugly or heavy to me. It functioned, and that was all I cared about. However, I could see now why Jesus called it a chain: in comparison to the exquisite piece of jewelry in my hand, the old one was hideous. His necklace was of finely wrought silver. On it was a silver phial, written over with shining letters that seemed to slide away from my vision.

"What's it say?" I asked.

" 'Drink and thirst not.'[29] The phial is filled with living water. You'll have to refill it, of course, but this will take care of you for now."

I fastened the necklace, then took a sip of the living water. Immediately, my ravenous thirst fled. I grinned up at Jesus.

He beamed back at me, then stood and offered His hand to help me up. "Now let's go take care of your bottle."

On leaden legs I forced myself over to the tree. There He helped me take the bottle down and wrestle it out of the leather bag. Even with renewed energy, I staggered under its weight.

He held out His hand for my poison. "It's time."

Cradling it in my arms, I stared at my precious bitterness, struggling to hang on to it, struggling to let go of it—unable to succeed in either. Despite my longing to be free, it felt like it would take a miracle to get rid of it.

"We are the God who performs miracles; We display Our power throughout the universe, among the nations, and within the depths of your heart,"[30] Jesus said.

I looked up at Him. "I want to believe that. Help my unbelief."[31]

Jesus placed a gentle hand on my own, and together we put my poison into His waiting hand.

His jaw tightened. "Let's go get the rest."

We were instantly transported back to my damaged cellar. It was only the glow Jesus gave off that allowed me to make out our surroundings. The very air seemed dark and heavy in comparison to where we'd been.

Jesus took a large stone cup out of His pocket. I was beginning to wonder about that pocket. He poured all the poison from the first bottle into the stone cup (evidently His cup was like His pocket), then set the empty bottle on the floor.

"Now hand Me another one," He said, still holding the cup. Time and time again, we repeated the process. Finally, we reached the end—no more bitterness except in His now brimming cup. He took a deep breath, then began to drink my poison.

"Stop!" I cried. "O my Lord, You'll be so hurt if You drink it all!"

He paused, panting. "What else would I do with it? I love you too much to let you keep poisoning yourself. If I were to pour it out, it would only injure someone else. I'm the only one who can get rid of it."

Tears streamed down my face as He drank and drank. Not a drop escaped Him. His light began to dim, starting with His extremities and moving to His core. He swayed. Sweat poured down His face.

"It is finished," He declared, like a soldier emerging from battle. Then He fell to the floor, His breathing ragged.

I stumbled over to Him, still sobbing. I hated to see Him so injured when He had radiated light and life before. A thought broke over me, chilling my very marrow. I had done this. All those years I had tended my bottles, I'd prepared poison for the One who loved me most.

"I'm sorry," I whispered.

Through my tears, I saw a faint light begin to flicker in His core. The glimmer turned into a steady pulse and moved outward, swallowing up the darkness. It grew and grew until I had to turn away. The light flared, then resumed the comforting glow to which I had grown accustomed.

I turned back to Him. Jesus stood, healthy as before. A grin lit His face. "See? This was the best way."

I clung to Him, thankful He was all right and overwhelmed by the depth of His love for me. He dropped His arm over my shoulder, and I looked around from the safety of His side.

My cellar had changed: The empty bottles and wine rack had disappeared. The air had been cleansed. All the stones, including those newly repaired, glowed, much like the meadow had. I'd no longer need a lantern. The whole place exuded peace and expectant life.

Best of all, the spring of living water was here. My wine rack had been covering it the whole time. I knelt down beside it and took a long drink. Health tingled through me, refreshing me. The water satisfied my thirst in a way I had never dreamed possible.

THREE

However, as Jesus sat down with me by the spring, I realized something was wrong.

"Jesus, why do I still hurt? I thought You were going to heal me."

He turned to face me. "Remember Jonah? Deprive him of his bitterness and where is he?"

I sighed. "With a new bottle in a different valley."

"We love you. We want you to become the person We made you to be. Suppose We heal your pain and snuff out your anger; what happens the next time someone hurts you?"

I lowered my eyes. Like an alcoholic, I'd end up right back where I had started, chained to my bottle.

"Exactly. A relationship with Us is the only place of freedom.[32] Fill up your phial every morning[33] so you won't be tempted to drink something else. Healing will come, but you need to grieve and to grow."

I stared at the bubbling water. At one time I would have felt cheated or deceived, but now I realized my own heart wanted Him more than I wanted healing. And it made sense that being forced to come to Him daily would keep me from ending up in some valley. Besides, He had guaranteed to heal me in the end.[34]

But still, if He could heal me, why did I need to grieve?

"We're not lightly allowing you to walk this road. Grief has a purpose," Jesus said.

I frowned. "What kind of purpose?"

"Describe grief."

It wasn't hard to do. I had only to listen to that keening part of myself. I closed my eyes and began.

"Grief is like an ocean—a grey, sullen, roaring sea of tears. It hungers to overwhelm and destroy you, like waves devour a cliff face, undermining its foundations. The ache lives down so deep that nothing can reach it. Grief refuses to be comforted; it wails ceaselessly. Sometimes I can't drown it out, and others, I can ignore it for days on end. Bottling my anger and hurt into bitterness seemed to help, to soothe them in some way."

A spray of salt water hit my face. Winds tore at me. My eyes flew open.

We stood near the edge of a cliff, overlooking the ocean. Fortunately, a guardrail bordered the lookout. I peeked over the edge. The waves, balked by the cliff, beat against the rocks.

"Where are we?" I shouted, striving to be heard over the howling wind.

"We're examining your view of grief," He yelled back.

"Well? Is it correct? Can we go back now?"

"Do you have it firmly fixed in your mind?"

"Yes!"

In an instant, we stood at the center of an overgrown field. The sun shone, but the earth lay barren. The crops had long since died and been covered in tall weeds, which had also died. The ground was a rock-hard mat of dead roots and bone-dry soil. Fertile fields bursting with crops lay on either side, only emphasizing this field's desolation.

"Where are we now?" I asked, brushing my damp, wind-swept hair out of my face.

"Still looking at grief. What do you notice about this field?"

"It looks pretty neglected."

"It isn't fruitful, if that's what you mean. But look at the fence."

He tramped through the waist-high, dead plant matter. Curious, I followed Him. At the edge of the field we came to a peculiar fence. Tall wooden posts stood at regular intervals. The air between them shimmered, creating a transparent wall. Jesus picked up a dirt clod and flung it at the fence. The clod exploded, showering us with bits of dirt. Rings of energy radiated out, like ripples in a pond. Was I imagining it, or had a strange wave of weariness passed over me at the same time?

"This is a high security area; nothing gets in or out. Someone's putting a lot of energy into protecting this field."

"From what?" I asked as I spat dirt and brushed pebbles off my clothing.

"The plow," He said and pointed to an old-fashioned plow that waited at the gate. Every so often it pressed in of its own accord, but the fence kept it at bay.

I looked from the plow, to the fence, to the field, and back again. "Why keep the plow out? It seems to me that plowing would do this field a world of good."

"How so?"

"Well, all this dead grass keeps anything else from growing. It's taking up all the space."

"So you're saying not plowing has kept this field dead?" He asked.

"I suppose so. Nothing new can grow, anyway—not until you get all this junk out of the way."

"Good insight. Grief is the process of plowing up the dead stuff.[35] In that sense, your earlier observation was right: grief is a destructive force. However, it's not destruction for its own sake. It turns over the dead and makes way for new life."

I took a step back. "What's it destroying?"

"What are you grieving?"

"A relationship, I guess."

He nodded. "You don't have the same relationship with Jack that you once had. Even changing a relationship involves some death, some grief. So, the object of your grief gets plowed up, whether it's a broken toy or a broken relationship. What else is dead?"

I looked down at the desolate ground. "I feel like—like a part of me died," I mumbled.

"Part of your identity did die."

"What do You mean?"

"You're no longer Jack's beloved. That part of your identity is gone. You've also lost the character traits you had anchored in your relationship with Jack."

"Like what?"

"You're no longer as innocent as you were before. You see yourself as less lovable, less desirable."

"How can that be? He left me years ago . . . . Why does it still hurt so badly?"

Jesus clasped my hands in His. "Death hurts. But what did you do with your hurt and anger?"

"I fermented them into bitterness . . . ."

"Thus this field lies dead, immobilized in agony. New things could be grown here. In fact, one of the beauties of death is that it can provide nourishment for new life."

My fingers tightened 'round His. "Why does it have to hurt so much though?"

"Grief tells you that there's a problem. You're plowing up the foundations of a relationship, an attachment between two image-bearers. That's no small thing."

I turned away. "I'd still rather skip the pain." Seeing my ocean had made me feel morose, like I had drawn its sullenness into myself. How could anyone expect to cry that many tears? If I begin, I'll never stop. No wonder I'd built the fence.

"How big is this field?" Jesus asked.

I shaded my eyes and looked around. "I have no idea. An acre? Ten acres?"

"So it has boundaries, an end?

I nodded.

"So does your grief. It isn't going to last forever.[36] And once you've plowed your field with tears, you can harvest with joy."[37]

"It's going to be so hard though, so much work," I moaned.

"Listen, is it more work to constantly maintain your fence, or to plow and allow new life into this field?"

"You're probably right. I just . . . . It's just too big for me."

"That's true. But you don't have to do it alone."

I smiled as I remembered how He had helped me with my bitterness. "Jesus, please help me with this monstrosity," I begged.

"Darling, you're looking at this all wrong. It isn't a monstrosity. It's an opportunity for freedom. Without grief, you would be doomed to carry the pain of your dead relationship forever. Plow it up, and you can move on."

All at once I began to see what He meant. I looked around with new eyes. The pain of grief had always been my enemy, but maybe it could be an ally, an instrument of healing even. I turned to Him, feeling more hopeful than I had in ages.

"Jesus, please resurrect my field."

"Plowing does take time."

"I know." I squared my shoulders resolutely.

"For the times when you're tempted to give way to despair," He said gently and put His hand on my shoulder.

The field blossomed. Lush green plants grew in an orderly profusion. Huge fruits I couldn't identify grew all around. Life thrived here. It didn't seem possible for something so beautiful to be birthed in such a dead place.

Jesus pointed to the ground. I could see a seed, hidden below the earth. It swelled. The root slithered forth questingly. The tiny leaves burst out of the husk and forced their way up to the sunlight. Once the process was complete, the seed had been destroyed, and a plant remained in its stead.[38] "Death doesn't mean the end,"[39] He said.

I nodded, too full of emotion to speak.

He took His hand off my shoulder, and the vision faded. "Shall we begin?"

"How?"

He pointed. "It's time to open the gate."

I broke out in cold sweat. One slow step at a time, I dragged myself over to the gate and lifted a trembling hand. With a sudden shock, the gate disappeared and the plow trundled in.

It tore into the dead ground, and I collapsed, weeping.[40] Jesus held me, quieting me with His presence. There is a time, when one is wholly beyond words, that silence is one's best comfort.

Some age later, the pain lessened—or at least I became accustomed to it. I lifted my tear-stained face to Jesus. He brushed my grimy hair out of my face and wiped a tear. "Let's leave grief to its work. We have our own work to do."

I nodded. Jesus stood and lifted me to my feet. We passed through the wide-open gate to the dusty road beyond.

As we walked, I thought about how far He had brought me—light-years from where I'd begun my day. Yet something nagged at me, a loose end still hanging.

"Jesus, what about my anger? I know I'm not supposed to get angry; I'm supposed to love, but"—a certain face flitted through my mind—"it just doesn't seem possible. I still want to lash out."

He turned to look at me. "Darling, what is anger?"

"An intense dislike of something? Or maybe an uncontrollable urge to beat something—or someone—and scream in frustration? I don't know, I can't explain an emotion. It just is," I said.

"Well, why are you angry right now?"

"Because he hurt me. Because what he did was wrong."

"Then your anger reflects the way We made the world to work."

I stopped. "Come again? I thought anger was bad."

He took my hand and walked onward. "Anger can be twisted and misused, or you can be angry for the wrong reasons. The point is not to sin in your anger.[41] However, a longing for justice is a longing for things to be the way We created them to be."[42]

"So I'm still angry because he hasn't been punished? Doesn't that just put me back where I was before?"

Abruptly He turned off the road. A newly mown lawn stretched before us. Straight ahead lay a stone wall with the wrought iron door to my cellar. A sudden clatter sounded to my left. There, a wild, black horse reared and plunged in his corral. His untamed ferocity terrified me, though there was something beautiful in his spirit and power.

Jesus led me right up to the corral, and we watched the stallion's frantic display. He pawed at the fence, searching for a way out. Dust covered his sleek, black coat, mute testimony that he'd been trying to escape for quite some time.

"This is uncontrolled anger: powerful, destructive, liable to lash out indiscriminately. It injures you and everyone else around you. We designed anger to be a tool. Do you think you would be able to use this tool?"

"No way! I couldn't even keep my seat on that horse."

"That's what happens when you ignore your anger or misuse it. It gets restive, like a horse without exercise. Now let's change the equation." He walked over and held His hand out in front of the stallion. Anger immediately calmed. "Good boy," Jesus said, patting his shoulder and neck. He pulled two apples out of His pocket, then gave one to the horse and handed one to me. "Give it a try."

I cautiously approached, expecting him to panic again. Now, however, he seemed gentle as a lamb. I caressed his neck and shoulder and fed him the apple. He remained quiet and even seemed to enjoy the attention.

"Now what would happen if you rode him?" Jesus asked.

"Well, I'm not much of a horsewoman, but if I were, he could take me places."

"Right. Anger is a defense mechanism. It energizes you to deal with the situation at hand. What does the presence of anger indicate?"

"That there's a problem?"

"Exactly. It's a tool and a warning light. So, how do you think you can get rid of anger?" He asked.

"Fix the problem?"

"And how would you do that?"

"I have no idea."

"Read Matthew 7:3–5," He said and produced my Bible from His pocket. He handed it to me.

I found the passage in question and read it aloud: " 'Why do you look at the speck of sawdust in your brother's eye and pay no attention to the plank in your own eye? How can you say to your brother, "Let me take the speck out of your eye," when all the time there is a plank in your own eye? You hypocrite, first take the plank out of your own eye, and then you will see clearly to remove the speck from your brother's eye.' "

I read back through it silently. "Are You suggesting that *I* was responsible for the problems in our relationship?"

"I'm saying that anger and hurt are opportunities for change. You can use them to shine light on something you've missed."[43]

"I see."

"Think about both the circumstances that prompted your feelings and how you've reacted to them. How did you contribute to the problem?"

I frowned. "I don't know." Taking a look at myself seemed too hard and too painful.

Jesus squeezed my hand. "Sometimes it's important to do hard things. You'll stay captive in that area of your life until you allow Us to uncover the truth there. You need to face those issues, so you can move on and stop repeating those types of relationships."[44]

"Right . . . ." I agreed in principle, but the reality felt out of my league.

"It'll be easier as you grow to know Us better."

"Don't I already know You?"

"You've started to get to know Us, but you have some mistaken ideas about who We are. For instance, your attempt to wreak vengeance shows you don't see Us as the one true Judge.[45] You don't trust Us to deal rightly with sin."

I knew it was true, but it sounded so shameful when put that bluntly.

"You also don't really understand grace, or you would be more willing to forgive."

"I think I am more willing, now that I know I don't have to condone his actions or pal around with him," I said. Maybe I understood more than He realized.

Jesus raised an eyebrow. "Suppose you had two people who owed you money. One owed you $5,000 and the other, $50,000. Neither could pay their debt, so you forgave them both. Which of them would love you more?"[46]

"Probably the one who owed $50,000."

"How many bottles of bitterness do you think I just drank for you?"

I gave up my mental count. "I don't know. Quite a few."

"Could you have taken care of them on your own?"

"No," I said, once again awed by His love for me—a love I clearly didn't deserve.

"Right. I just forgave all your bitterness, so who are you to withhold forgiveness from Jack?"

"But what about him? How many bottles does he have?"

He held up a hand. "That's not the point. Let's look at it another way: if you were both trying to cross the Grand Canyon and one of you had a thirty-foot ladder and the other had only a twenty-foot ladder, would it matter? The distance is still insurmountable. You don't need to compare sin or 'good works' with other people. You will all equally fail if you try to cross on your own."[47]

"Okay . . . ."

"When you truly grasp the hopelessness of your situation and the depth of Our grace in rescuing you,[48] you'll naturally forgive and love others."[49]

"I'm still confused," I admitted.

"Let's go back to your cellar."

I gave the horse a final pat and trooped back down the stairs. Jesus knelt down next to my spring. I sat beside Him. "Take this cup." He pulled a red plastic cup out of His pocket. "Now, if I pour water into this cup, what happens?" Using His stone goblet, He poured living water into the cup. It filled, but He continued to pour.

"It overflows."

"Correct." He set the cup down. "We've poured Our infinite love and forgiveness into you.[50] When you forgive others, it's a natural overflow of Our forgiveness. It's not because you're somehow mustering up forgiveness and grace for Jack, or anyone else who's wronged you. Instead, you're merely passing along *Our* forgiveness and grace."

Understanding flooded my brain. I gaped at Him. "No wonder I couldn't love him on my own! It's not just him—I can't love anyone. You do the loving.[51] That's Your job, not mine."

"That's right! You're getting yourself stuck trying to do it on your own."

I made a face. "Like clogging my spring with a wine rack."

"Exactly."

"Then how does anger fit in?" I asked.

"Once you've examined yourself—pulled the log out of your own eye[52]—you can turn your attention to the other person and how best to love them. For instance, if you had tried to put down healthy limits with Jack, you could have said something like 'I really want to have a healthy relationship with you. Therefore, if you're going to talk down to me, I'm going to leave the room until you're ready to treat me with respect.' It varies from situation to situation."[53]

I pictured the dark horse, realizing maybe he had been my ticket out.

"Yes, anger can take you places you can't go alone. It's a protective emotion. It displays part of how valued you are as an image-bearer. You are precious to Us, and it's a significant offense to injure you."[54]

That made sense. I didn't feel livid when someone swatted a mosquito or ate chicken.[55] Getting injured myself and watching other humans be injured was another story. It all made sense.

But what if I just don't want to forgive?

"What do you think you can do about that?" Jesus asked.

"I guess I could ask You to help me want to. You are the God of miracles . . . ."

"Darling, you've already taken the first step; you gave Me your bitterness. And, like with your bitterness, you have a choice. We've already told you to love Jack with Our love.[56] Part of that is forgiving him:[57] There's no middle ground. Either you choose Us and love him, or you give in to sin and don't love him."

I scowled. He was right. Loving was the practical outworking of my decision to give Jesus my bitterness—a difficult, painful outworking, but still simply a logical result. Unless I wanted to remake my decision, my course was clear.

"All right. I want You more than I want to not forgive him. I can't love him on my own. Please help me." At once I felt better, though not perfectly charitable towards him. Another huge weight had lifted.

Jesus' eyes lit up. "We will help you. It's a process though. The choice to love is a discipline made up of a multitude of small decisions. For starters, pray for him and anyone else who hurts you.[58] Do the work of love first, rather than waiting for loving feelings to motivate your actions."[59]

I reluctantly thought of what I would wish someone to pray for me. "Okay, please help him to have a good day today." To my surprise, I felt much better praying for his good day than I had wishing for him to have a horrible day.

"Love is always better, though rarely easier," Jesus said.

"I guess that's another misconception I had. I expected loving and forgiving him to somehow become easier if I waited long enough."

"You're right. Time is not the key factor in this equation—We are. And We're always ready to help you practice passing along love."

Practice? I have to do this more than once? Praying any more good on him felt impossible.

"I'll have to take Your word for that," I told Him.

Jesus looked at me seriously. "Jack was hurt too."

I flinched. Had I ever even considered that possibility? The thought of his pain created just the tiniest bit of compassion for him.

"How was he hurt?" I asked.

"That's between him and Us."

"Okay," I said. Somehow I was content with that answer. I trusted Him to give me more information if I needed it.

Jesus stood up. "Now, darling, I believe you have a day to get back to."

I got slowly to my feet. "I would rather stay here with You," I said, fearing my anniversary pain would re-engulf me the moment I left.

"This isn't goodbye. Come meet Us every morning.[60] Remember to fill up your phial." He hugged me, then gave me a gentle push towards the stairs.

I started up the steps. The door at the top swung open, and a heat haze momentarily obscured my vision. When it cleared, I saw the landing of subway stairs. People hurried by. I sighed and stepped through.

I stood there, blinking in confusion. How long had I been gone? I checked the time. Still 7:16 a.m. Odd, hallucinations take time . . . . Maybe it *was* divine intervention.

Finally, the jostling and stares reminded me I should move. The train! I still need to make the train! I hurried down the stairs.

Today had been transformed. Maybe it was no longer the anniversary of destruction. Maybe now I could celebrate it as an anniversary of change, of life. I decided to test out this newfound life.

God, change my heart towards him. Please use his pain the way You've used mine.

Jesus was right! It seemed easier this time to do things God's way. I wondered if I'd see Jack today. Wow. It felt so strange to think his name. Jack. Maybe things had changed more than I realized.

I checked. The old anger was still roiling around. "Steady there," I said. "I'm not going to leave you to simmer anymore. I have plans for you." I wasn't exactly sure how to use my anger, but I figured I would just wait and see what came up. Well, that and ask for some serious guidance from God.

My grief had remained as well. How long would it take to plow my field? At least an end was possible, if not closely in sight. I chuckled. A horse and plow. At this rate, I was becoming a regular farm girl.

The train arrived. I sat by the window and stared out at my newly-made day. A fellow commuter plopped herself down next to me. "It's such a beautiful day," she commented.

I smiled at her. "Yes. Yes, it is."

Therefore, since we are surrounded by such a great cloud of witnesses, let us throw off everything that hinders and the sin that so easily entangles, and let us run with perseverance the race marked out for us.

~ Hebrews 12:1

1 Deut. 32:35; Rom. 12:19

2 Mal. 3:2

3 For the sake of readability I've used both the singular and plural pronouns with regards to the Trinity and the Persons therein. When talking about the Trinity, it's almost impossible not to emphasize either the oneness of God or His threeness. Since the American church tends to emphasize God's oneness, I've used the plural pronouns in places to emphasize God's essential relational nature. In no way do I wish to imply that God is not one (Deut. 6:4–5; 1 Kings 8:60; Isa. 45:5–6, 45:21–22; James 2:19) or to stray into Tritheism (Matt. 28:19–20; 2 Cor. 13:14; Eph. 4:4–6; 1 Pet. 1:2; Jude 20–21; John 1:1–2, 1:9–18, 17:24, 14:26, 16:7; Acts 10:38).

4 Jon. 4:2

5 Ezek. 18:30–32, 33:10–11; 2 Pet. 3:9

6 Isa. 61:1–4; Luke 4:16–21

7 Matt. 6:14–15, 18:21–35

8 A helpful distinction for me has been to learn that forgiveness has to do with the past, but reconciliation is related to the future. See Henry Cloud and John Sims Townsend's book *Boundaries: When to Say Yes, When to Say No to Take Control of Your Life* (Grand Rapids, MI: Zondervan Pub. House, 1992), 251–252, 262–264.

9 e.g., 1 Cor. 5:9–11

10 Isa. 64:6

11 Luke 6:45

12 Gal. 5:22–23

13 e.g., 1 Thess. 5:19; Matt. 23:37

14 John 8:31–32

15 Rom. 6:16

16 Matt. 6:24

17 Ps. 51:4

18 Ps. 9, 67, 75, 96:10–13, 98:9; Isa. 11:4–5; Ezek. 18:29–32; Nah. 1:3; Acts 17:30–31; Heb. 10:30

19 Rom. 2:6; Col. 3:25; Ezek. 18:30

20 See John 4:1–26, especially verses 13–14; John 7:37–39

21 Eph. 5:18

22 Isa. 55:1–3

23 Acts 3:19

24 Ps. 18:19

25 Isa. 30:8–18

26 Ps. 103:10

27 Mark 9:23

28 Matt. 7:7

29 John 4:14

30 Ps. 77:14

31 Mark 9:24

32 2 Cor. 3:17

33 We can meet God anytime, but starting our day full makes a huge difference. e.g., Mark 1:35; Ps. 90:14, 143:8; Isa. 33:2; Matt. 6:33

34 Rev. 21:3–4

35 In grief, our brains literally break down the connections we built up in that relationship. We unlearn our emotions toward the person. Cathy Clough and Linda Pouliot, *Grieving Forward: Death Happened, Now What?: A Practical Guide for Healing & Understanding the Grief Process* (Mustang, OK: Tate Pub & Enterprises Llc, 2011), 25.

36 If you find grief continuing to be your main focus years after the event occurred, please get professional help. Grief is not designed to become a life-sucking stronghold. e.g., Ps. 30:5; Isa. 61:1–4; Matt. 5:4; 2 Cor. 1:3–4

37 Ps. 126:5–6, 30:5

38 John 12:24

39 1 Cor. 15:21–26, 15:52–57; Rev. 21:4

40 While talking to Mary about Lazarus' death, Jesus wept, even though He knew He would be raising Lazarus from the dead, and even though He knew Mary & Martha's sorrow would turn to joy (John 11:32–35). How much more do we, who don't know the future, need to grieve? For a summary on the mechanics of tears and how important they are, see Clough and Pouliot, "Tears Contain the Miracle of Healing." In *Grieving Forward.*

41 Eph. 4:26; John 2:13–17

42 e.g., John 2:13–17; Ps. 73; Isa. 11:4–5; Ps. 9

43 For further information, see Robert S. McGee's work "Chapter 13: The Trip In." In *The Search for Significance: Book and Workbook,* rev. ed. (Nashville, TN: W Pub. Group, 2003), 141–151. See also Leslie Vernick "Chapter 7; The Truth About Choices: They Have Not Been Taken from You." In *The Emotionally Destructive Relationship: Seeing It, Stopping It, Surviving It* (Eugene, OR: Harvest House Publishers, 2007), 133–144.

44 Prov. 26:11; For more information, check out Vernick, *Emotionally Destructive Relationship,* as well Cloud and Townsend, *Boundaries*, especially 272–274, Nancy Groom's book *From Bondage to Bonding: Escaping Codependency, Embracing Biblical Love* (Colorado Springs, CO: NavPress, 1991), and Dan Allender's book *The Wounded Heart: Hope for Adult Victims of Childhood Sexual Abuse,* rev. ed. (Colorado Springs, CO: NavPress, 1995).

45 Rom. 12:19

46 Luke 7:41–43

47 Rom. 6:23

48 Eph. 2:8–9

49 1 John 4:7–12, 4:19; John 15:9–12; Gal. 5:22–23; Matt. 18:21–35

50 Rom. 5:5

51 Gal. 5:22–23; 1 John 4:19

52 Matt. 7:5

53 For more examples, check out Cloud and Townsend's book *Boundaries*. Obviously, anger is beneficial only when harnessed by God's love. Godly boundaries, likewise, are not an opportunity to lash out, but an instrument of true love.

54 Gen. 9:6; Luke 15:4–7; Matt. 22:35–40; John 3:16; Rom. 5:6–8

55 I'm not advocating the mistreatment of animals, merely emphasizing the fundamental difference between animals and people—we're made in God's image. However, God cares for all His creation (Matt 6:28–34; Luke 12:6–7), and we ought to do likewise (Prov. 12:10; Deut. 25:4).

56 Matt. 5:43–45

57 Matt. 18:21–35; Eph. 4:30–32

58 Matt. 5:43–45

59 1 John 3:18

60 e.g., Mark 1:35; Ps. 90:14, 143:8; Isa. 33:2; Matt. 6:33

The Sculptor's Lair

ONE

And we, who with unveiled faces all reflect the Lord's glory, are being transformed into his likeness with ever-increasing glory, which comes from the Lord, who is the Spirit. ~ 2 Corinthians 3:18

"Beautiful," I murmured, struck by the elegant simplicity of the sculpture. A marble maiden sat on a log, staring dreamily into the distance. She had been carved in the classical style. After going through the museum's modern art wing, I was ready for something I could recognize.

"It's pretty amazing what a talented sculptor can do," my friend Lydia agreed.

I stared at the sculpture a moment longer. The girl looked as though she hadn't a care in the world—a state I couldn't remotely relate to. The past few years had been a relentless onslaught of never-ending days, full to the brim with cares.

Part of me longed to trade places with her. I wouldn't mind just sitting there, day after day. No demands. No decisions. I shook myself a little. Get over it. Life isn't that way, not for you anyway.

I wandered over to an exhibit detailing types of marble. Lydia was already there. "Look at this," she said, pointing to the accompanying quotation.

"In every block of marble I see a statue as though it stood before me, shaped and perfected in attitude and action. I have only to hew away the

rough walls that imprison the lovely apparition to reveal it to the other eyes as mine see it." ~Michelangelo, 1475–1564.[61]

She smiled. "I love that quote. It always makes me think about God as a sculptor."

"How so?"

"Well, I like to think of Him freeing the person I was designed to be out of all my brokenness, remaking me into His image."

"Oh, right . . . ." I turned away, feigning interest in a nearby statue.

I knew what she was talking about. Someone at church had compared my string of troubles to "God's chisel at work." I wanted to cry out on behalf of the rock. Stone might not feel resentful or hurt, but I did. Didn't God care? Or was He, like Michelangelo, so focused on the end result that He disregarded the pain of His chiseling?

I smiled at Lydia and nodded in response to some comment about another sculpture. I was so tired of pretending to be cheerful. Getting out of the house had been a good idea, but not here, not with someone else. *"You need a break. It'll be fun,"* Lydia had said, yet here I was, in another painful discussion about God's character. Right. Loads of fun.

"I think I'm done looking at sculptures. Shall we move on?" I asked.

"I want to look around a bit more. How about we meet back at the main entrance in half an hour?"

"Sounds good to me." I glanced around, trying to decide where to go from here. Tortured rocks met my gaze in every direction. The room seemed far too small and close. I bolted back the way we had come.

There had to be a faster way out. I turned down a promising hallway. This corridor was deserted, void even of art, and the omnipresent shuffling and muttering had faded. The lights were set farther and farther apart, leaving most of the hall in deep shadow. The hair on the back of my neck prickled.

Where was everyone? I hesitated, scanning the hall. There was nowhere to turn off. I hurried forward, my footsteps echoing on the polished concrete. Surely I could find someone to point me in the right direction.

At last the hall curved around and opened into a room—full of sculptures. You've got to be kidding me! I pressed on, hoping it was a small collection. The statues themselves varied in form and style, but I soon realized they all had the same sunken visage. A modern art series, perhaps?

I came to an archway with double doors. I could hear the ringing sounds of chisel upon stone and the clatter of shards falling to the floor. Maybe the sculptor could give me directions. But did I really want to see someone beating up stone right now? I decided to risk it, rather than continue my aimless wandering.

I pushed through the doors and found a large workspace. It was dark concrete and bare, empty of all but the sculptor and a single statue. Bright lights illuminated the piece in progress. The rest of the studio remained lost in gloom.

The sculptor stood on a ladder, working the piece with a chisel and mallet. He had black hair and pale skin. His form looked normal, but his face reminded me of a plastic mask, void of humanity. Not even a flicker of emotion showed in his dark eyes.

Everything in me demanded I slip away unnoticed, but then I recalled I was lost. I took a deep breath. What's the worst that could happen?

I waved to get his attention, but he appeared unaware of my presence, or perhaps he was ignoring me. All at once I recognized him. Those were his sculptures in the adjacent gallery, and it was his face they bore.

I moved to better see the statue taking form beneath the artist's calculated blows. It stood about nine feet tall and was obviously a woman. She wore a long, flowing gown, and her straight hair hung loose down her back. Another step brought her face into view. I gasped. It was my face the sculptor was obliterating in favor of his own.

"What are you doing?" I yelled.

He turned, and his cold gaze slid over me. "I am the Creator. Worship me!" He returned to his work. Now I could feel the blows he so skillfully directed. When he chiseled the image, my own face burned with furrows of fire.

"Stop! It hurts!" I screamed.

I felt something running down my cheek and put a hand to my face. I stared in disbelief at the liquid on my fingers: it was blood. More and more gushed onto my clothes. I began to feel faint. On shaking legs, I ran to him and grabbed his arm. His muscles were like cords of steel.

"Stop! Can't you see what you're doing?"

He wasn't even fazed. As he raised his arm for another blow, my strength gave out, and I fell into a crumpled heap on the floor. I lay there, sobbing, bleeding all over. "Please," I whimpered, trying to see him through a haze of pain. "Please . . . stop . . . help me . . . ."

Suddenly a tall man stormed in. "Stop!" he roared.

The sculptor's eyes widened, and he stumbled down the ladder. Everything went black.

I came to, still on the concrete floor. The man knelt next to me, his hands cradling my head. I moaned and put a hand to my aching head. I felt like I had been hit by a truck.

"Where am I?" I licked my dry lips, tasting blood. It all came flooding back. My heart began to pound. I looked around wildly for the sculptor.

"He's gone," the man said. "Just lie still for a moment."

I lay back. The room spun, and the pain threatened to steal my consciousness once more.

The man began caressing my face, tracing the furrows left by the sculptor. My pain gradually eased. I watched him, wondering what sort of man had come to my rescue. Where the sculptor's gaze had been cold and lifeless, this man's eyes sparkled. Just now he was studying me, concern writ large across his features.

"Who are you?" I asked.

"I'm not sure you're ready for that. How do you feel now?"

I assessed my pains—physically, they were gone, as was my perpetual exhaustion. "Much better, thank you."

"Good. Try to sit up," he said, then gently raised me.

I sat there for a moment, nauseated by my surroundings. It was like a horror film: the dark room, the mutilated sculpture, my blood pooled on the floor. At least the sculptor is gone.

"Would you like to go somewhere else?"

"Yes, please!" I begged.

A smile lit his features and his eyes flicked heavenward. "All right," he said, then held out a hand. I took it, and he escorted me through a rear door.

We stepped out onto a flagstone terrace where a crescent moon glowed in the sky. Stairs led down to a large flower garden. A balmy breeze, delicately perfumed by the garden, caressed my skin. I could hear a fountain bubbling companionably to our right. I took a deep breath and relaxed my shoulders.

The man led me over to the fountain and filled the tethered water dipper. "Here, you look parched."

I swallowed hard. "Thank you." I swished a mouthful of the crisp water around, then gulped the rest. Once my thirst had been quenched, I couldn't stand the stickiness on my hands and face.

I began to dab my face, expecting to find deep wounds. Instead, my face felt smooth. The fountain water wavered too much for me to see my reflection, but my fingers told me I was whole, without even a scar. I remembered the man's gentle touch on my injuries. Did he heal me, or had I only imagined the injuries? I turned and found the man seated on a nearby bench. He seemed to be studying me.

"Feel better?" he asked.

"Yes, much. Where are we?"

"We're in my garden."

I looked back at the door.

"We're outside the sculptor's reach. Don't worry. I just temporarily attached that door to the garden."

"I see," I said, though I did not see at all. He talked about the door as if it were a tent to be moved about willy-nilly. Please don't be crazy, I silently begged him. No more crazy people today.

I flashed back to that awful moment when I had realized the statue was me. I shuddered.

"Do you want to talk about it? Pull up a bench," he said, indicating the seat opposite him.

I sat down. "What was that place? Who was that awful sculptor?"

He looked grim. "That was a prison of lies, and the sculptor was one who decided to take advantage of it. What happened in there?"

I recounted how I had seen the other statues, and finally the statue of myself, all being carved to look like the sculptor—a sculptor who identified himself as the Creator. I shuddered again.

"I know that as a follower of Jesus, I'm being remade into His image.[62] I just wish it didn't hurt so badly. It's making me rethink whether I even want God to change me. Maybe I'd be better off if He just left me alone," I said, a little shocked I had been so forthright with a stranger.

"Then the impostor has done his job well. Do you really think God works that way?"

"Doesn't He? I feel like I've had one painful growing experience after another, and I'm tired of it. I wish that just once He could feel my pain."

His eyes softened. "How do you know that He hasn't?"

"Hasn't what?"

"Hasn't felt your pain. What about Jesus? Didn't He experience pain while He was on earth?"

I shrugged. "I don't know. Even if He did, He wasn't forced to go through pain—He chose it. Plus, as God, how could He get hurt, other than on the cross when He chose to be injured?"

He shook his head. "Don't you think you're negating, or at least downplaying, His humanity? Jesus became human. The Word became flesh.[63] Don't you think He ever got tired[64] or had sore feet or got dirty?[65] And what about the cross and the pain of betrayal[66] and desertion[67] beforehand?"

I frowned, trying to picture a dirty Jesus. "I don't know. I've never really thought about it. It seems somehow sacrilegious to say Jesus was dirty or sick. He's God. I picture someone much more put-together than that."

"Isn't that such an ingenious lie? It implies that Jesus is less than fully human." His jaw muscles rippled.[68] "I hate it!"

I edged away, shocked by his vehemence. Maybe I'd been too quick to stay with him. Was he any more trustworthy than the sculptor? I glanced around, noting potential avenues of escape. If nothing else, I could probably stay out of reach. Just try to work the conversation back around to leaving.

He leaned forward and rested his elbows on his knees. "If Jesus isn't fully God *and* fully human, can anyone be saved? Can anyone be rescued from God's coming destruction of evil?"

I took a deep breath. Keep things low key. I shrugged. "Why does it matter if He's fully human? Jesus had to die to pay the penalty for sin.[69] Didn't He have to be God to be able to bear the full weight of His own wrath?"

"Yes, but only a human could be born under God's law and under the consequence of death. And only by living a perfect life, and not deserving death, could His death count for others.[70] Not only that, but how else could He give you a spotless record? After all, it's because of His righteousness that you're able to come to God. If you get rid of Jesus' humanity, His work on the cross is no longer effective."

I supposed what he said made some sense. In any event, if I agreed, maybe I could get out of here.

I smiled at him. "So maybe Jesus does understand my pain. After all, the Bible says He came to do the will of His Father.[71] He probably knows what it's like to be pushed around by God too."

The man stood up and began pacing in front of me, hands clasped behind him. "You sound like you feel 'pushed around by God.' Can you give some specific examples?"

"Well, I've had some very painful experiences, which I suppose are growing opportunities—"

The man stopped and held up a hand. "Wait. You keep equating pain with harm. What about love? What about purposeful pain?"

I scoffed. "Is there pain that isn't harmful? Isn't the point of pain to alert you to injury? Like touching a hot stove and being burned."

"Let's find another way to look at this. Come with me." He held out a hand to help me up, then led me back through the door.

TWO

No art studio lay beyond the door this time. Instead, I found myself in my own bedroom. I sighed in relief. Home at last. I reached out to touch the bed. It felt solid, but my hand appeared transparent. I looked down at the rest of me. Also transparent.

I looked around the room and then back at the man. "This is just a memory of yours," he said, "like watching a recording, so feel free to move about and interact." His eyes twinkled. "You won't disrupt the space-time continuum."

I attempted to nod wisely, as though I did this all the time.

"There's something important for you to see here, so pay attention," he said.

I scanned the room, hoping it wasn't anything horrible. I'd filled my quota of horrible for about the next forever.

Before long, I watched myself enter the room, holding a long needle and rubbing alcohol. My husband followed, carrying our youngest daughter. He put her on the bed and angled a light towards her.

I remembered this well. She had fallen on the deck a few days earlier and scraped the backs of her thighs. Though the injuries appeared scabbed over, she complained off and on that her legs still hurt. Finally, we had laid her on our bed and examined her legs under a bright light. We discovered she had several small splinters that were now badly infected. The resultant pain was affecting her sleep, play, and overall mood. In short, those slivers were making her life miserable. They had to come out.

My husband explained to our precious two-year-old that we had to remove the splinters and that we would be as gentle as possible. She didn't understand. He turned her over onto her stomach so that I could dig out the slivers.

As soon as she felt the needle on her legs, she began screaming and trying to get away. "Mommy! Mommy! Stop!! Daddy! Daddy! Stop!! You're hurting me!!!" My husband tried to soothe her, which is difficult to do while holding down a screaming child. I began digging out the splinters.

It was all I could do not to weep and take her into my arms. Even watching it happen this second time, the tears streamed down my face. My hands bunched into fists. Why? Why did this have to happen to my baby? The man put a comforting hand on my shoulder.

I saw myself desperately rushing to finish my task as painlessly as possible. I looked grim and almost uncaring. I had been afraid that if I listened too closely to her cries I would be unable to go on, or that my subsequent tears would have kept me from seeing clearly.

Our daughter finally stopped begging us to let her go and lapsed into inarticulate cries of rage and pain. I longed to take the pain for her. At least I understood why it was happening.

Abruptly, the memory froze. The man stepped around the bed, and pointed to the "memory me." "Were you trying to harm your daughter?"

I dashed tears from my eyes and scrubbed my face, trying to view the scene objectively. "No."

"Were you hurting her?"

I looked over at my child, frozen in her agony, and nodded, trying not to cry again. "I never wanted to hurt her. But I couldn't just leave those stupid splinters in there. What else could I have done?"

The scene dissolved and shifted. I saw myself on the bed, jagged splinters sticking out all over my body. A figure sat where I had, looking grim and uncaring, working to remove my splinters.

Like my daughter had, I screamed bloody murder. "Why? Why are you doing this? Stop! It hurts! You're hurting me! If you loved me, you wouldn't do this to me! You're a monster!"

The figure remained silent, allowing me to pour out my vituperation on him. He did not, however, even pause in his work, no matter how I railed.

Suddenly, he looked directly at me and smiled. I half-turned, expecting to see someone behind me. Was he looking at me?

"I love you," he mouthed. Then he returned to his work. I felt suffused with his love, warm and safe. It made me want to curl up in his lap forever.

The scene dissolved. Once more we stood on the moonlit terrace. I silently walked over to the bench, wondering if I had correctly interpreted what I had seen. The man sat down across from me.

"Who was that?" I asked my rescuer.

"My father."

I started. "*Your* father? That was your father? It looked like some kind of picture of God. Are you saying God is your father?"

"I am."[72]

"Wait a minute, does that mean you're Jesus?"

He smiled, His eyes dancing. "I am."

I shifted, surreptitiously checking for exits again. "Why didn't You say so earlier?"

"You weren't ready to hear it."

"Oh, really? And I am now?"

"Maybe. We'll just have to see," He said, still smiling.

I frowned. "Why wasn't I ready before?"

"You were in your prison of lies. Given your view of Us,[73] would you have even listened, let alone come with Me?" He asked, giving me a knowing look.

"Um . . . ." Did I really want to answer that? I didn't know. I still wasn't sure I wanted to be with Him now. But then, God had seemed so different from how I usually imagined Him. So loving and trustworthy.

"Sometimes it takes putting the familiar in a strange setting to recognize the truth. What did you think about what we saw?" Jesus asked.

"I don't know. I guess I can see Your point: not all pain is harmful. I never wanted to hurt my baby, but her wounds couldn't heal with those stupid splinters in them . . . ."

Strange—the agony of being chiseled didn't seem to fit with the picture of God removing splinters. The first belonged in a horror gallery, whereas the second was colored with love. Dare I trust Him after all? I studied Jesus' face.

"Yes?" He asked.

I flushed. "You don't look at all like the sculptor. Who was he?"

Jesus stared into space for a moment, frowning. I remembered His fury when He'd come to my rescue. "He was an impostor taking advantage of your prison of lies,"[74] He said.

I tried to recall if I'd seen anything unusual when I entered the sculptor's lair. Nothing. "You called it that earlier. What does that even mean?"

"Well, suppose I told you that this terrace"—He pointed to the flagstones—"is not actually above a garden, but is instead on the edge of a deep chasm. In fact, the stairs end in a steep drop, one that would probably kill you if you fell. If you believed Me, would you walk down them?"

I looked over at the few stairs down to the garden, and wondered nervously if it was an illusion. "Not if I believed You. Perhaps not even if I only half-believed You. The risk wouldn't be worth it."

"You're right, depending on what you were missing out on. So My lie[75] would keep you away from the stairs just as securely as if I shackled you up here."

As He spoke, He stood and began drawing a picture in the air. Where His finger disturbed the air, He left shimmering lines of emptiness. I had never thought of air as "full," but the picture remained crisp, as though He had directed all the surrounding atoms to steer clear.

First, He drew the terrace with a deep chasm below, and then me, standing in the center of the terrace. Next, He drew a wall of iron bars blocking off the stairs.

"Now, what if I, or someone else, told you a second lie about this part of the terrace?" He drew another wall on the left side. "And suppose you heard the sound of the fountain and mistook it for a raging river. You decided that it was clearly unsafe over there." He drew another wall to my right.

I snorted.

"Happens all the time," He said.

"What? People confusing fountains with raging rivers?"

"No, people, even you, misinterpreting part of the truth to their own detriment."

I sighed. "All right, I guess I can see that in a more general sense."

"And finally, suppose Satan sends someone to twist the truth in some other way."[76] He fenced in my image the rest of the way. There I stood, securely enclosed in a box. He erased the chasm and filled in a beautiful garden. "Do you think you'd ever get to the garden?"

I walked 'round the picture. "No."

He pointed to the drawing. "That's a prison made of lies—much less visible and just as secure. It's also more effective than a physical prison, because you can unknowingly carry it with you every day of your life, wherever you go."

I studied it, frowning. So the sculptor had somehow made my prison into reality? Or was this all an illusion?

"How did I get into the sculptor's lair?" I asked.

"Truth is still truth," Jesus said softly.

"What?"

"Even if you learn truth in unusual ways, that doesn't make it less valid."

I nodded uncertainly. "I suppose You're right."

He sat, and the drawing vanished. "You've been in that prison for a long time. You got there by believing some lies and half-truths."

I rolled my eyes. Well that's specific. "Such as?"

He looked up at the sky, "Oh, let's see. How about 'all pain indicates harm'?"

"Okay, what else?"

"Well, think about it. What else did you see? What was different between the sculptor and My Father?"

What *was* different? Both had appeared uncaring, but there was a different quality to God's impassivity: pain. The sculptor's disregard extended down to his very soul, if he had one. God, on the other hand, only appeared impassive from my vantage point.

"Well, I think You're trying to show me that You're not uncaring. If my pain bothers You even half as much as it bothered me to cause my daughter pain, You still care. The sculptor didn't care about me at all."

"True. We aren't indifferent to your pain. Do you really think I would have died for you if I was indifferent?"[77] Jesus asked, a tender light in His eyes.

I paused, struck by the thought. Could duty alone have driven Jesus to die for me? "I've never really thought about it. I know You love me, but You *are* God; You don't have a choice. Plus, isn't the cross more about escaping judgment than about love?"

Jesus shook His head. "It's both. And We don't just love you, We delight in you. Our love is not forced. You never have to doubt that. Does a healthy mother have to force love for her newborn child? It just springs up. We wouldn't have rescued you otherwise.[78] Nor do We permit pain pointlessly. If you allow it to, every single hurt can teach you something—remove some splinter."[79]

God loved me. Somehow, in that moment, my doubts fell away, and I knew He really loved me. It was a strange feeling, contrary to everything I had believed for so long. He had said it Himself: He wouldn't have rescued me otherwise. And here I was, rescued out of my prison of lies.

My eyes filled with tears. "Jesus," I reached out and put a hand on His arm, "thank You. Thank You for loving me enough to rescue me."

He covered my hand with His own. "You're welcome, darling."

I squeezed His hand, then sat back, turning His last comment over. "So what is a metaphorical splinter?"

"It's anything that hinders you from living life to the fullest."[80]

Such a broad definition! I was sure there were myriads of splinters in my life. Maybe I was like my daughter—unable to run or play or be the person I was supposed to be. "So You use painful experiences to get rid of splinters in my life?"

Jesus nodded. "Or to make you aware of them."

"All kinds of pain? Even the pain I've gotten myself into?"

"Definitely. Often the pain and guilty feelings[81] associated with those things are a gift from Us to show you that harm is occurring so you'll stop doing whatever it is."

"Wait a minute." I sat up straight. "Is that really fair? What if I like what I'm doing?"

"Would you be a loving parent if you let your children play in the street, even if they really wanted to?"

I tried to come up with a situation where it would be appropriate for my children to play in the street, but I couldn't. I slumped back into the bench. "No."

"Likewise, My Father disciplines you out of love. It shows that you're a true child of God."[82]

"It's still not fun," I muttered.

He smiled. "That's kind of the point, isn't it? It isn't pleasant at the time, but it changes your direction, helping you cultivate something else. Instead of ending up with heartbreak, it produces something wonderful in you, like peace and righteousness."[83]

"So You're saying that when You discipline me, it's not because I made You angry? You don't enjoy punishing me?"

"The old 'killjoy view'?" He shook His head vigorously. "No, We're not eagerly watching for an opportunity to punish you. We don't delight in anyone's punishment.[84] We're slow to anger.[85] And yes, it's loving discipline—the real thing," He said, speaking directly to my fearful heart.

The fear lessened, but refused to leave. "But what if I don't notice it right away, or what if I don't want to change my direction? Don't You turn up the volume or something?" I worried

He would get as fed up with my willfulness as I did with my children's. Maybe He'd eventually give up on me. Or zap me.

"It depends. We won't give up on you.[86] But sometimes We let you continue in your sin until it reaches its logical end.[87] Then you can see for yourself how bankrupt the ending is."

"Morally bankrupt?"

"No, just bankrupt," He said, His eyes bleak and distant. "Everything good and perfect comes from the Father,[88] so when you look elsewhere, you find a counterfeit." He turned to me. "Does a counterfeit ever satisfy?"

"Probably for a while, or at least until you realize it's fake."

"Then what?"

"Then you're back where you started."

He tilted His head. "Are you?"

"Why wouldn't you be?"

"Because hope deferred makes the heart sick.[89] Suppose you're cold, but your sole blanket only covers part of you at a time. Does it warm you up or just underscore how cold you are?"

A chill wind blew off the garden, and I shivered. "Oh, I see what You're saying. With the counterfeit, you're worse off than you were before. You thought it would meet your need, but instead it emphasizes how unmet the need is."

"Right. So sometimes We give people over to their sin until they're sick of it and miserable.[90] Obviously, whenever you decide to turn from your sin toward Us, you can be forgiven,[91] healed,[92] freed,[93] and restored."[94]

I nodded. There had been times when I had experienced that very thing. "Then what about the painful things other people have done to me?"

"What about them?"

"What good are they? Can You use them?"

He gave me a slow smile. "Beloved, if you grasped how wide and long and high and deep Our love is, [95] you wouldn't have to ask. Yes, We can use them. You are a child of God. If you're going through pain, it's because We allowed it in your life for a purpose."[96]

My mouth twisted. "That doesn't seem very evident when I watch the news. What about all the awful things in the world, like genocide? Is that purposeful too? How can You be good and still allow it? Are You not able to stop it?"

Jesus leaned forward. "This is a broken world under the control of the evil one.[97] Evil is part of that. And yes, We allow it to continue for now. Its end is certain, and the time is set![98] We're not unwilling to destroy evil, or slow to do so. Instead, We're being patient. We love people. We don't want any to be swept away when We get rid of evil; We want everyone to turn to Us."[99]

I had hoped for an answer that would explain evil and somehow justify God's inaction. This wasn't it. Even though Jesus' answer made some sense, it seemed inadequate when compared to the pain suffered by millions.

"You've got to stop thinking about people as a group," Jesus said.

"Huh?"

"You were just thinking about 'millions.' That isn't how We view people—as the great mass of humanity.[100] People are really a collection of individuals so different that you can't abstract them into a group." He smiled. "Or at least you wouldn't if you knew them better."

"I think I'll have to take Your word for that."

"Think about your children. Are they the same?"

I chuckled. "Not at all. I remember being surprised by how different they were, even as babies."

"We know them a lot better than you do. We know everything they do, every thought that flits through their minds.[101] We know their beginnings and ends.[102] We know every atom of their bodies inside and out. We can see their souls through and through. We knit them together, hardware and software,[103] when they were in your womb.[104] They're completely unique individuals.

"The same is true for every person. There's no one like you, or anyone else for that matter."

"I guess You're right. But back to genocide and such—"

He held up a hand. "Actually, if you're going to deal with evil, you need to start by dealing with the evil in your life and the ways you feed and coddle it, rather than the abstract concept of evil."[105]

I squirmed in my seat. Sometimes I love that God knows me inside and out, and sometimes I hate it. His eyes bored into me. There was nowhere to hide.

"Stop worrying about how We're dealing with everyone else. Worry about yourself. I died so you could be free from sin.[106] We've already done something about pain and evil. It's done. Just as surely as water solidifies when you freeze it, pain and evil will cease to exist when the time is right. They're already in the freezer. Evil has been overcome.[107] You have to decide what you're going to do."

"What do You mean? I've already asked You to forgive my sin.[108] What else is there?"

"All these painful experiences we've been talking about—how are you going to handle them?"

I shrugged. "It depends on the experience, I suppose."

"How have you dealt with them in the past?"

I thought back over recent years. "Probably tried to escape the pain . . . ."

He nodded. "Or numb it. But pain in life is like pain in childbirth."

I winced. Who wants to be reminded of labor?

"As long as you try to escape it, you prolong the pain. You preserve the wound instead of allowing it to heal. But if you work with the pain—if you work with Us to remove the splinter—something wonderful is birthed, and the pain ends."

I had to admit I longed for the pain to end. If nothing else, that carrot would pull me almost anywhere at this point in my life. But after my encounter with the sculptor, the thought of being chiseled made my blood run cold. I scuffed my feet. "So what exactly does it look like to work with You?"

Jesus smiled, as though He could see straight into the heart of my question—come to think of it, He probably could. "To believe that if We allow pain, it's out of love. To trust Our character when you can't see exactly how something will work out. To cooperate in the transformation process. It's not something you can do halfway."

I stared into the distance. Cooperate? I wanted to weep. How could I cooperate with something so painful?

Jesus put a hand on my arm. "What's wrong?" He asked.

I hesitated, trying to think of the best way to explain. "You have a nicer face than the sculptor does . . . ."

Jesus threw back His head in a full laugh. It was rich and uninhibited. "Yes, I do. But not one you would like to share, eh?"

I smiled back sheepishly. "Not really . . . it's not that I dislike Your face, but I don't want to lose all of myself."

A thought seared through my brain: He was just like all the other perfectionists in my life. I jumped up. "Isn't any part of me good enough for You?"

Jesus stood up as well, His face serious. He put a gentle hand on my shoulder. Something passed between us, and suddenly I knew that He had seen all those times of failing to measure up. He knew my wounds and wasn't discounting them. He loved me.

Love. It kept coming back to that. I dropped my eyes.

Jesus lifted my chin, drawing my gaze back to His own. "Why do you think you have to lose all of your self to gain My image?"

"I don't know. Doesn't the Bible say that I'm being transformed into Your image?"[109]

"Why do you think that involves destroying every part of who you are?"

"Your Word says that I'm a new creation—that the old things have gone.[110] Or what about those places where You say that You replace people's hearts with new ones?"[111]

"Just because you have been and are being made into My image, doesn't mean there's nothing of you left. Maybe you should read some other verses," He said with a smile and pulled my Bible out of His pocket. "Take a look at Genesis 1:26–27. What does it say?"

I took my Bible, and we sat back down. "Let's see . . . ." I flipped to the front, glad it was an easy reference to find. " 'Then God said, "Let us make man in our image, in our likeness, and let them rule over the fish of the sea and the birds of the air, over the livestock, over all the earth, and over all the creatures that move along the ground." So God created man in his own image, in the image of God he created him; male and female he created them.' " I stared at the passage some more, still mystified. "What am I looking for?"

"You're noticing that when We made humans, you were specifically created to bear Our image."

"Okay . . . . What does that have to do with anything?"

"It means Adam and Eve bore Our image. You're talking about a loss of personality when you refer to changing your face, right?"

I nodded.

"Adam and Eve have plenty of personality," He said dryly. "Being image-bearers doesn't mean that they stopped being individuals."

"But that was them. What about me? Did You see those statues? How can I still be myself with Your face on me?"

"We created you in your inmost being. We knit you together in your mother's womb.[112] We didn't forget to include Our image. You wouldn't be human otherwise."

I wrinkled my brow. "Are You saying that You made me with Your face? Then why do I need to be transformed into Your image if You've already made me so?"

He looked at me sadly. "Think of it as a restoration project. We created Adam and Eve perfect. They bore Our image 100%. But then they tried to decide what was best for them—to assert that they too could see all their options and know what was best.[113] And so, they broke the world. Satan became ruler.[114] And the image was marred, though not destroyed. Even you put yourself in Our place regularly and further mar Our image in you.

"Being changed into My image means becoming the person We created you to be. You are more yourself when you are in My image. Not less."

More myself. I wondered what that would look like. "Then that's another lie, isn't it? That I'll be less myself when I'm transformed into Your image?"

He nodded.

Argh! I had been shooting myself in the foot all along. "How in the world am I supposed to see these lies? I mean, if I believe they're true, I won't examine them unless I hear something contradictory. Maybe not even then," I added ruefully.

He smiled. "Ask for help from someone who can see everything for what it is. That would be Us, in case you didn't know."[115]

I smiled back.

"And study the truth." He tapped my Bible. "As you learn what's true, the lies become more obvious—like the 'baloney grid,'" He said, citing an example from one of my teachers.[116]

This teacher would draw a grid of dots, pinpricks of knowledge against a background of ignorance. The more you learned and understood how things were related, the more dots could be connected, creating a fine mesh. Then if someone tried to throw a piece of baloney at you, it would come out as mush on the other side, preventing you from swallowing the untruth whole.

"Right," I said. It sounded like so much work.

"Remember what G. K. Chesterton said: 'The Christian ideal has not been tried and found wanting. It has been found difficult; and left untried.'[117] It isn't easy, but it is worthwhile." His eyes sparkled. "This restoration project with Us can take you on the adventure of your life."

I grimaced, thinking back to my prison of lies. I felt more alive and more myself when I was with Jesus than ever before, but was it worth it? "It's already been a pretty adventurous night. I'm not sure I can handle the excitement."

Jesus chuckled. "It won't always be this out of the ordinary. But, it will always be abundant life."

"Will I ever end up in the sculptor's lair again?"

"Not if you hang on to the truth—the truth will keep you free."[118]

I nodded "Right. The truth . . . ."

"Do you remember the truths you learned tonight?" He asked, smiling with the air of a teacher to a favored student.

I stood and began pacing. "Let's see . . . ." I felt like I had just lived through about a week's worth of input. "Um, that You're not impassive to my pain and that not all pain indicates harm."

"Right. Anything else about pain?"

I remembered the figure removing my splinters. I was still awed that God really loved me. How had I tolerated a lie for so long? "That pain is allowed in my life by my loving Father, and I can choose to avoid it and prolong it, or work with it and grow."

He nodded.

I stopped in front of Him. "Also, that lies can keep me captive, but since You can see the truth, I need to come to You and Your Word for help seeing the lies."

"Correct."

"Is that it? Did I miss anything?"

He smiled and pointed to His face.

"Oh! Right. I don't lose myself when I'm made into Your image. Rather, I become more myself, because I grow into the person You created me to be."

"Yes! And on that note, there's something I'd like to show you. Come with Me," He said, heading towards the door.

I followed close at His heels. What did Jesus have in store now?

THREE

This time the door opened into a different art studio. "This is *My* studio," Jesus said and gestured for me to enter. I felt a little apprehensive given my previous experience, but I went in anyway. This workplace looked vastly different: light poured in from huge windows and a glass ceiling. The floor appeared to be made of a single piece of richly-stained wood. Brilliant flowers bloomed in pots. The room was filled with sculptures and a scattering of tools.

Jesus led me to an unfinished statue in the center. "This is what I'm working on right now."

I circled it, feeling a touch of déjà vu. It was a statue of me. Some places on it were pockmarked and portions rough-edged. I could easily discern which section He had been restoring because it was smooth and beautiful.

"Look over there," He said and pointed to an easel I hadn't noticed. "There's the design."

On it stood a portrait of a woman, beautiful and poised. She seemed somehow more human, as though every person I had seen before was just a shadow of humanness. She radiated health and beauty. I couldn't even fully comprehend or describe her. Every time I focused on some aspect of the portrait, I had the feeling I was missing something. I couldn't take my eyes off her.

"She's beautiful."

"That's you," Jesus said, "as We created you to be and as you will be someday. You can't apprehend the full picture because you don't have access to all the reality it's been painted in. But you get the basic idea."

Startled, I looked closer. It *was* me. Me, without the flaws and brokenness engendered by my willful sin and this broken world. I could see a resemblance to Jesus, some indefinable likeness—perhaps in the very exultant aliveness and wholeness she radiated. It was so strange, so upside-down, to think that He could use pain and brokenness to create wholeness. I wished I could be her.

I turned to Jesus. "How long?"

"Well, that depends on you. Are you going to cooperate with My Spirit in the restoration process?" He asked, watching me intently.

The very daily-ness of all the hard work rose up to swallow me. It still sounded like so much time and energy and just plain hard work!

Then again, how many women put just as much effort into changing their looks to conform to society's standards? I would be putting my effort into attaining God's standards. And it wasn't as though I'd be doing it on my own. God was only asking me to surrender to His work in me and to obey Him.

I turned to look at the picture again. I could become her. That decided me. I wanted it. Badly. Even if it did hurt. I smiled a little. I was ending up like Michelangelo—all focused on the end instead of the means.

I turned back to Jesus. "Yes!"

He smiled. "All right. Lesson over for now. Down to the life learning lab."

"How long?" I repeated.

"For some of it, you can change now. See?" He said and pointed to the statue again.

It had changed. My small decision to be obedient today had made me more like the woman in the painting, more like the God who loved me and had come to rescue me from my lies. I looked back at Jesus, realizing I would never think of God in the same way. I was falling for Him.

"It won't be complete until you come to live with Us forever,"[119] He said.

I sucked in my breath. A lifetime. It was daunting. Then the last part of His sentence sunk in: forever with Him. It was a whole different prospect than it ever had been. I loved the idea of being with Him every day.

Jesus shook His head, smiling a little. "My Spirit is already with you every day."[120]

The door swung open of its own accord. I sighed. It was time for me to leave.

"That's the way back, but you won't leave alone. Remember, this isn't good-bye." He pulled me into a hug. "We love you. Now, go. Lydia is waiting for you."

I clung to Him a moment longer, then walked through the door.

"And that's when I ran into you."

"Literally," Lydia said with a laugh.

I was glad to see her laugh. She had been shaken by my sudden appearance, especially as I was still blood-stained and disheveled. When I stepped through the door into the foyer, I had walked right into her. She had asked what had happened to me, and I'd suggested we talk about it over coffee (after I changed my shirt).

I laughed with her, my first real laugh in a while. I felt like my crazy adventure had awakened me from the nightmare of my life. "I wonder how long I was trapped in those lies," I murmured, staring into my coffee cup.

"You've been fighting with God for a long time."

"How do you know?"

She smiled. "Just a hunch. You know you always run when the conversation turns to trusting God."

I blushed. "Really? Me?"

"I don't mean physically, at least not all the time. You just sort of shut down. Plus, look at how upset you've been lately."

"With good reason," I replied, half-heartedly. "At least, it seemed like good reason before . . . ."

"And now?"

I leaned forward. "Now I'm excited to see how these situations pan out. I've never trusted God the way you do, but, somehow, now I do."

"Hang on to that!"

"You mean I won't always feel this way?"

Lydia shook her head. "It's like Jesus said, you have to keep coming back to Him for the truth. It's easy to drown in your own life if you aren't focused on Him and anchored in His Word."

"That makes sense."

"So, where shall we go next time?" she asked slyly. "Maybe you can pick, and I can have the adventure."

I smiled. "I'll have to get back to you."

And we know that in all things God works for the good of those who love him, who have been called according to his purpose. ~ Romans 8:28

61 Henry Wadsworth Longfellow, *Michael Angelo, A Dramatic Poem* (Boston: Houghton, Mifflin, 1884–1883), 166. See also John Addington Symmonds, *The Life of Michelangelo Buonarroti Based on Studies in the Archives of the Buonarroti Family at Florence,* 2nd ed. (Philadelphia: University of Pennsylvania Press, 2002), 109.

62 Rom. 8:29

63 John 1:14

64 John 4:6

65 Luke 7:44

66 Matt. 26:17–25

67 Matt. 26:31–35, 26:69–75

68 John 2:13–17

69 Rom. 3:22–26; 1 Thess. 1:10

70 Rom. 5:19; 2 Cor. 5:21

71 John 5:30, 6:38

72 Matt. 3:17; Mark 14:36; Luke 9:35

73 For the sake of readability I've used both the singular and plural pronouns with regards to the Trinity and the Persons therein. When talking about the Trinity, it's almost impossible not to emphasize either the oneness of God or His threeness. Since the American church tends to prioritize God's oneness, I've used the plural pronouns in places to highlight God's essential relational nature. I in no way wish to imply that God is not one (Deut. 6:4–5; 1 Kings 8:60; Isa. 45:5–6, 45:21–22; James 2:19) or to stray into Tritheism (Matt. 28:19–20; 2 Cor. 13:14; Eph. 4:4–6; 1 Pet. 1:2; Jude 20–21; John 1:1–2, 1:9–18, 17:24, 14:26, 16:7; Acts 10:38).

74 I am indebted to Beth Moore for introducing me to this concept in her Bible study, *Breaking Free,* updated ed. (Nashville, TN: LifeWay Press, 2009). See especially "Video Session 3" and "Week 9: The Steadfast Mind."

75 God is incapable of lying. Num. 23:19; 1 John 1:5

76 John 8:44; 1 Pet. 5:8

77 Heb. 12:2; Rom. 5:8

78 Ps. 18:19; Matt. 7:7–11; John 3:16, 14:21

79 James 1:2–4

80 John 10:10–11

81 This does not refer to our legal standing before God. Before we've accepted Jesus' death on the cross, the Holy Spirit convicts us of our guilty standing (John 16:8–11). After we've come into a right relationship with God, the Holy Spirit convicts us of sin so we can confess it and move on (Acts 3:19; 1 John 1:9). We are no longer guilty in the legal sense, however, as there is no condemnation for those in Christ (Rom. 8:1–2).

82 Heb. 12:5–8

83 Heb. 12:10–11

84 Ezek. 18:30–32

85 Exod. 34:6–7

86 Phil. 1:6

87 Ps. 81:11–12

88 James 1:17

89 Prov. 13:12

90 Ps. 81:8–12

91 1 John 1:9

92 Isa. 53:5

93 Isa. 61:1–4; Ps. 119:32, 119:45

94 Luke 15:17–24; Zech. 1:3

95 Eph. 3:16–19

96 Rom. 8:28

97 1 John 5:19; Matt. 4:8–10; Col. 1:13; Eph. 6:11–12

98 Rev. 20:10–15, 21:1–5a, 22:3

99 2 Pet. 3:9

100 One has only to read through the numerous genealogies in Scripture to see that God cares for individuals (e.g., Gen. 5; 1 Chron. 1–9; Matt. 1). Even though we become part of His Church, He calls us to follow Him as individuals (e.g., Mark 8:34–38).

101 Ps. 139:1–4

102 Ps. 139:16

103 Chuck Missler, "Whence Our 'Reality?'," *Personal Update NewsJournal* (December 2003), accessed October 26, 2012, http://www.khouse.org/articles/2003/498/

104 Ps. 139:13

105 Though I have refocused the question back onto the individual, I in no way wish to make light of the problem of evil. For more information see: C. S. Lewis, *The Problem of Pain,* Macmillan Paperbacks Edition (New York: Macmillan, 1962), and John S. Feinberg, *The Many Faces of Evil: Theological Systems and the Problems of Evil,* rev. ed. (Wheaton, IL: Crossway Books, 2004).

106 Rom. 6:6–7, 6:11–14; Gal. 5:1

107 Heb. 2:14–15; 1 Cor. 15:16–28

108 Rom. 3:20–26, 5:6–8; 1 Tim. 2:3–6

109 Rom. 8:29; 1 John 3:2

110 2 Cor. 5:17

111 Ezek. 11:19, 36:26–27

112 Ps. 139:13

113 Gen. 3:1–7; Rom. 5:12–19

114 Matt. 4:8–9; 1 John 5:19

115 God alone is transcendent, completely *other* than everything else. As Creator, He is outside of all else (Heb. 1:10–12; Gen. 1:1; Col. 1:16). As sovereign, He has a full knowledge of what He planned (Job 42:1–2; Isa.40:22–28, 46:9–10; Jer. 29:11; Dan. 4:35; Eph. 2:10) and a full view of time (Ps. 90:2–4; 2 Pet. 3:8; Isa. 46:9–10).

116 Illustration courtesy of John Baltes, Front Range Alliance Youth Group, Front Range Church, Colorado Springs, CO, e-mail message to author, April 1, 2011.

117 G. K. Chesterton, *What's Wrong with the World?* (New York: Dodd, Mead and Co., 1910), 48.

118 James 1:25; John 8:31–36

119 1 Cor. 15:50–57; Phil. 3:20–21; 1 John 3:1–3

120 1 Cor. 6:19; Eph. 1:13–14

The Resting Place

ONE

God will speak to this people, to whom he said, "This is the resting place, let the weary rest"; and, "This is the place of repose"—but they would not listen. So then, the word of the LORD to them will become: Do and do, do and do, rule on rule, rule on rule; a little here, a little there—so that they will go and fall backward, be injured and snared and captured.
~ Isaiah 28:11b–13

I lay in bed, trying to sleep. My mind had other plans though: replaying the day's events, checking off what I'd accomplished, trying to figure out how to be more efficient tomorrow. Insomnia had become a fixture in my life. I used to think if you were tired enough, eventually your body would have no choice but to sleep. Sadly, it didn't work for me; I was constantly exhausted. My relationship with coffee had gone from enjoying an occasional cup in high school to requiring a pot or more to get through the day. I frequently joked that I needed a caffeine IV.

I decided to get up and fix some chamomile tea. Maybe writing out my list for tomorrow would let my mind relax. Thank God tomorrow was Saturday! I tripped over some toys on my way down the stairs and bit my tongue to keep from swearing. I froze. Had I awakened anyone? Silence reigned. I glared at the toy, then sighed. Tomorrow. I'll make time for housecleaning tomorrow . . . .

At least everyone else was still asleep. The one thing I loved about insomnia was the quiet. It seemed I was the only one alive in the world, blissfully free from the demands of daylight.

I grabbed the kettle, moved a stack of dirty dishes, and filled it. Tea—check. Stove on—check. I slumped against the counter and stared unseeing at the kettle.

Once brewed, I took the tea to the kitchen table and opened my folder of lists. One of the kids had a soccer game tomorrow. Or was it later today? I checked the calendar, then flipped past "Church," "School," "Work," and "Housework," until I found "Kids' Activities." I made a note to verify that her uniform had been washed.

I stared at my stack of lists. When did life get so busy? I used to be able to complete most of the things on my single to-do list. I'd never been able to finish all of them all the time. No-body's perfect, not even me. It used to be easier, though—and it will be again! This is just a stage of life we're in while the kids are young.

I finished my tea and stacked my lists, finally beginning to feel sleepy. Time to beg. Some nights it worked. Others, not so much. I wasn't sure when God was listening, or if my problems were big enough to bother, but it couldn't hurt. "God, I'm so tired. Somehow give me the energy to get through tomorrow. Please let me sleep." I laid my head down on the table while I summoned the energy to get back upstairs.

One sphere. Two spheres. Catch the third. Catch and throw. Catch and throw. Careful! If one drops, the rest will too.

I walked slowly, my eyes riveted on the spheres. My feet told me I traveled a dirt road, or a path of some sort, but I didn't have a glance to spare. From the corners of my eyes, I noticed distant trees and fields. Sunlight flashed off my spheres, bright against the blue sky. I could tell it was going to be a hot, muggy day. The motionless air smelled of dust.

It was eerily quiet. Nothing but the *thwack*, *thwack* of the spheres hitting my palms. I mentally shrugged. At least I can focus. Then someone started talking to me, but I had no time to look at him or even to listen. After a while, he seemed to take the hint.

Catch and throw. Catch and throw. Practice makes perfect. Hours later, juggling my few spheres became less difficult. The day remained hot and still, but at least clouds had rolled in, mitigating the sun's blaze.

I noticed that the spheres had names on them that corresponded with different areas of my life. As I handled them more and more, it was as though I had tuned into a strange medley of radio stations. Every time I touched a sphere, I could hear voices. The spheres began to glow brighter and brighter as I continued.

Add another. Keep practicing. Add another. Keep practicing. Add another. More and more voices. Somewhere nearby the man's voice intruded again, but I steadfastly ignored it. I had to focus. After a while, the voice left. The road, on the other hand, stretched on and on, as did the day. The sun never seemed to move.

Catch and throw. Catch and throw. Nothing mattered but the spheres I was juggling. I trudged on. Sweat beaded my face and dripped down my body. I longed for a breeze.

Catch and throw. Catch and throw. My arms screamed, and my muscles shook. The endless heat sapped my strength. My mind was numb from concentrating for so long, and my head ached from the din of all those voices kaleidoscoping through my tired brain. I shook my head. Nope. Not going to quit.

I didn't even know how many spheres I was juggling. I had been adding them as I walked, largely by instinct rather than any real desire to juggle more. If I stopped, they would all collapse, and then where would I be?

How long have I been here? Hours? Days? Years? I shook off the uncomfortable thought as it slithered into my gut. No time for thinking. Only concentrating. Only juggling.

Catch and throw. Catch and throw. I was so hot and tired and thirsty and dirty and smelly—Concentrate! Things will calm down soon. Then I can rest.

"Would you like some water?" the same voice asked. The man was probably nearby, but I couldn't risk looking for him. He seemed like a nice man, given the offer and the kindness in his voice. The thought of cool, refreshing water tantalized me. I stopped walking for a moment, so I could devote that extra bit of brain power toward deciding what to do.

"When will you rest? Will you keep juggling until you drop?"

Rest . . . . I closed my eyes for a second and imagined it. No! My eyes flew open. "No! Just until things calm down."

"What if that never happens?"

I faltered and almost dropped a sphere. What if he's right? I shook my head. What does he know anyway? Water did sound good, but what if I couldn't get all my spheres back in motion when I stopped? It wasn't worth the risk. I carefully continued down the path.

Catch and throw. Catch and throw. How much longer can I keep this up? The pain in my head was getting worse. The man's voice returned with more urgency than before, but I ignored him.

My left foot came down hard in a hole. I lost my balance. My arms windmilled as I struggled to regain my footing. The spheres fell, hitting me like a shower of fist-sized hailstones. I fell backward and cracked my head on something hard. The world went black.

I awoke with a cool cloth across my forehead and a blinding headache. My headache had been bad before, but now even breathing hurt. I breathed shallowly, trying to keep still. It didn't seem to matter. The pain pounded relentlessly against my consciousness. I moaned, wishing I could pass out again, or throw up, or something—anything to feel better. At least whatever I lay on felt soft, and the room was dimly lit.

I heard footsteps in the hall outside. Someone must have heard my faint groan, or maybe it hadn't been that faint. I could barely hear past the roaring in my ears and the *thud, thud* of the pain in my head. And then I knew that I was going to vomit, regardless of whether or not it would make me feel better. I pulled the cloth off and leaned weakly over the side of the bed.

A man hastened in to hold a wash basin in front of me. I managed to vomit into it despite my wavering vision. He set the basin down and gently wiped my mouth. "Would you like a drink?" he asked. I instantly recognized his voice as the man from the road.

"Yes," I croaked. My mouth tasted awful. He settled me back in bed, then dribbled water into my mouth with a spoon. I swallowed feebly. "Where am I?"

"You're at my workshop. You hit your head."

"I remember," I said, though the memory was a little hazy. All at once I realized my hands were empty. "My spheres!" I exclaimed, sitting up. Bad move. The sudden, violent movement caused the pain to explode like a bomb inside my skull. I groaned.

"Lay back," the man said as he gently resituated me. "I brought your spheres too. If you still want them, you can have them when you're strong enough." He laid a cool, work-hardened hand against my forehead. "Rest now. We can talk later." He took the basin and left.

I lay there in the semi-darkness, wondering about this strange place. After a while, I must have fallen asleep. When I awoke, it was still mostly dark. My head ached, though now I could shift it without overwhelming pain. I looked around. The small room had space for little more than the bed. A dirt floor, wooden walls, and a slanted wooden ceiling all made me feel like I had been transported into a pioneer shanty. A rough wooden table stood next to my bed, and opaque cloth covered the only window. Perhaps the man had darkened it in consideration for my injury.

I must have made some noise, because the man peeked into the room. "How do you feel?" he asked, his eyes mirroring the concern in his voice.

"Better than earlier."

"Do you think you can manage some broth?"

"Maybe." I worried my stomach would rebel.

"Then I'll be right back," he said and closed the door behind him. Moments later, he returned with a steaming bowl of broth on a tray. He set it down on the little table, then grabbed some extra pillows out of a wooden chest at the foot of the bed.

"All right, nice and easy. Don't rush." He carefully propped me up with the pillows. The room swam a bit, but that seemed to be the worst of it. He spoon-fed me as though I were a helpless baby. I thought about protesting, but my arms felt like lead. My pride was already smarting—I didn't need to pour broth all over myself in addition.

So I docilely ate my broth. I could only manage half a bowl. "I'm done now, thank you. It was delicious," I said, my voice still rusty with disuse.

"You're welcome." He set the bowl back on the table. We repeated the laborious process of getting my fatigued body situated. I could barely keep my eyes open. "Call me if you need anything," he said, taking the bowl and leaving. I'm not sure if I said anything in reply; I might have fallen asleep before he even made it out the door.

I awoke again, this time in pitch black. I ached all over, though my head felt increasingly better. I lay there thinking about my spheres: Would everything fall apart without me, or, even worse, would things continue on without a hitch?

I pushed the thought away and tried to think about other things. I landed on the man as a safe subject.

Who is he? What kind of work does he do? Why did he talk to me in the first place?

My face burned as I remembered how I had ignored him. Yet he had rescued me. He could have left me on the road, but instead he was sheltering and caring for me. I didn't know if I would have done the same thing if our positions were reversed. And His questions . . . .

When will I rest? How many spheres do I have to juggle to merit a break? What if things never calm down?

Perhaps this wasn't a safe topic after all. It was making my headache worse. I rolled over and tried to get comfortable. If I quieted my body, maybe my mind would follow.

Why was that blasted hole in the road anyway? I had been happy, content with my carefree juggling as I traveled . . . except of course for being so weary, and hot, and thirsty, and having a headache, and having to listen and cater to all those demanding voices from my spheres . . . and not being able to drown out the niggling sense that I wanted more out of life.

Argh! Why couldn't I just think about something less confusing and stressful? Think about wood. There's lots of it around. Wood. Wood. Wood. Eventually, I fell back to sleep and dreamt of wooden balls with faces chasing me and demanding I juggle them.

When I woke up, daylight peeked around the edges of the curtains. I felt better, though still sore and about as strong as a limp noodle. We repeated the events of the previous day: I slept and ached in bed, endeavoring to push disturbing thoughts out of my brain; the man checked on me, ready with water and broth.

As I tossed and turned, I couldn't help grappling with this concept of rest. I felt exhausted, though obviously not as much as some people would have been if they had been in my shoes. If only I could get things aligned in my spheres, then I could rest while juggling. Or at least maybe I could take short breaks, or a long vacation every couple years to recharge.

Why did the man suggest that things might never calm down? Everyone knows that life has cycles—sometimes you're busy and sometimes not so much. I'm in a busy time. So what?

The next time he came in, I voiced my question. "Why did you ask when I would rest? Doesn't rest just come naturally in the ebb and flow of life?"

He sat down on the stool by my bed. "That depends. What do you mean by 'rest'?"

"Well, what did *you* mean?" I countered, not prepared to answer.

He leaned back against the wall and stretched his legs out. "I asked you first," he said with a smile.

"Okay. Um, I guess when I think of rest, I think of a vacation, or a break of some sort."

"So you're saying rest is the absence of work?"

"Right."

"Do you feel rested now? You're not juggling."

Was that a question I wanted to answer? I weighed my options. "No, not really."

"Why is that?"

"Too much time on my hands?" I began pleating the blanket. "I feel restless, antsy to get away from my thoughts. I need a distraction."

"So in order to rest, you have to take a break from labor *and* from burdensome thoughts?"

"Maybe . . . ."

"Almost sounds like you're waiting for death to find rest," the man said, laughter lurking in his eyes.

"Why do you say that?"

"Is there another time in the normal course of your life when you won't have any worries or activities?"

I smiled airily. "You never know. I could become independently wealthy. My financial worries would be over, and I could simply pay people to take care of things for me."

"Right," he said sardonically. "First, you would have more 'financial worries' than you do now, because you would have a lot more financial choices to make. Second, how boring to pay other people to live your life for you."

I frowned at the blanket. "I suppose you have a point."

"Anyway, if it's based on circumstances, can anyone truly rest while they're still alive?"

"What do you mean?"

"I mean, can any human ever control external factors—their circumstances—well enough to bring internal rest?"

"I don't know. I've never thought about it that way."

He hopped off the stool and pulled a book out of the chest at the foot of the bed, then opened it. "Here, look at it like this." The page depicted a two-tiered fountain on it.

I squinted at it. Was the illustration getting bigger? All at once the picture swelled, filling up my vision.

My bed and I now sat on a terrace beside the fountain. The sun shone brightly, and birdsong filled the air. The grass surrounding the terrace glowed, like a day in late spring. The man remained sitting next to me, still holding his book. The page now displayed a picture of the empty bedroom. We had traded places like Alice through the Looking Glass.[121] I blinked at the book. After all, I had spheres that acted like radios. Why not a simulated-reality device disguised as a book? The man touched my arm and I realized he'd been talking.

"I'm sorry—I was distracted. What did you say?"

He smiled. "That's all right. I just wanted to draw your attention to the fountain."

I studied it. It seemed like a pretty standard fountain. The top tier was smaller than the bottom. It looked like water would come up through a pipe in the center, fill the top basin, and then cascade out into the bottom. The fountain was off, and the top tier appeared empty. The bottom tier, however, had been filled about three-quarters of the way.

A young man came dashing up the three steps to the terrace carrying a bucket of water. He wore round glasses, and his dark hair hung lank. His slacks and collared shirt had seen better days. A ragged beard completed the general unkemptness of his appearance. He poured the contents into the bottom tier, then ran back down. An overflow drain kept the water level from rising.

"Hello, Saul," my rescuer called after him.

The young man seemed only vaguely aware of our presence. He moved out of my field of vision, but reappeared shortly, carrying another bucket of water. He dumped it into the fountain as well, then hurled himself back down the stairs. "No time, no time," he muttered in our direction as he left. Carroll's white rabbit immediately came to mind.[122]

I looked up at the man. "What's he doing?"

"He's trying to fill the top tier," he said, as though it should have been obvious.

"Oh . . . but how will filling up the bottom help? It doesn't somehow spill up into the top, does it?"

He shook his head. "No, it doesn't."

"Oh. Well, I guess he'll figure it out eventually."

"Perhaps. Saul's been working on it for quite some time."

"How long?"

"Years."

My stomach twisted at the poor man's plight. Gravity and the overflow drain meant he could spend the rest of his life on this impossible endeavor. "Hasn't anyone tried to tell him? You obviously know him—why haven't you stopped him?"

"Oh, I've informed him, but he's not a very good listener while he's working, and he never stops. Kind of like someone else we know."

I blushed. Just watching the young man run up and down with his bucket tired me out. I hoped I hadn't looked that frantic.

"So what is this fountain? Does it really exist?" I asked.

"What do you mean 'really exist'?"

"I mean, does it exist in the physical world?"

He raised an eyebrow. "Do your spheres?"

"Of course."

All of the sudden I remembered my normal life. Where am I? How will I get home? What about my lists?

Then I remembered my insomnia and exhaustion. I took deep calming breaths and tried to reassure myself: this was probably all a dream, a way for my subconscious to wrestle through my recent busyness. I wish my brain had used this dream on something nicer, like a vacation in Tahiti.

I shifted. "Actually, I suppose if you want to get technical you could say they're representations of something in the physical world."

He looked at me piercingly. "Like lists?"

What in the world? *Is* this a dream?

He pointed to the fountain. "This fountain is also a representation."

"Of what?" I asked, schooling my features into apparent interest.

"The bottom tier represents the external factors in Saul's life. The top tier is his internal reality. Like you, he believes that if he can control enough of his external factors, it will translate into internal fullness: satisfaction and rest."

"Maybe he's just trying to control the wrong external factors," I said. Since this was just a metaphor, one couldn't assume it applied universally, right?

"What do you think he should focus on?"

I shrugged. "We all have things we control. Otherwise, we wouldn't be able to change our environment."

"I think you're mistaking influence for control, but even then, the list is pretty short."

My chin came up. "Are you sure?"

"Well, if we're going to discuss environments, what about yours? Can you control the weather?[123] Or did you decide when you would be born?[124] Or pick your family? Can you control what the people around you do? What about other creatures? Or time? Or even your own thoughts or tongue?"[125]

I squirmed. I knew he had just landed a facer, but I was loathe to acknowledge the hit. "Speaking of rest and environments, I think I'm ready for a nap. Can we change our environment?"

He smiled knowingly. I could tell that he knew what I was up to and was letting me get away with it. "All right." With that we were back in the bedroom. "Have a nice nap," he said on his way out the door.

I tried to find a comfortable position and to keep my mind blank enough to sleep. Maybe talking to the man hadn't been one of my better ideas.

TWO

After a restless night, I decided I was desperate for a distraction. Since this place was short on distractions, the man was my only prospect. I'd just have to steer the conversation carefully, very carefully.

As he was carrying me back from the outhouse, I looked around, scrounging for a harmless topic. I couldn't see much because the outhouse had been built on the back side of the house, which from here looked like a small wooden shanty. The size didn't exactly tally with my perception of the interior, but I'd never been very good with eyeball measurements.

"So what do you do here?" I asked.

"I'm a carpenter."

"Did you build this place?"

"I did, though I don't usually build a lot of houses."

"What do you build?"

He studied me. "Do you feel up to sitting for a bit?"

"I think so, at least for a while. I'm getting tired of that bed—though it's a lovely bed," I added, hoping I hadn't offended him.

He chuckled. "Then would you like to see my latest project?"

"Sure!" I smiled back.

He carried me through the interior hallway, past my room, then opened another door. The smell of newly-cut lumber greeted us as he stepped into the workshop.

It was much, much larger than I had imagined possible. Fresh wood shavings covered the floor, although I had the impression he was the type of guy to sweep up every night. Tools hung on various nails and hooks. Huge windows let in plenty of light. Potted plants dotted the room. The floor was dirt, but the walls had been sanded and stained a golden honey color. I imagined it felt light and cozy, even on the darkest of days.

Several split logs lay in one corner. They reminded me of the sort used for dugout canoes. Squarish beams of various sizes were arranged in another area. Large wooden sticks had been tied to a wooden frame, trapping them in a U-shape. Further in, I saw a couple of beams, rounded and smoothed. Heavy iron hoops hung from one wall, like the links of a giant chain.

He settled me in a rocking chair with some pillows, then held up something like a wooden beam. "This is what I'm currently working on." I could tell he had done some carving and shaping, but I had absolutely no idea what it was.

"Very nice," I ventured, then curiosity won out over pride. "But what is it?"

He smiled. "It's a yoke."

"A yoke? What's it for?"

"Well, a yoke is a device that's used to harness an animal or animals to something. It enables them to bear a load, like a plow or a wagon."[126]

I lost interest immediately. "Oh, I see. What else do you make?"

"Well, right now yokes are the main thing." His eyes lit up. "It's a fascinating and challenging job. Those other pieces of wood are in various stages of being steamed, or dried, or shaped for different yokes. There are different types, you know. Even within those types it's important to create each yoke specifically for the creature that will be using it."

"Why?" I asked, his enthusiasm piquing my interest even if the topic did not.

"Because no two burden-bearers are alike. If the yoke isn't fit exactly to them, it can cause injury."

"How so?"

"Well, look here," he said, pulling a book off a low shelf in the corner. He grabbed a stool and sat down next to me.

As he opened the book, a gust of dusty wind blew out of it. I braced myself for the rushing picture. Instead, without any sensation of movement, I found myself sitting in the middle of a prairie. Hot, gritty wind ruffled my hair. The sun beat down on us. The man and his stool remained next to me.

He pointed. "See those oxen?"

To my left, several yards away, stood a yoked team of oxen hitched to a cart full of supplies. "They're, um, very nice," I said.

"These are some of mine. They have an individualized yoke and burden. I'll drive them around so you can see."

"Wait! How do I know what to look for?" I shouted, as he walked over to the oxen.

"Don't worry about it. Just watch." He gave the oxen a quick pat before getting into the cart and taking the reins. "Easy girls," he said, as they fairly quivered. He drove them around in a circle a few times. They walked quickly, pulling as though the cart weighed little. It seemed like the yoke fit, though I had no clue how a proper yoke should fit—like this one, supposedly. The man stopped the cart in front of me. "What do you think?"

I tried to come up with something intelligent to say—not an easy task when one is totally ignorant of the subject in question. "They seem to enjoy your driving," I finally said.

"Yes, they're a good team, well-trained. Do you see where the yoke beam is sitting?" he asked, jumping down from the cart and walking up to the oxen.

I studied the contraption, then nodded. The wide beam rested on the oxen's necks with curved U-shaped pieces passing under their necks to secure them in place.

"Did you notice what part of their body they're using to pull the cart?"

"Well, it looked like they used their necks to push on the beam and their shoulders to push those U-shaped pieces."

"Very good. Those U-shaped pieces are called 'bows.' We'll make a yoke expert out of you yet," he said with a grin.

I smiled back. I may not have wanted to be a "yoke expert," but I was definitely not opposed to basking in approval.

"I'm going to borrow someone else's team now. See if you can spot some differences," he said as he sprang back into the cart. I looked around for another team of oxen or a barn. Instead, he drove to a sort of door frame: two posts set in the ground with a third post across the top. I watched in amazement as he passed through the doorway, becoming invisible for a moment. He emerged with a new team hitched to the same cart. Both oxen were larger than the previous ones.

I studied them, interested in spite of myself. I was enthralled by this man's magnetic intensity, by the passion and care he had for such an inconsequential object. I wanted to understand what he found so significant about yokes.

There were differences in the second team. The first team had stepped cheerfully, keeping up a much faster pace than I had expected. This team plodded, dragging their feet, straining to pull the weight of the cart, despite their larger size. They also held their heads differently, though I couldn't quite pinpoint how. More still or stiffly, perhaps?

The man drove the oxen around a bit, then stopped them in front of me as before and hopped out. When he asked what I had observed, I filled him in and asked why the oxen held their heads differently. "Look at the yoke beam," he said, "Do you see how narrow the wood is?"

I examined it, trying to recall how wide the other beam had been. This one did appear thinner. I still didn't see why that mattered and told him so.

"It means that the weight from the full cart is on a smaller surface area of their necks," he said. "It takes more work to pull the same weight. They're tired, unnecessarily overworked by the wrong yoke."

"I see. Is that why they don't move as much?"

"Partly. Look at the bows." He pointed to the U-shaped pieces. "They're not properly fitted to these oxen."

"How can you tell?" I craned my neck, but still couldn't see any difference.

"Well, look at this one," he said, putting a hand on the closest. "It's too tight." As he slid his hand between beast and bow, I realized the bow left little room for the ox's neck. "It's chaffing this steer, pinching and rubbing, like a too-small shoe. If left untreated, the injury will get worse. Eventually, the ox won't work in the yoke anymore. He could end up permanently burned out."

I had recently dealt with ill-fitting shoes and blisters. When I had to wear them I didn't want to do anything either. "Poor ox," I murmured.

"Indeed. It's not worth the lesser amount of work they can accomplish in this yoke." He patted the oxen, then crouched down in front of me. "They need rest: a short break from work while they heal up. But, more importantly, they need the rest of a new yoke."

I blinked at him. "I suppose that's true."

He looked at me intently, as though measuring his next words. "If they keep using this yoke, they'll never be the creatures they were trained to be, created to be."

"It does seem like that yoke is preventing them from functioning well," I said, confused by his intensity. "Wait a minute! I thought rest was an internal state. You just linked it to an external reality."

He returned to his stool. "That's because this external reality gives us a picture of the internal reality. Internal yokes are just as real as internal rest."[127]

"I see . . . . I'm just glad I'm not an ox." I said, staring thoughtfully at the team.

"Why's that?"

"I'd rather not wear a yoke, thanks anyway. I like being free." I said, surprised it wasn't obvious.

He quirked a smile at me. "Only God is free."[128]

"I'm free!"

"Oh really?"

"Well, I'm no one's slave, if that's what you mean. Nobody makes me work myself to exhaustion. I go where I want, when I want."

He raised his eyebrows.

"What? You don't believe me?"

"Well, those spheres of yours seemed to work you pretty hard. I don't think you realize how spent you were."

"It is true that I'm a hard worker," I agreed piously.

"And why did you say you work so hard?"

"Because I take pride in what I do."

"Okay, but why?"

I thought about it for a moment. "I suppose because it's what I've been taught. I don't know how many times I was told, 'If it's worth doing, it's worth doing well.' I can still hear that in my head every time I even think about doing something halfway."

"All right, if that saying is true, how do you know when you've done 'well'?"

"Because I feel like I've done well. I guess that goes back to the standards I've been taught."

"So you're trying to fulfill standards set up by other humans? You're trying to keep all those voices satisfied?"

My eyes narrowed. Did he know how my spheres acted like radios? Maybe he wanted them for himself.

"Where are my spheres?" I demanded, even while part of my mind informed me I was being ridiculous. If he had wanted to steal them, he could have just done it and left me on the road.

He sighed. "They're in a safe."

"May I have them?" I asked, doing my best to keep my tone even.

"I'm not sure you're up to that yet."

"I really want them," I insisted sweetly, trying not to clench my teeth.

"All right." He slowly picked up the book, then closed it. Immediately we were back in the workshop. He walked over to a low cabinet on the interior wall and opened the door. A high-tech safe was inside, complete with keypad and thumbprint scanner. It appeared so utterly out of place that I felt the comfortable security I had developed here slipping away. The man pulled out a lumpy bag and re-locked the safe. He held it in front of him, as though it contained a live snake.

My heart began to race. My palms ached for the caress of the smooth, glossy spheres. I imagined the peace and rejoicing that would follow once hand and spheres had been reunited. It would probably even do my body good. They say a positive attitude can promote healing.[129]

He set the bag down on the stool so I could reach it. I put my hand in and pulled out a sphere. Instantly, I heard the clamor of a strident voice: "How could you leave me for so long? I bet you didn't even think about me. What's wrong with you? You're so lazy!" As I lifted the sphere off the stool, I almost dropped it. My muscles strained under its weight. My head hurt more and more as the voice continued berating me. The sphere flickered feebly.

Maybe he was right.

I put the sphere back into the bag. Blessed quiet followed. My arms shook. I felt exhausted, as though the sphere had somehow drained my small reserve of energy.

"I think I will rest for a bit longer," I said shakily. "Will you take me back to bed, please?"

He eyed the bag of spheres. "Where would you like me to put these?"

"Do you mind putting them back in the safe?"

"Not at all," he said and shoved them in.

I tried to sleep, but my mind kept racing. I had the feeling that all his talk of yokes had been somehow significant, if only I knew the key. My head ached, reminding me of the recent criticism from the sphere. Why even bother? Could I ever do enough? What if juggling is a waste of time?—No, it's important!

I tossed and turned, drifting in and out of sleep as the questions whirled in my brain until they no longer even made sense. Finally, I gave up on sleep. I scooted into a sitting position and massaged my aching temples. Maybe since this mysterious carpenter seemed to give voice to my inner dissatisfaction, I just needed to talk about it more with him. If I could persuade him that juggling was important, maybe my doubts would be laid to rest, and I could return to my life. It certainly made sense. Therefore, the first step was to marshal my own arguments. Then I could get him to talk with me. Once I'd convinced him—voilà! Good sleep, and then back to my old life.

I frowned. What were my arguments anyway? Yes, the voices disturbed me, pushed me, and often criticized. No denying that. But I accomplished more with them than I ever would have alone. How dare he disapprove of my juggling! Had he seen the size of that bag?

Plus, with my spheres I was never alone. Lots of people complained of loneliness. They just needed to channel their complaining energy into accomplishing something—like I'd done with my spheres of influence. I was significant. Needed. They missed me. It warmed the cockles of my heart to know they had noticed my absence.

A knock sounded, and I jumped.

"Come in."

The man entered, carrying another steaming bowl. "I brought you some more broth."

"Thank you," I said, hoping my arguments had been sufficiently marshaled. When I had finished the broth, I cautiously introduced my topic: "Thank you for keeping my spheres safe."

"You're welcome."

"I got the impression that . . . you don't like them?"

His face hardened. "No, I don't like them."

"I don't think you understand how helpful they've been to me."

"Really? How so? By sucking you dry? Or the perpetual negativity of some? I can see how both those things would definitely enrich the quality of your life."

"They are a lot of work, but they give me purpose. Some of them tend to be hard on me, but look what I've accomplished! If they hadn't been pushing me so hard, I'd never have juggled this many. I used to struggle with just two spheres. Now I can do so many more than that."

"And why is that a good thing?" he asked.

"What?"

He put a hand on the bed. "Suppose instead of juggling, your job was to dig. Every day you dug and dug. Your goal was to dig a hole five feet long, five feet wide, and five feet deep. After you finished it, you had to fill it back in with the exact same dirt you removed. Eventually you got good enough to dig multiple holes a day. But would it matter how good a digger you were if you never accomplished anything? Think about Saul. Is his work meaningful?"

I straightened. "How can you compare juggling to digging or to Saul? My work is much more rewarding and meaningful than that!"

The man leaned forward. "Is it? Is it meaningful to wear an ill-fitting yoke that sucks the life out of you?"

"I told you—I don't wear a yoke. I'm free!"

"And I told you: only God is free. Look at the way you craved those spheres—how you snatch the crumbs of attention they throw you and try to feed your need for approval and love. Attention is not love!" he thundered, towering over me even though he still sat. "Don't you know that you become the slave of anyone whose approval you seek?"[130] He rubbed a hand across his brow. "Everyone wears a yoke. It's part of the human condition. You can only decide whose yoke you'll wear.[131] And I'm telling you that the yoke you're wearing right now is wearing you out. It doesn't fit properly. And to add insult to injury, you're not even bearing the right load. Can't you see? Don't you realize how spent you were?"

I felt like I was drowning in the onslaught of his words, mostly because they resonated with something deep inside me. I fought to find something to grapple with, something to dispute, something to silence the traitorous part of me that agreed with him.

"I'm not spent!" The man snorted, and I took a firm hold on the blankets. "Okay, it's taken me a couple of days to recover, but I wouldn't be in this condition if someone had marked the stupid hole in the road!"

"A couple of days? You've been here for over a week."

"Over a week?" I shook my head slowly. There was the day I woke up, and then the day after that when we saw Saul, and then today, which was not going so well. "I count three days. Not over a week."

"Three days you were conscious. You were so dehydrated and exhausted—not to mention that head injury—that you were delirious for the first five days. Tell me that doesn't indicate you had been sucked dry."

"Again, I say if the road had been marked, I wouldn't be here, trespassing on your precious hospitality!"

"The road was marked! I even warned you about the hole, but you were too enthralled with your spheres to listen."

I looked down at the bed. I couldn't argue, because I had no idea what he'd said before. He was right; I hadn't listened.

We sat in silence, as the uncomfortable moments stretched on. "I'm going to go take care of a couple things now," the man said at last. "In all your thinking, start asking yourself if you're truly content. How do you feel about juggling for the rest of your life, even if things never 'calm down'? Now that you know how draining your spheres are, consider if you want to keep obeying them. Ask yourself if you ever want true rest." He took the empty bowl and left.

I glared after him. Right. Trying to convince the dissatisfied part of me that I'm content is how I got myself into this conversation! The man's words had only lit a fire under that portion of my soul.

I sagged against the wall. Is my work pointless, purposeless? Do I ever really accomplish anything, or am I simply digging and refilling endless holes? What *am* I trying to accomplish? My only measure of how well I was doing was the number of spheres I juggled, a number of which I didn't even keep track.

I suddenly realized that if my goal was to satisfy all the voices, I might never reach it. I could sometimes please some of my spheres, but only at the expense of the others' well-being. "Aesop's right," I muttered. "'Please all and you will please none.'"[132]

And I rarely made a quality difference in my spheres, even though I poured so much of myself into them. I was always struggling to keep up, to catch up, running around putting out one fire after another. Did I really want to spend the rest of my life that way?

I had a sudden, awful picture of my life: the juggling stretching on for years upon years, and with it, the indefinable yearning and perpetual exhaustion. It was all right for a short time, while things were less settled in my spheres, but what if things never calmed down? What if rest was just the proverbial carrot at the end of a stick? What if I ended up like Saul, so pre-occupied that I couldn't see the truth?

Years from now, would I still be refusing to take a break? Was it worth it? That was the crux of the matter: Was I laboring in vain? I was willing to sacrifice for something significant. But how can I know if something is truly significant?

The question echoed in my brain, growing stronger. I pushed it back for the time being. I was getting quite good at that since coming here. But it was getting more and more difficult.

I needed someone to help me, to reason it out with me. I felt that if I didn't get these questions settled, I might go crazy. I wanted the man to come back, though the idea terrified me. What if the part of me that hated juggling grew strong enough to take over? Where would I be then? At least I wouldn't be stuck in this awful limbo. I just wanted to get back to living my life, whatever that looked like.

THREE

Just when I thought I would drown in my confusion, the man knocked on my door. I invited him in, and he sat down on the stool next to me. "Ready to talk some more?"

"Yes. Maybe. I don't know."

He scooted the stool closer. "You sound confused. What's going on?"

"I don't know. I never questioned my life before. I just followed the path that seemed right to me."[133] I sighed. "Part of me hates juggling and never wants to go back. But part of me loves it, even though it's hard. I do long for rest. But I'm not even sure what rest looks like, or if it even exists in the real world."

"Well, as you said, you've already proved in your time here that external inactivity doesn't always translate into internal rest. What do you think internal rest looks like?"

"Peace, maybe? Not having such stressful thoughts or struggling to figure out what's important. They wear me out even when my circumstances don't."

"It sounds like you're saying rest comes from not needing to prove your own worth, not having to worry or wonder about the significance of what you're doing."

"Right."

He leaned back against the wall, once more looking as relaxed as a cat. "So did you decide if rest is a state you can attain while you're juggling?"

The question, along with his laid back manner, irritated me. This man was the most rest-full person I had ever met. It simultaneously fascinated me and repulsed me. I surreptitiously studied him, trying to decide what exactly it was about him that exuded the peace I so desperately desired.

"Well, I can't find rest with things so hectic in my spheres."

"I thought we'd already established that true rest isn't dependent on circumstances."

"Oh, right. In that case, whether I juggle or not has nothing to do with it," I said, sure I'd won my right to continue juggling.

"Unless juggling causes you to neglect the things that can give you true rest."

"Huh?"

He straightened. "Let's say you're getting ready to eat something. You have a limited appetite so you can only pick one selection. On one plate there are doughnuts, or something else equally nutritionally deficient, and on the other there are vegetables, fruit, and some steak. You can't eat both. The first will appease your hunger, but it won't satisfy your body's needs. The second may be less appealing in light of the first, but it'll nourish you. Juggling promises to meet your internal needs but fails to deliver. It masks the true need by appearing to meet it."

I mulled over that concept for a while. "I guess I can see that," I said rather begrudgingly. "I suppose if it was really providing what I needed, I wouldn't be so dissatisfied and confused."

He smiled "Very astute. Would you go so far as to say juggling chafes at your soul?"

"Are we back to the yoke thing?"

"Why does that bother you so much?" he asked, his face alight with concerned interest.

"I can run my own life better than anyone else."

"I can see that." His eyes sparkled. "I'm sure you fell in that hole intentionally, so you could have a nice break."

"What are you getting at? That was an accident. They happen to everyone."

"True. They are unforeseeable to anyone within the bounds of time," he said.

Did I just give away a point?

He sobered. "Is there a reason you don't want someone else 'running your life'?"

"I've had some very bad experiences with people running my ship aground when I've given up control." Just the possibility of yet another repeat made me leery. Some might say I was a paranoid control freak. The way I saw it, I was just someone who had finally gotten wise.

"It is wise to avoid giving power to those who will abuse it, but haven't you just traded one bad situation for another?" He asked.

I tensed. "How so?"

"Your spheres. Don't they abuse their power over you?"

"They don't force me to do anything I don't want to."

"But they take your time and energy, making it impossible for you to find true rest. They tell you what to do, and you do it because you've made them your master. *They* run your life, not you."

With those words, I flashed back to the yoked oxen. It hit me like a ton of bricks. My spheres did hold the reins. I was letting a myriad of conflicting voices pull me in as many different directions. I sat there dumbly, overwhelmed by the sudden paradigm shift. It had advanced in small degrees, but his words had been the final shove. It was a lot to take in. How had I gotten myself back into a situation with someone else running my life? I clenched my fists, trying to keep from crying.

He laid a hand on my arm. "So what are you going to do?"

I looked up at him, my eyes straining to focus. "Do? Do about what?"

"Your spheres. Are you going to keep that yoke or find another master who can provide rest?"

I shook my head slowly. "I don't know. I have no idea how to go about finding another master in general, let alone one who can give me rest."

"If you don't intentionally choose someone else, you'll either return to your current master or slide into another bad situation.[134] You know that, right?"

"Yes," I whispered.

"It's not something to be ashamed of," he said gently. "Again, the need for a master, for a God, is just part of being human.[135] Would you like a suggestion?"

"Okay," I said, still numb as I sat amongst the shattered pieces of my former reality. Then hope flared as I realized this man might actually have an answer. If anyone would know something about a restful master, it would be him: the yokemaker who exuded peace.

"Take my yoke upon you. It's an easy yoke and my burden is light. Acknowledge me as your master."[136]

"What?" Did I miss something? I suddenly realized that, in my preoccupation with my own situation, I had never gotten around to asking his name.

"What about one of my yokes?" he repeated.

My cheeks burned. "Who are you?"

"Jesus."

It made perfect sense. In fact, it was the piece that illuminated the whole. How did I miss that? I simply hadn't expected to meet Jesus here—or anywhere, for that matter. In fact, it had been quite a while since I had spent much time with Him. My face continued to radiate embarrassment. "I'm sorry."

"For what?"

I looked down at the bed. "For ignoring You before. For being so focused on myself."

Jesus moved to sit on the bed, and I looked up at Him. "I'm[137] sorry too. I hated to see you suffering." I held His gaze for a moment and found only compassion at my plight. There was none of the scorn and condemnation I had expected to see.

Maybe that's part of why He exudes rest: He's so comfortable in His own skin. I had rejected Him, but He felt no need to prove me wrong, at least not for the purpose of feeding His ego.[138] Yet He didn't just let the incident go, either. My pride, on the other hand, had been dealt a severe blow. Things were changing so fast I felt as though I couldn't find any ground to stand on. In fact, I was starting to feel panicked.

"Take a deep breath." He inhaled and exhaled slowly. "Focus. Let's just finish this conversation."

"Okay." I took several deep breaths. Then grasping at whatever straws were about, I asked the first question that came to mind. "So what are Your yokes like? What's the difference between my juggling and Your yoke?"

"Well, how do your spheres function?"

"In what way?"

"Is there a lead sphere that runs the others, or is it just a cacophony of voices, all vying for your attention?"

I grimaced. I didn't even have to think about that one. Just the word "cacophony" instantly reminded me of the perpetual headache I had acquired from so many conflicting instructions.

"I can see by the look on your face that it's the latter," He said. "So how do you think it might be different with My yoke?"

"I guess if it's Your yoke, there'd only be Your voice, right?"

"That's right.[139] Can you see some potential pros and cons to having only one master?"

I smiled ruefully. "Fewer headaches."

He nodded. "At least ones caused by lots of yelling. What else?"

"Um, no struggling to sort through conflicting information and pick the right path. Just listening to Your instructions."

"Do you think that works with any single master or just with Me?"

I stared at the blanket. What if my single master was as ignorant of the road ahead as I was? Or what if the person found it humorous to watch me fall or led me into bad situations? Or what if they didn't know me well enough to know what I really should be doing?

Jesus smiled. "Those are all good thoughts. You're right. You need someone who isn't limited by space or time, so they can always see the road ahead. Then they can know which things are truly significant, and which only appear significant at the time. And you need someone who's good, who loves you, and who always wants your best. They need to know you inside and out. Otherwise, how will they know what's in your best interest?"

"That makes sense . . . but—" I gulped, "how do I know *You're* those things?"

"How do you know anything?"

"Um, by observing, doing my own research, or finding a reliable source?"

"How can you tell if a person is a reliable source?"

My brow wrinkled. "Maybe by watching for a while to see if their actions match up with their words. Testing their words against reality."

"You can also check their track record with other people. Of course, it's hard if everyone's reliability is suspect."

"True," I said, my head whirling. I decided to cling to my previous question until I had an answer I could understand. "So how do I know You're outside of time and space, good and loving, and that You know me?"

"Think of it like testing the ice on a skating pond.[140] First, you do some research to find out the proper equations. For instance, you find out how many inches thick the ice has to be to hold your weight. Then you get a hatchet and a ruler and go measure the ice's thickness. Then maybe you talk to some other people who are approximately the same weight as you and have been out on the ice. You've collected data: the odds are that it will hold you. But you still can't definitively answer the question, 'Will this ice hold me?' until you test your hypothesis. So based on the 90% of the puzzle you've got filled in, you step out on the ice in faith."

I blinked at Him. "Faith? I thought faith was blind."

He shook His head. "No, faith is taking action on the information you have, once you've collected a reasonable amount. It's not foolishness."[141]

"So how does that play into this situation?"

"Do you have enough data to start putting together the puzzle? Can you begin to form a picture of who We are?"

"Well, You've treated me kindly so far, and You did rescue me from my sins, but what about those other things? And how do I know You won't change tomorrow?"

"Study Our Word and Our actions through history.[142] You've talked to other people who've been on the ice. Take as much action as you can with what you know so far. Sometimes you can't see further until"—He mounded up a bit of the blanket and walked two fingers up to the top—"you take a step forward.[143] And as you're sifting through information, ask for help from the One who's transcendent and able to recognize the truth—that would be Us."[144]

"What about tomorrow?"

He was clearly unoffended by the question. "We're not bound by time, remember?[145] We're the same every day."[146]

His words helped, but I still wanted more data. "So Your yoke has a different master. What else?"

He stretched, then asked, "Did you notice that your sphere flickered when you held it last time? Does it normally do that?"

I shifted in bed, trying to adjust to the abrupt subject change. "No, normally they glow the whole time I juggle them."

"Where do you suppose they get the energy to do that?"

I stared at the wall. I'd never even considered that question. "Well, I guess it can't be from friction since the ball flickered when I held it still."

"Do they ever glow on their own?"

"No, only when I'm juggling or holding them . . . ." I frowned. "It must somehow be from me. That's what You've been talking about when You say they're 'sucking me dry,' isn't it?"

"Exactly. They're like lightbulbs. They need a power source, and right now they're feeding off your energy—physical, mental, emotional, and spiritual."

"So what's different about Your yoke?"

"You have My Spirit inside you. He powers My yoke."[147]

"Are You serious? You mean it won't exhaust me?"

"Does it exhaust your children when they cling to your legs?"[148]

"No. Sometimes they get tired from hanging on, but I'm the one who does all the work, so I'm the one who gets exhausted."

"Right. It is work to cling to Me,[149] to stay yoked to Me, especially since you've been attempting to control things. It takes work to submit. But, as long as you keep My yoke on and stay connected to My Spirit, it won't exhaust you."

Just the thought of expending someone else's energy made me feel giddy.

"It'll take some time to practice using that connection,"[150] He cautioned.

Like air from a punctured balloon, my excitement drained away. "Why?"

"Because you're broken. Because any time you do something outside of what We tell you to do, it'll interrupt the connection.[151] And there's still a part of you that wants to be your own master or choose someone else as your master."

I knew He was right—if inactivity hadn't forced me to pay attention to my longing for true rest, I probably would have continued to ignore Him. I would have kept juggling.

"Would I have to give up juggling forever?" I asked.

"Do you want to?"

"Yes. No." I tried to find words to explain my ambivalence. "Some of it I love. I love the challenge and the sense of accomplishment—seeing people and situations change for the better. I love that sometimes I feel so useful and important. But I hate being so exhausted all the time." My jaw clenched. "I hate feeling put down and abused by some of my spheres. I hate feeling taken for granted!"

He stroked my hand. "There's good news and good news. Which would you like to hear first?"

"The good news?" I said.

"Most of the things you love about juggling are because it allows you to touch the edges of who We created you to be.[152] You hate other things about it because it's an ill-fitting yoke that prevents you from being the person We created you to be."

"So if I take Your yoke, I still get to fulfill those parts of me that were fulfilled in juggling?"

"Right, and you won't be hampered by the yoke. Instead, you'll be hooking all those things up to Our power. You have enough energy to light up some spheres, but We have enough energy to power everything in the universe simultaneously, without even breaking a sweat."[153]

"Wow," I blurted. I'd been barely plodding along, but if I took Jesus' yoke, I would be able to soar.[154]

"That's right. Just remember that My Spirit only powers the things We want done.[155] So you'll be on your own if you do anything else. In fact, if you have My yoke and you're perpetually exhausted, you should ask yourself if you're doing extra things that are stealing your energy."

"I'll have to remember that. What's the other good news?"

He leaned forward, holding my gaze. "You've been eating doughnuts, but you can eat real food instead. Some of the things you love about your spheres are ways they almost fill your needs. And some of the things you hate are ways they absolutely fail to meet your needs. You don't have to stay in this place. You can get your needs met in Us."[156]

I couldn't believe it. I could have a yoke that fit and true rest. No more striving to fulfill rules I didn't even fully comprehend. I could learn from the man who literally knew everything[157] and who took the time to answer my questions gently, without getting angry or making me feel stupid. Longing swept over me, but was brought up short by a sudden thought.

"This yoke of Yours, how much does it cost?"

"Everything and nothing. I don't need anything from you,"[158] He said matter-of-factly.

"Ouch," I said.

"Ah yes, pride does get in the way, doesn't it? It also exhausts you far more than you think."

"How so?" I asked, struggling to maintain an even tone. My pride was all I'd had sometimes, and it was hard to think of letting go.

"Suppose you do well. Your pride gets stroked, and then you exhaust yourself trying to repeat your achievement. If you do poorly, pride is injured, taking the poor performance onto yourself. Suddenly, it's a reflection of your character—you fear you're worthy of rejection. Pride drives you to expend all your energy, endlessly attempting to prove the mistake was a fluke."[159]

"I guess that makes sense." It felt so strange to see pride as an enemy, rather than the constant friend that helped me up and covered the nakedness of my shame. Parting with it was still almost unthinkable. It rankled nearly as much as His saying I didn't have anything He needed.

"'Nothing' is the highest price a proud person can pay.[160] In that sense My yoke costs you dearly."

I shivered, thinking about the first half of His price. "What about the 'everything' part?"

"You give up the illusion of control for the reality of Us being in control.[161] You give up your exhausting attempt to fill your own needs for the energy of being filled with My Spirit and letting Us worry about your needs."[162]

I sighed. "I was going to call that giving up my freedom, but I suppose we've already established that I'm not free anyway. When I think about having You as a master instead of my spheres, it's a no-brainer. But when I think about the cost—" How can I give up so much?

Yet on the heels of that thought, my hunger for rest and for Jesus Himself swelled once more. "Maybe the cost isn't that much compared to what I gain," I said quietly, shocking myself a little.

"Definitely. You need to consider that before you decide. Following Me isn't easy.[163] It's not always what you'll want to do. But the benefits are worth it. That's the same reason I could die on the cross for you, because I kept in mind the end result, the benefits."[164]

I thought about it some more. I wanted it. Desperately. I wanted rest from the longing, from the perpetual striving to prove my worth, from the cacophony of voices. Rest from the constant question of whether my labor was significant. Rest from the fear that I would end up in another hole somewhere, injured and alone. Rest from labor that drained every part of me, leaving me an exhausted shell of who God designed me to be.

I suddenly realized that with Jesus' yoke, I didn't have to fear inactivity. I could enjoy physical rest, because I would have internal rest.

Jesus sat silently, seeming to watch my internal struggle.

"Okay." I was still terrified at taking the plunge, but I willed myself to continue. "I want it. What do I have to do?"

"You'll have to let go of your pride first, otherwise you won't be able to tolerate My yoke."

"How do I do that?"

He stepped over to the chest and pulled a book out of it. "The only antidote for pride is humility,"[165] He said, seating Himself on the edge of the bed.

I immediately began having second thoughts. "Humility?" I had been humiliated quite enough lately, thank you very much.

He chuckled. "Humility, not humiliation. The former is a change in perspective: showing you who We are and who you are.[166] The latter is just an injury to your pride. Are you willing to get a small glimpse?"

I hesitated, but at this point I needed His yoke. I could almost taste the rest. I cleared my throat. "Y-yes."

He opened the book to a picture of stars, and we were transported into space. I could see a shimmering ball of beauty below.

Jesus pointed at it. "This is the earth. If you look closely, you can see your home."

I stared for a moment where He'd indicated, and my vision telescoped in, zooming past cities, streets, and homes. I could clearly see my own house. It was amazing.

He turned, pointing the opposite direction. "Now look out that way."

I obeyed, turning to look. This time my vision expanded, planets and stars whizzed past, turning into galaxies. Everything was so huge in comparison to my house, to me. It seemed to take hours for us to zoom out enough to see the hugeness of the universe. By the end, I felt tiny. Insignificant. How had I thought my own life so important? Then we were back in the bedroom, out of the book again.

"We created all that.[167] We're bigger than all that, in ways you can't even imagine right now. We're fully capable of running your life."

I looked down at the bed. "It's such a small life compared to all those people and all those stars."

"True," Jesus said, tenderness in His voice. "However, smallness does not equal insignificance. You are a person I died to rescue.[168] Me, the God who is bigger than everything. That fact alone demonstrates your significance to Us."

I sat awestruck. He was right. Humility did wonders for pride. My pride looked ridiculous next to who He was. I didn't care what it cost anymore; I just wanted Him—the God who had died to rescue me. I wanted to give Him everything I could, even if He didn't need it.

He smiled. "Now you're ready. Let's get to work." He stood, gesturing towards the workshop door.

"Wait a minute. I have one question. You live in a shanty?" I asked incredulously.

He laughed. "No, I built one just for you. You needed somewhere free of distractions, so you could think about what was really important."

"Wow, thanks," I said. He had seen my need for rescuing before I had been aware of it. He had designed the perfect situation to give me the opportunity to choose life. "Now I'm ready." Leaning on Him, we headed into the workshop.

"Honey. Babe, wake up," my husband said, gently shaking my shoulder.

"Huh? What?" I sat up and pulled a paper off my face.

"It's almost time to get up. Were you down here all night?"

"I guess so." Lists littered the space in front of me. My neck ached from sleeping on the table. I remembered I had a new yoke now—one that should hurt my neck less. I smiled.

"Do you want me to start the coffee? Is today a two-pot day?" He asked, rubbing my back.

"Actually, I'm going to start cutting back. But I'd love a cup." I stood up, stretching to work the kinks out. I gathered my lists into a single pile and stashed them on the counter. I wanted to rework them, to condense them into just one list—the things I thought God wanted me to do. Thankfully, it was Saturday so I had a little time.

He sighed. "I suppose you need to rush off somewhere."

"Not right now."

"Maybe you should go get some rest then, since you slept out here. I can keep an eye on the kids when they wake up."

"Actually, I got plenty of rest last night."

He raised his eyebrows at me. "Oh really?"

"Yup! Want to hear about it?" I asked, sitting back down at the table with my coffee.

"Sure." He grinned and sat down.

Come to me, all you who are weary and burdened, and I will give you rest. Take my yoke upon you and learn from me, for I am gentle and humble in heart, and you will find rest for your souls. For my yoke is easy and my burden is light. ~ Matthew 11:28–30

121 Lewis Carroll, *Through the Looking-glass, and What Alice Found There,* ed. Florence Milner (Chicago: Rand, McNally & Co., 1917), 20.

122 Lewis Carroll, *Alice's Adventures in Wonderland* (London: MacMillan Publishing Co., 1865), 1.

123 For a more extensive list of questions, see Job 38–39.

124 Acts 17:26

125 James 3:7–8; Matt. 12:34–37

126 For more information on yokes, Tillers International has a great website: http://www.tillersinternational.org/. They also have some fascinating booklets on the mechanics of yokes and yoke building: http://www.tillersinternational.org/oxen/resources_techguides/BuildinganOxYokeTechGuide.pdf, http://www.tillersinternational.org/oxen/resources_techguides/ImprovingOxYokesTechGuide.pdf.

127 John 8:34; Rom. 6:16–18

128 God alone is the unmoved mover (Saint Thomas Aquinas, "Question 2: Article 3," in *Summa Theologica*, trans. Fathers of the English Dominican Province [New York: Benziger Brothers, 1947], accessed October 26, 2012, http://www.ccel.org/ccel/aquinas/summa.txt/). As the Creator, He alone has the freedom to change reality (Gen. 1–2). So, if one is talking about the ability to make decisions without being affected by other factors, God is the only one in that category.

129 Prov. 4:20–23, 14:30, 15:30, 17:22

130 Gal. 1:10

131 John 8:34–36; Rom. 6:16–18; Matt. 6:24

132 Joseph Jacobs and Richard Heighway, "The Man, The Boy, & The Donkey," in *The Fables of Æsop: Selected, Told Anew and Their History Traced* (London: MacMillan, 1894), 151.

133 Prov. 14:12

134 Part of being designed with a need for a transcendent God means we'll keep trying to fill that need with one thing after another until we fill it with God (e.g., John 4:1–32). See also Beth Moore's "Video Session 6" in *Breaking Free,* updated ed. (Nashville, TN: LifeWay Press, 2009).

135 Eccles. 3:11, or as Blaise Pascal put it: "What else does this craving, and this helplessness, proclaim but that there was once in man a true happiness, of which all that now remains is the empty print and trace? This he tries in vain to fill with everything around him, seeking in things that are not there the help he cannot find in those that are, though none can help, since this infinite abyss can be filled only with an infinite and immutable object; in other words by God himself." *Pensèes,* trans. W. F. Trotter (Grand Rapids, MI: Christian Clas-

sics Ethereal Library, 1944), Section VII: Morality and Doctrine: 425, accessed October 26, 2012, http://www.ccel.org/ccel/pascal/pensees.txt/.

136 Matt. 11:28–30

137 For the sake of readability I've used both the singular and plural pronouns with regards to the Trinity and the Persons therein. When talking about the Trinity, it's almost impossible not to emphasize either the oneness of God or His threeness. Since the American church tends to prioritize God's oneness, I've used the plural pronouns in places to highlight God's essential relational nature. I in no way wish to imply that God is not one (Deut. 6:4–5; 1 Kings 8:60; Isa. 45:5–6, 45:21–22; James 2:19) or to stray into Tritheism (Matt. 28:19–20; 2 Cor. 13:14; Eph. 4:4–6; 1 Pet. 1:2; Jude 20–21; John 1:1–2, 1:9–18, 17:24, 14:26, 16:7; Acts 10:38).

138 Job 41:11; Acts 17:24–25; "Feeding an ego" implies need and insecurity. God is inherently relational within the Trinity. His relational needs are already met (John 17:5, 17:24; C. S. Lewis, *The Problem of Pain,* Macmillan Paperbacks Edition [New York: Macmillan, 1962], 29.) He calls us to bring our lives into alignment with the way He designed the world to work so that things will go well for us. John 10:10–11

139 John 10:27

140 This illustration courtesy of James Bates, e-mail message to author, April 2, 2011.

141 Rom. 10:17; You also see Jesus providing basis for faith (Luke 7:18–23, 24:13–35) and the apostles explaining the gospel throughout Acts, rather than telling people "just trust Jesus" (e.g., Acts 2:14–41, 3:11–26, 7:2–53, 8:26–39, 10:1–48, 13:13–43, 13:48–49, 14:3, 14:14–18, 16:13–40, 17:2–4, 17:10–12, 17:16–34, 18:4–5, 18:24–28, 19:1–10). Information precedes faith, rather than an appeal to ignorance (Gal. 3:2–7).

142 Deut. 18:21–22

143 John 8:31–36; As Anselm puts it, "I seek not, O Lord, to search out Thy depth, but I desire in some measure to understand Thy truth, which my heart believeth and loveth. Nor do I seek to understand that I may believe, but I believe that I may understand. For this too I believe, that unless I first believe, I shall not understand." Clement Charles Julian Webb, *The Devotions of Saint Anselm, Archbishop of Canterbury* (London: Methuen, 1903), Proslogion: Chapter 1, accessed October 26, 2012, http://www.ccel.org/ccel/anselm/devotions.txt/. See also Millard J. Erickson, "Contemporary Issues in Christological Method: An Alternative Approach," in *Christian Theology,* 2nd ed. (Grand Rapids, MI: Baker Book House, 1998), 689–691.

144 If you're not a believer, a helpful technique can be to ask "The Transcendent One" for help discerning truth. If you aren't sure if the Bible is true, it's a way to sort through religions without committing yourself to Christianity.

145 Ps. 90:1–4; Isa. 44:6; John 8:57–59; Eph. 3:21; Jude 25; Rev. 1:8

146 Mal. 3:6; Heb. 13:8

147 Luke 4:14; Acts 1:8; 2 Cor. 12:7–10; Gal. 2:20, 5:22–25; Phil. 4:13

148 I am indebted to Beth Moore for this example. *Breaking Free,* 235.

149 John 15:1–11

150 Rom. 8:1–17; Gal. 5:16–18, 5:25

151 1 Thess. 5:19; Eph. 4:30; Acts 7:51

152 God created us to glorify Him (Isa. 43:7) by knowing Him (Isa. 43:10). He has also gifted us for specific tasks (Rom. 12:6–8; 1 Cor. 7:7, 12:7–10, 12:28; Eph. 4:11). When we do the things on His agenda (Eph. 2:10), we will be most happy (Ps. 16:11, 4:7; Prov. 10:28). See also C. S. Lewis' books *Mere Christianity* (New York: HarperCollins, 2001), 48, 50, and *The Problem of Pain,* 52.

153 Gen. 1–2; Col. 1:17

154 Isa. 40:29–31

155 The Holy Spirit is not a force, but rather a person (John 14:16–17, 14:26, 15:26, 16:7–15; Luke 4:14; Acts 5:1–11, 10:38; Matt. 28:19–20; 1 Cor. 12:4–6; 2 Cor. 13:14; Eph. 4:4–6, 4:30; 1 Pet. 1:2; Jude 20–21); therefore, He won't empower outside of His will. 1 Sam. 19:18–24; Acts 8:9–25; 1 Cor. 12:11

156 Isa. 55:1–3

157 1 John 3:20; Heb. 4:13; Job 28:24; Matt. 10:29–30; Isa. 42:8–9, 46:9–10

158 Job 41:11; Acts 17:24–25

159 Bruce B. Barton et al., *Life Application Bible Commentary: Matthew* (Wheaton, IL: Tyndale House Publishers, 1996), 230, quoted in Beth Moore's Bible study *Breaking Free,* 171.

160 Dan B. Allender and Tremper Longman, *Bold Love* (Colorado Springs, CO: NavPress, 1992), 39.

161 Peace is linked with submission throughout the Bible (e.g., Isa. 9:6–7, 48:18; Col. 3:15).

162 Matt. 6:24–34

163 Mark 8:34–38; Luke 9:57–62

164 Heb. 12:2

165 Job 40:12; Prov. 16:9, 29:23; Jer. 13:16–17; Dan. 4:37; James 4:6, 4:10; 1 Pet. 5:5–6

166 See "Week 9 'Gentle Giants': Day 2 'Selfless Humility' " in Beth Moore's Bible study *Living Beyond Yourself: Exploring the Fruit of the Spirit* (Nashville, TN: LifeWay Press, 1998).

167 Gen. 1–2; John 1:1–3; 1 Cor. 8:6; Col. 1:16; Heb. 1:1–2

168 Mark 10:45; Col. 1:13; 1 Thess. 1:10; Heb. 9:25–28

The Wounded One

ONE

. . . by his wounds we are healed. ~ Isaiah 53:5

His mouth twisted into a sneer. A moment ago he had been my beloved. Funny how wide a gulf words could create between two people.

"I don't want you. No one will ever want you," he repeated slowly, as though savoring the words. And then he left.

Shock held me transfixed. My lungs seemed broken, along with my heart, and I could barely breathe. *I can change! You don't have to leave*, my heart cried. But no words seemed adequate to bridge that aching chasm he'd dug.

Instinct took over. I retreated. Like a child returning to her mother's womb, I ensconced my soul in a small, dark cocoon.

My days went on. The seconds, minutes, hours passed. Day by day, I dragged myself through my life, supposedly moving on. In reality, every time I closed my eyes, I was instantly here . . . alone . . . bleeding . . . trapped in the moment of my betrayal. I looked down at my chest. With every beat, my heart gushed. So what if I was bleeding? Maybe someday, if I was lucky, my heart would simply stop. Then I could find release in death. Can you die of a broken heart?

I marked through another day on the calendar. Death was taking far too long. I had long since given up on healing. Time hadn't done a thing for my wound. Some days I longed to move on. Others, I relished this state—if I couldn't have his love, his rejection was better than nothing.

And yet, was this it? An eternity of agony? I was dying while he was off enjoying himself, probably snickering at the swathe of broken hearts he'd left behind. And here I was, yet another heart still broken.

No! I won't be anyone's pawn. Hot fury clawed through my chest, demanding vengeance. I would prove him wrong! I'd have my revenge, somehow.

I thought furiously, envisioning scenarios and trying to decide which would cause him the most agony. One stood out. I steepled my fingers. Yes, I'd make him want me and then reject him as he'd rejected me. I pictured him weeping as I had wept, a look of disbelief on his face as I left him.

An unwelcome thought broke into my lovely daydream: What if I never saw him again? I didn't even know where he lived anymore. He could be in Timbuktu for all I knew. I chewed my lip, then nodded. I could still reject him and anyone like him. I didn't have to see him to reject him. I'd reject him with my every breath. I'd never let anyone break my heart again.

Step one was to protect my heart. I had long since put my interactions with the world on autopilot and focused my energies here. I began fortifying my cocoon. I'd chosen my location carefully: in the middle of nowhere, surrounded by a brown, barren wasteland as far as the eye could see. Lonely. Safe. I made the cocoon's surface brown to camouflage it, in case someone wandered by.

Outwardly, I appeared more vivacious and alive than ever. Inside, I felt more isolated and dead than ever. But I was strong. I was secure. I ignored the bleeding of my heart and created a hard crystal breastplate to guard it. No one could breach my defenses.

I had long since convinced most people that I had "moved on." My projection of false togetherness usually entertained them in a more suitable location. I preferred it that way. The few times I had interacted with someone here, they embarked on a program to "rescue me." It usually involved a lot of empty platitudes about time and pain—platitudes that only illuminated and labeled my brokenness. They widened the distance between me and the speaker, leaving me even more hurt and alone.

Someone knocked on my cocoon. I jumped. Who in the world? No one knew I was here.

I thinned my cocoon's door to near-transparency. It would stand up to an assault but allowed me to examine this new threat. After my eyes adjusted to the light, I saw a man outside. He was disfigured, scarred. I couldn't imagine wounds that deep ever healing. Yet he wasn't bowed by the weight of his pain. He stood tall, waiting.

"Hello," he called.

I held my breath, wondering who he was and what he wanted. Perhaps, if I stayed quiet, he would find someone else to bother.

"Hellooo."

I added a small speaking slit to my cocoon. "What do you want?" I demanded, trying to infuse as much bravado as possible into the question.

He gave me a disarming smile. "I came to see you."

"Why?"

"You've been in there for quite some time. I thought I would see how much longer you plan to stay."

"Forever!" I shoved the opening closed and slammed opacity back into the cocoon.

Come out? My limbs trembled uncontrollably. The outside world was dangerous. Full of tricky folks who would betray you in a heartbeat. Who was this man anyway? How did he know how long I'd been in here?

I glanced back at my door. Now I could just make out the man's outline as he stood there. He sighed, then settled himself on my doorstep. Minutes passed. Hours passed. Days passed.

The man just sat there, occasionally taking short breaks to walk about.

I tried to ignore him, to get back to my life, but I couldn't. He had said he'd come to see me, to discover when I would come out. But what did he really want? I tried to think of a way to make him leave, so I could suffer in peace. Others I had driven away with harsh words and withdrawal. Somehow I couldn't bring myself to injure someone so obviously battle-scarred.

Those scars haunted me. The more I thought about them, the more I couldn't think about anything else. Finally, I couldn't take it anymore. With a thought, I cautiously thinned a section of my cocoon, making it transparent as a window, and added a speaking slit. The man still sat just outside. I stared, spellbound by the wholeness those scars somehow exuded.

"Hello again," he said, smiling at me, as though only seconds had passed.

"H-h-hello . . . ."

"You look lost," he said.

I started. Me? Lost? Couldn't he see I had constructed this cocoon with the latest in defensive technology? I lived in the middle of nowhere. My cocoon was a destination. You didn't just happen upon it.

"Actually, I was wondering if you were lost," I improvised.

"No, I'm not."

"Oh." I licked my dry lips, then took the plunge. "I noticed that you have scars. If you don't mind me asking, where did you get them?"

"Someone I love betrayed me," he replied steadily.

"Do they still ache?"

He shook his head. "No. Only wounds hurt.[169] You look like you have your own wound. How did you get it?"

"Someone I loved betrayed me." I glared at him, daring him to mock my pain, or to gloss over it and talk about the weather.

Instead, his eyes softened, as though he truly empathized. "I'm sorry; I know that pain. What happened?"

And so I sat down on my side of the wall and told him about it. Somehow his scars made me want to share. Maybe there would be release in the telling. It had been so long since I'd told anyone the truth.

He listened to my tale of rejection and pain without judging—no jollying attempts to help me "buck up," no suggestions for fixing the problem, just quiet identification with my wound through his own obvious wounding.[170]

"And now, here I am, in this state-of-the-art haven of safety." I spread my arms wide. "Now I can never be hurt again."

He shook his head, looking grave. "I don't think so. I think you got lost."

"Got lost?" I scoffed. "No, I planned my location very intentionally."

"No, you yourself got lost in the wounding. You're upside down. Is there any part of you left outside of your injury? You're no longer a person with a wound. You're a wounded person."

I frowned. "I don't know. I'm not sure what that even means."

"Who are you?" he asked, his voice patient.

"I'm myself."

He smiled. "That isn't a real answer. That's the answer of someone who doesn't know herself or who refuses to respond honestly."

I thought, and thought.

He pointed to my cocoon. "You live in this bunker—that should tell you something about how you see yourself."

I looked down. "I suppose I'm vulnerable on my own, and I don't like it."

"An honest answer. Why do you see yourself that way?"

I smiled bitterly. "You've seen my wound. I know it's true, down to the tips of my soul. I'm not one of those naïve saps who thinks people won't hurt you. They will," I said, breathing raggedly as the pain engulfed me once more.

"I too know that people sin, but I'm not holed up in a bunker."

"I wouldn't be here either, if that, that person hadn't driven me to it!"

"No, you wouldn't be here if you didn't want to be," he said calmly.

"Do you think I *like* living here all alone? Do you think I enjoy feeling the agony of a broken heart every waking minute? Do you think I like dreaming of things the way they were, only to be hit with the loss every single time I wake up?"

"Why do you stay here then?"

"Where else would I go? There's nowhere else safe! I suppose that's the one benefit to all this. My betrayer taught me well: love is a myth." I slumped back against my cocoon.

He looked at me for a moment, his eyes full of sadness, then asked, "And so you created this bunker?"

"Yes, he forced me to."

He raised an eyebrow. "Your betrayer stuck around after wounding you and forced you to build this place?"

"No! Not literally forced me. He simply made any other choice ludicrous."

"So he wounded you, but you decided what to do with that pain?"

"I suppose so," I said, wondering what he was getting at.

"Then it's your fault you're here," he said quietly. "You chose this place."

My fingers dug into the floor. "Where else would I have gone?"

"Somewhere to find healing. Why spend so much energy lying to the outside world and hiding in this cocoon? Why preserve your wound? Why not take the energy of your pain and find healing?"

I sputtered, trying to drum up a suitable reply. None came to mind. I decided to turn the pressure on him instead. "'Energy of my pain'? What exactly is that?"

"Pain is like rocket fuel," the man began.

As he spoke, an image took shape in my mind's eye, as vivid as if I were there. I stood in the middle of a plain under a vast night sky, naked of my breastplate. The stars shone so brightly that they seemed close enough to touch. My wound glowed. The dripping blood looked like rivulets of molten lava streaming from my heart. A small, one-person, rocket-propelled ship stood to one side.

"Pain's energy doesn't just go away," he continued. "You have to do something with it. You can put it in the rocket and go somewhere—closer to God or farther from Him."

I saw myself scooping the liquid energy into a pitcher and filling up the fuel tank. I sat down in the ship.

"*You* decide where to go, though. You aim the ship," he said. I whimsically aimed it at the brightest star and fired the ignition. In a blink, there I was, light-years from where I had started.

"On the other hand, you can try to bottle it up, to pretend it isn't there," he said.

Immediately, I was back on the starlit plain with the ship beside me. Now my crystal breastplate sat snugly over my wound. As the energy bled out, my breastplate kept it close to my body. Physical pain intensified as the energy increased. It began to eat a hole through me.

"Eventually, it will destroy you."

I clawed at my breastplate, trying in vain to remove it. Then I was back in my cocoon, in my own body, as though I had never left. Maybe I hadn't. My hands dropped and I shook myself a little, averting my eyes from my familiar breastplate and trying to regain the thread of our conversation.

The man leaned forward. "You aimed the wrong direction. You got lost far away, and now all that energy has nowhere to go."

My wound seemed to burn in response to his pronouncement. "Wh-who are you?" I asked.

"Jesus."

I didn't even wonder if He was lying. Who else could find me here?

"So You've come to rub it in," I said. "How could You let this happen to me? How could You leave me to that monster? Don't You care?"

I imagined myself back on the starlit plain. Jesus stood nearby. This time I put the energy squarely into His outstretched hands. I poured and poured, wanting to vent my hurt, my anger, and my hatred on the One who was in league with my betrayer. He had failed me more deeply than anyone else, because He could have stopped the wounding. I was powerless, caught unaware, but He was neither powerless nor ignorant. And so His culpability was great.

As I continued to pour, His flesh burned and burned. A part of me stared aghast at the damage, but I was unable to stop. At the end, when I had drained my pain to the dregs, His wounds healed before my eyes, leaving Him as before—scarred yet whole.[171]

"Of course I[172] care, beloved. That's why I've come."

I glared at Him. "If You really loved me, You wouldn't have let this happen. I would still be whole."

"No, you wouldn't. You weren't whole before your wounding."

"What? I wasn't?"

"If you had been whole, you wouldn't have given that person the power to wound you so deeply," Jesus said. "No, the wounding just exposed your brokenness, though I know that it hurt."

Looking into His eyes, I realized that He did know my pain, both as I saw it and as He had experienced it. Tears filled my eyes. I lifted my chin and dashed them away.

"Then why didn't You stop it?" I caught my breath in a sob. "Did You want me to end up here?"

"No, I didn't. You let your betrayer set your aim and got lost. Now you're the one staying lost, preserving your wound. I'm the One who came to find you."

I pictured the rocket ship, my betrayer maliciously aiming it into a nearby sun, then shook my head. Jesus was wrong—I hadn't let him anywhere near me after he'd so callously destroyed my heart. My eyes narrowed. "What do you mean that I let my betrayer set my aim?"

"You said that your betrayer taught you well. You also thought that We were in league with him. You're viewing everything—Us, you, and everyone else—through the lens of your betrayal."

I shrugged. "So?"

"Why should any human, let alone a person who betrayed you, have the right to change your perception of truth? Would he even recognize truth if it hit him over the head?"

I didn't have an answer for that. I couldn't deny that my own view of reality—the ridiculously fragile security I thought I had possessed—had been shattered in the moment of my betrayal. I suppose that meant my betrayer did, in some sense, determine my perception. The bile rose in my throat and I grimaced. Yet . . . if it was true, didn't I have to swallow it, regardless of my preferences? And as much as I hated the thought of being grateful to him for anything, hadn't my betrayer opened my eyes to truth? I would never have seen my vulnerability and taken steps to protect myself if it weren't for him. Perhaps he had set my aim. But maybe, just maybe, he'd done me a favor.

"Yes, yes, and no," Jesus said.

"What? I forgot the question."

"Yes, truth remains true no matter how anyone feels about it. You can't save the elephants by writing new statistics.[173] Yes, this wounding has the potential to pry your eyes open to truth. But that's not the truth that you should learn—it's not true that you ought to take steps to protect your vulnerability."

"Oh," I said. I forgot: He can hear my thoughts.

"I noticed," He said, a teasing glint in His eyes.

My eyes widened. "So anyway, what am I supposed to learn?" I asked, trying to change the subject before I really thought something I oughtn't.

"Having Us know your thoughts is not a new development, you know. It hasn't changed Our love yet, and—speaking as someone who knows all of eternity—it's not going to," He said, looking me directly in the eye. I dropped my eyes before long. I couldn't bear the love and knowing in His gaze. "You can't learn until you change out your lenses," He continued. "Get rid of the ones you've fashioned from your betrayal."

"How do I do that?"

"Start with what you know is true, rather than what you feel is true. View the things that change in light of the things that never change. You once knew that Our Word is truth,[174] that We are truth.[175] Will you allow Us to give you new lenses?"

I clasped my hands tightly. Allow Him to give me new lenses? Now? Even after He'd failed me? The answer seemed obvious, yet my heart yearned to believe Him. I used to trust God before my betrayal, or at least I had thought I did. But now that I wasn't sure He was—or had ever been—good, trusting Him seemed absurd.

"Why would I die in your place if I'm not good?" Jesus asked. "If I'm not good, I wouldn't care about right or wrong, perhaps at all, or at least not enough to sacrifice Myself.[176] Or maybe I wouldn't care about you, depending on how you're going to define 'good.'"[177]

"Why would You allow this betrayal if You are good?" I shot back.

Jesus reached a hand towards me. "Don't you see what you're doing?"

"What? What am I doing?"

"You're viewing Our character through the lens of your circumstances, rather than understanding circumstances through the lens of Our character and perspective. That's visional priority—wherever you begin will set the tone for the rest of your worldview. Right now, you're imputing character traits on Us that are based on your interpretation of the betrayal, which is based on your betrayer's view of reality. You have bottom-up lenses. You need to change them out for top-down lenses."

"That doesn't answer my question!" I said, morbidly sure I had somehow won against God, and feeling the tiny flicker of hope for healing die.[178]

"I already answered it. Pain has a purpose—We work all things out for the good of those who love Us.[179] You, however, can't see that purpose right now, because you're stuck with the wrong lenses." Suddenly my cocoon grew opaque, and I couldn't see Him anymore. "Once you've changed your lenses,"—the door grew transparent again—"you'll expose this pain's purpose as you grow, peeling off each deeper purpose like the layers of an onion."

I frowned. "How is that an answer? I want something specific."

"I know you want something concrete right now, but you can't understand anything more specific until you change your perspective to line up with truth, rather than trying to fit truth to your perspective. You have to grow past this first." He looked at me seriously. "I ask again, will you allow Us to give you new lenses? You've already said you don't like your current situation. What do you have to lose?"

I shook my head and started to say something about not feeling like I could trust Him, but He interrupted me, "There comes a time when trust involves taking action on what you know is true, rather than on how you feel about the truth."

"Fine. What does this new perspective look like?" I didn't want Jesus to leave, but I wasn't sure I liked Him right now.

"Like this," He said and pulled a pair of glasses out of His pocket. The lenses shimmered. Briefly I could see shining silver words written over them: *Your statutes are my delight; they are my counselors.*[180] Then the text faded. I widened the slit in my cocoon, and Jesus passed the glasses through. I turned them over and over, then polished the lenses. Finally, I exhaled deeply and put them on.

"Now what?" I asked, looking down at the floor and trying to adjust the glasses so they would stay on.

"Now look around. What do you see that's different?"

I looked up to see Jesus standing in front of me. Intense light stabbed at my eyes, more bright and terrible than any I had ever seen. I took the glasses off and mopped my streaming eyes.

"Try again," Jesus said. "It's just the first shock. Your eyes will adjust."

Right. I barely refrained from rolling my eyes. I got to my feet, then, bracing myself for the pain, I put the glasses back on. I began at the edge of the light. Gradually, I could look directly at Him. He seemed exactly the same as before, and yet wildly different, as though I'd only ever seen the faintest outline of His shadow.

I stared at His scars, mesmerized. No longer a disfigurement, they adorned Him. Beauty where I had least expected it. Those were for me—from when He died for me. He had allowed Himself to be betrayed to rescue me.[181] My heart felt as though it would burst with the knowledge.

I remembered how I had poured the pain of my betrayal and my hatred on Him, and marveled that He could still love me. I caught my breath, overwhelmed by the wonder of His sacrifice. God, betrayed and dying for a lowly human—someone He could have snuffed out as easily as a candle.

How had I dared to rage against God? I knew now, beyond a shadow of a doubt, that Jesus was God.[182] Thin lines of energy streamed away from Him, holding the world around us together. He had created everything, and sustained its existence, moment by moment; He upheld time itself.[183] Absolute power clothed in humanity, God's essential nature on display for all the world to see—a mystery far beyond my ability to grasp.[184]

But how could absolute power not corrupt absolutely? Could that explain my betrayal?

All at once, I could see His goodness. He was pure, without even a speck of darkness. I knew deep in my being that He could never be in league with evil.[185] It was literally impossible for Him to tolerate evil, like asking light to become dark without losing any of its brightness. He could never have allied Himself with my enemy. It wasn't in His nature to take pleasure in pain for its own sake.[186]

I also saw that my pain grieved Him. He entered into my woundedness on a level I couldn't begin to grasp. It must have been love that caused Him to take on my pain as His own. As I had this thought, my vision shifted, and somehow I could see His love.

I knew it was love, yet it was so different from anything I'd ever imagined. I'd always thought of love as something I did or felt. The comparison left my poor imitations of love lifeless. He didn't just love relentlessly—He *was* love, in the very essence of His being.[187] He could never stop being love, any more than He could stop being good.

I shuddered, terrified by the strength of that love—love that was irrevocably committed to my best, regardless of my feelings in the matter.[188]

All this passed in what could have been the blink of an eye. Then again, perhaps it had been years of gazing. I only knew that I longed to behold Him thus forever, yet couldn't bear to continue for a moment longer.

Then He looked me in the eye, laying my soul bare before that piercing gaze. As He had said, it was nothing unusual for Him to know me inside and out. On the other hand, I had never been so aware of His knowledge. I cringed away from that look, cognizant of my flaws, of the hatred I had for Him—in short, of my sin. I fell to my knees with the weight of it.

His light pulsed, growing brighter and brighter. My eyes watered profusely, finally closing of their own accord. My face bowed to the floor. The light flashed so intensely that I felt it in my bones. Then everything dimmed. I stayed there, prostrate before a Majesty I no longer dared to address.

TWO

"Come out," Jesus commanded.

I scrambled up, quaking at the thought of leaving my cocoon, at the thought of being so close to God. Cautiously, I obeyed, my eyes downcast. A blast of fresh air hit me. God's presence beat at me. Nowhere to hide. I knew I was safe with Him, safe from everything but perhaps Himself. Still, I felt exposed, and somehow bereft, as though in leaving my cocoon, I had lost a part of myself.

He moved to stand in front of me. Tenderly, Jesus raised my trembling gaze to His own. He smiled down at me. "Beloved."

In that moment I knew that He had seen every part of me and loved me, not in spite of my flaws, but *with* all my flaws. A glow spread through my chest, battling against my icy terror. I wanted to stay with Him, dreaded being sent away, and loved being this known—and yet, I also longed to run away and hide.

"It's a start. Shall we continue?"

"With what, my Lord?" I asked, trying to still my wildly beating heart.

"With a change in perspective. You've begun at the top, with the unchanging, with Us.[189] Are you ready to discover who you are?"

"Y-yes, my Lord," I said through chattering teeth.

He clasped my hands. "Now, as We alone can see your true self, you'll have to use My eyes as a mirror.[190] Focus on your reflection."

I concentrated on His pupils, trying to filter out everything but my own image. There I stood, dazed and disheveled. It had been ages since I'd seen myself. I had grown gaunt, and there was a tightness to my features that I didn't remember. The black of my mourning only emphasized my pallor.

Suddenly, my reflection rose up, growing larger and larger. I fell forward into the blackness of Jesus' pupils. With an abrupt jolt, I stood in a cavern. Burning torches lined the cave walls. In the center stood a collection of art. Pieces I recognized—the *Mona Lisa*, the *Venus de Milo*, the *Winged Bulls* of Sargon, *Starry Night*, and others—were interspersed among a host of others I didn't know.

Jesus stood next to me. I surreptitiously studied Him. Here He looked so ordinary, so human. My heart rate slowed. Maybe being this close to Him wouldn't be so bad after all.

Jesus gestured to the art. "What are these?" He asked, His voice echoing against the stone walls.

"Works of art?"

"Right. These are all priceless works of art. Why are they priceless? Look at this one." He walked over to the armless Venus. "It's damaged. How can damaged goods be priceless?"

I studied the piece thoughtfully. Was He really looking for such an obvious answer, or was this a trick question? Only one way to find out.

"Because they're irreplaceable. They're one of a kind."

"Why?"

"Um, because the artists are dead. I suppose even if they were alive, one could argue that they could never exactly duplicate their art."

"But what about all the other 'irreplaceables' that get thrown out like junk? Why are these works any different from them?"

I thought for a moment, trying to dredge up my Art History class notes. "These were created by masters of their craft. Plus, people want them, so throwing them away is unthinkable."

"It sounds like you're saying that their value is based on supply and demand. These items are unique and irreplaceable, and they have inherent value because of who made them. Also, people would go to great lengths to obtain them. Is that right?"

I nodded.

"All right, just something to keep in mind."

I glanced back at the collection. Just something to keep in mind?

Jesus smiled. "One step at a time. Now, look at this."

As He spoke, the art collection vanished and was replaced by an enormous painting. The artist had painted a young woman in the left foreground. She stood on packed earth under a dingy gray sky. Behind her, to the right, the artist had positioned a large group of people.

Vivid red blood stained the front of her dirty, tattered shirt and pooled on the ground below, drawing the observer's eye to her heart. In fact, it was the most colorful part of the painting. She wore a dark cloak with the hood up. Her hair hung in matted strings on either side of her face. Haunted eyes looked out of an emaciated, almost expressionless face. On her back she carried a burden secured with chains; the weight of it bowed her. Her hand rested open at her side.

A bright red rose lay in the dirt, as though it had slipped out of her fingers only moments before. The rose had been so intricately painted that it almost seemed alive. On the rose's stem was carved a single word: *Beloved.*

A brightly colored image on the back of her cloak drew my eye. It was the only other color in this emphatically drab setting. As I stared, a phantom wind spread her cloak wide, so I could see it fully. It was another portrayal of the same woman. In this picture, she laughed, clothed in color and gaiety. Her hair shone, and every part of her seemed to radiate poise.

A sob caught in my throat as my attention returned to her broken heart. Something about the whole painting resonated with me, creating instant sympathy with the woman's plight.

Jesus put a gentle hand on my shoulder. "What can you tell me about this woman?"

I took a deep breath and tried to distance myself, to examine the painting objectively. "Well, you can tell from the coloring that her broken heart is the first thing you ought to notice."

"Right, her woundedness is the central facet of her existence. What about the rest of her?"

"It seems unimportant. She's designed to blend in with her surroundings; even her skin tones are in the same color family as the sky and the dirt."

I paused, re-examining the painting. *It's so dismal. No wonder the poor girl is miserable.*

"How do you know she's miserable?" Jesus asked.

"I guess I don't. But look at her! Her heart's broken. Everything around her seems barely alive, as though the only real things in her world are her heart, the rose, and that cloak—maybe it's just her eyes that make me think she's sad. They're so bleak and pained, like she's sobbing inside." I tapped my chin. *Where had I seen that look before?*

"I agree. What else do you notice about her?"

My eyes roved over the painting, this time alighting on the woman's bent posture. "She's tired. That weight seems to exhaust her." I looked up at Him. "Why is it tied on with chains?"

"Because she's allowed her burden to become a prison," He said. "What do you think of the cloak?"

I shifted uneasily, glancing back at it. "I don't know. There's something about the flamboyance in the cloak's picture that seems to suggest disingenuousness. Maybe something forced in the gaiety and bold colors? It makes her seem less than trustworthy."

He nodded. "Anything else strike you?"

"She's utterly alone. Not only does she stand alone, but no one can see the real her. Her back is turned to those people, so even though her wound is the first thing I see, it's invisible to them."

"And what about the rose?"

I scrutinized the painting. What had the artist been trying to communicate with that fallen rose? The deep red almost glowed, rivaling the pooled blood. Dewdrops sparkled on the delicate petals. "It seems out of place. This woman doesn't look like she would be given, or even buy, roses. Also, you can tell that the artist put a lot of effort into making it beautiful, but the woman . . . well, she's unlovely. Having the rose there only emphasizes her dreary neglect. It's hard to believe it could be hers."

"No, it was hers. But she couldn't carry it *and* her burden."

I stared at the lumpy mass tied to the woman's back. "What is it?"

"Rejection." Jesus pointed to the woman. "Perhaps you should take a closer look at her face."

I stepped toward the painting, then gasped. It's me! I couldn't take my eyes off it, struck dumb at the pitifulness of this representation. Pain bubbled up to catch in my throat. How can this be me? I held my breath, trying to keep the tears at bay.

Jesus gestured to the painting. "This is how your betrayal has painted you. This is how you see yourself. Wounded. Alone. Cloaked in pride, with a false self you display to everyone else while keeping them at a distance. No longer the beloved. Unwanted. Bowed with the weight of rejection. You've lost yourself. Look at me." He laid His hands on my shoulders and swung me around to face Him. "This is not who you are."

A tear spilled down my cheek. I dashed it away. "I don't know anymore," I choked out, barely able to keep from looking back at the painting.

Jesus tenderly brushed away another wayward tear. "I know you don't—that's why you need a history lesson. You can't know who you are unless you understand where you've been."

The torches went out. It seemed pitch black, although somehow . . . different, as though my eyes were simply missing the substance all around. The air pressed in on me. I opened my eyes wide and strained to see something, anything.

"This is a history lesson? Where are we? I can't see anything," I said, still gulping air to keep from crying.

"That's because it isn't a place you can experience or comprehend. We're before. Outside."

"Before? Outside of what?"

"Time and space. This is when—though obviously there's no such thing as 'before' or 'when' here—We planned to create you and to rescue you. This is when We purposed to get you back for Our own."[191]

"Oh," I said. I was important to the God of the universe before my birth?

"Yes, before We had even made the world. Always. Now, fast-forward through time."

All at once, light exploded into the darkness. Temporarily blinded, I blinked and shaded my eyes, trying to make out where we'd ended up. Though we remained in the cavern, it had been transformed into something like a theater. Images played 360 degrees around us. Space stretched out. Planets, stars, and galaxies were set in place. The images played, faster and faster, until there was nothing but a blur of coruscating light. Then the image froze on a small baby lying in a manger as angels rejoiced.[192]

Jesus pointed to the baby. "Here I am, infiltrating enemy territory."

I half-turned. "Infiltrating enemy territory?"

He nodded somberly, and His eyes grew pained. "Yes. When Adam and Eve followed Satan's advice, and took themselves out from under Our authority, this world We created became enemy territory.[193] Humans became slaves to sin.[194] For this We had planned a rescue mission. It was in becoming human that I triumphed."[195]

"Oh, right." I turned back to the screen.

The picture moved on, then paused again at the crucifixion of my Lord. I shuddered. Such a gory, gruesome tragedy.

Jesus laid a hand on my shoulder. "Not just a tragedy. An accomplishment. Never forget that I came for this purpose: to die in your stead, to rescue you.[196] My love for you was why I stayed on that cross.[197] It was not just a tragedy, but a triumph!" He exclaimed as the image showed His empty tomb.[198]

"Now, skip ahead." The picture darkened to display a splotchy red-tinged black. "Where do you think this is?"

I squinted and turned around and around. "I don't know. Should I?"

"It's your mother's womb." His voice dropped. "Here is where We knit you together[199] soul and body, software and hardware."[200]

I pictured Him seamlessly integrating my soul and body, orchestrating each cell of my development. "Hmm, I like that."

Then the picture flashed to stop at a day familiar to me: the day I had first realized my own need for a rescuer and called out to God. I recalled all the agony of lostness[201] and the subsequent joy of being found. My heart softened. God had done something miraculous then. Maybe He could work another miracle in me now.

"On this day, you knew that you were loved, though the knowledge was limited." He turned to me and smiled. "Let's expand it." With that, the film ended and the torches returned.

Along with the torches, a procession of huge frames had appeared. More paintings? Inside each frame, grey mist swirled about, as though someone had framed fog.

Jesus held out an arm and escorted me over to the closest frame. Once we were near enough to examine it, the mist oozed away, and I could see the painting clearly. I gasped and hugged my stomach, trying vainly to still the fear and disgust humming through my being.

There I stood, absolutely naked. Not physically exposed—that would have been infinitely preferable, almost insignificant compared to this exposure. I was naked of the excuses I used to cover my sin. Laid bare before the gaze of the Almighty.

I saw my sin, and it was great. Huge streaks of darkness flowed through me, like giant veins. Wrapped around the veins were words, shimmering with a darkness so deep it dazzled. I closed my eyes. Of their own accord, they popped open and I read the words: *There is no God,*[202] *I run my life, I can decide what's best for me.*[203]

I turned my back on the painting. This can't be me. How can that be me? Surely it was a portrait of me before God rescued me. I couldn't still have that much sin in my life. I paused, struck by a thought. Deep in my being a small voice reminded me of my betrayal and subsequent actions. I wanted to protest, to proclaim my innocence—I hadn't betrayed him, he betrayed me.

But you hated him, and wanted to hurt him back, the voice persisted. *The sin is still there.* I thought back over the words. I had been trying to run my own life, to decide what was best for me. And rather than aiming my ship towards God, I'd lived like He was the enemy.

I recalled when I used to wonder at people who struggled with hatred; I'd questioned if they had ever fully experienced God's love and forgiveness. But how was I any different? I hated too. However, unlike those poor souls I had once judged, I hadn't tried to suppress my hatred or battle it. No, I had gleefully fed it, coddled it, and allowed it to run my life.

I turned back to the painting, desperate to escape the knowledge that flayed my soul bare. At my heart, I could see a black, gaping emptiness. Chains locked me in place, the same chains I had used to bind the burden to my back in the first painting. Even in such a horrible state, humility did not cause me to bend my knee. I stood tall, unbowed with shame, my fist raised in rebellion towards the God whose existence I refused to acknowledge.

Maybe I wasn't technically in bondage anymore, but this was how I lived: rejecting my betrayer and rebelling against God with my every breath. When had I gone astray? Looking at the portrait, I yearned for something to cover me, to be defined by something other than my sin. Pride and a false self had sufficed in the face of human inquiry, but they were useless before the God who sees.

Jesus put a gentle hand on my shoulder. I kept my eyes fixed on the painting, unwilling to meet His gaze in the face of such sin. We stood there in silence for long moments. My stomach knotted. Color came and went in my face as shame and horror warred within me.

He put a finger under my chin and lifted my gaze to His own. "You're not this woman anymore—you don't have to live like you are. Would you like to see who you really are?"

I recalled the portrait of me, bowed by rejection. Could I handle any more self-revelation? I glanced back at the portrait in front of me. Anything had to be better than this.

"Please."

We walked up to the next frame, and the mist curled away in intricate traceries. I stared at the painting, devouring it. Could this really be me? I look so, so beautiful.

The artist had painted me facing Jesus. No longer naked, I was clothed in garments of pure light. A band of light encircled my ring finger—a token of my betrothal to Jesus? It was like a fairy tale gone wrong. A Cinderella who hated and defamed her prince still ending up as His beloved. This portrait seemed wildly impossible in light of the previous one.

In this painting I gazed up at Jesus unabashedly, my face radiant. There was no reserve in that look, only love. And Jesus Himself was looking at me as though I were His beloved.

"You are," Jesus said.

I turned to Him, "I am what?"

"You are My beloved."

I looked up at Him, searching His eyes for falsity, half-expecting to be the butt of some incomprehensible divine joke. Suddenly, I realized He wore the same expression from the painting. In fact, He'd worn it all along. How had I missed that?

I thought back over my experience with Him. His every look, every word, every action proclaimed His love. How could I question God's love for me? I'd been a mistress of disguise, deceiving even myself. Unloved. Unwanted. Neither of these terms applied to me when I looked into Jesus' eyes. But could it really be true?

I looked down. "I know that . . . yet it seems so hard to believe."

"Why do you think that is?" He asked, compassion in His voice.

"I suppose it's because I don't see myself the way You do."

"Darling, look at me." I raised my eyes, and He continued. "You are so beautiful and desirable to Me. Helen of Troy launched a thousand ships with her beauty. But I, the God of the universe, died to rescue you, to have you for My own. Look at this painting. Do you see someone who is unwanted, worthy of rejection?"

I turned back to the painting, poring over it. "N-no, but this picture seems less real than the first." I sighed. "Let's face it, he did reject me. I live like the woman in the first painting—that's me."

He cupped my chin. "No, just because you're living a lie doesn't make it true. You have to choose your visional priorities and stick with them, no matter how you feel. Think about a ship. Suppose the captain decided to navigate based on where he *felt* his ship was. Would he ever arrive at his destination?"

I pictured a storm-lashed ship being whisked off to who knew where. "Probably not," I said, "particularly if he ever got caught in a storm and was unknowingly carried away."

Jesus nodded. "You're right. It's much wiser to pick something constant to sail by; hence, sailors use the stars or instrumentation. You've transferred your betrayer's view of you as though that's how We see you. Do you think he knew you nearly as well as We do?"

I recalled my "history lesson" then said, "No, I suppose not."

"Then why do you let his picture inform Ours? Why not let Ours inform his?"

My brow creased. "I don't know." It did seem ludicrous the more I thought about it, but only on a cognitive level. Why did I let him call the shots? I turned back to the painting again. Why couldn't I be this woman instead? Clothed in mourning or arrayed in light, was it as simple as a choice? My eyes wandered back to my garments of light. I loved seeing myself clothed in them instead of covered in sin. Jesus did that for me, I realized.

I turned to Him. "Thank You for covering my sin and nakedness."

He gave my hand a quick squeeze. "You're welcome, though actually I didn't just cover up the sin—I took it away. You're clothed with Me, with My righteousness,"[204] He turned serious, "so when you label yourself as 'the rejected one,' you're rejecting Me."

I turned the idea over and over in my brain. I'd never thought of it that way, but I'd already discovered I'd been rejecting Him since my betrayal.

"C'mon," He pointed His chin at the adjacent painting, "let's look at the next one." He began walking towards it; I trailed along, loathe to leave this view of myself.

When we reached it, the mist vanished all at once. A rushing sound filled my ears, like a multitude of voices or the wind rustling through the trees. In this painting, I stood against a black background. In the core of my being I saw a figure: someone made of live coals with small tongues of flame licking about him. It almost looked as though the flames really flickered. Perhaps it was a trick of the wavering torch light? I took a step closer, squinting at the painting. They *were* moving.

As I examined the painting, I could see that every bit of light moved. Lines of liquid fire raced out from the figure, creating a tracery throughout my body. The blazing fire reminded me of my pain's lava-like energy. I stepped back. Here and there, stagnant pools of darkness quenched the fire and left gaping holes in the overall pattern.

I shivered. "What's that sound?"

"Instructions. It's the sound of My Spirit, the teacher, instructing you in truth."[205]

I gaped. "The Holy Spirit? Instructing *me* in truth?" I pointed to the figure in the painting. "Is that, that fire Him too?"

He smiled. "Yes, that's a representation of My Spirit."[206]

I stared at the figure, wide-eyed. I knew I was "a temple of the Holy Spirit,"[207] but somehow seeing Him like this made that concept vastly different—like the difference between reading in a history book that Rome existed and actually walking through the city.

I traced the lines of fire with my eyes, stopping abruptly at one of the dark pools. The thing bubbled over, spreading its muck like a tumor. I swallowed convulsively. "What are those dark places?"

He held my gaze. "Rebellions. Things you're hanging on to, areas of sin that are quenching Our power."[208]

"How is that even possible? You're much more powerful than I am."

Jesus looked grave. "My Spirit won't go where He's not invited. We won't force ourselves on you."[209]

The idea settled into my brain, at once comforting and terrifying me. Though I wasn't reduced to a robot, I could also maintain those pools of darkness indefinitely. I could choose my sin over Him, even if it destroyed me. I looked back at the darkness. I wish the fire would just burn it out of me.

"Not 'the fire'—We are a person, not a force," Jesus corrected.

I blushed. "Sorry."

"I forgive you," He said with a smile.

I shifted my attention back to the painting, mesmerized by the flickering fire. "Why fire?" I asked.

"Just like your pain has energy to be used, My Spirit provides energy. It's only through Our power that you can accomplish meaningful things—the things We've called you to do."[210]

I blinked at Him. Use God's power? Thank God I couldn't misuse it; I hadn't exactly done very well with my pain's energy.

"And, like fire purifies gold, My Spirit can refine you,[211] convicting you of sin and providing opportunity to act differently.[212] We won't force you to change, but neither do We allow you to be comfortable in your sin."

I breathed a sigh of relief. So maybe I'm not doomed to keep my sin . . . .

"You're right—you don't have to hang on to your sin, nor do you battle it alone. You have Our power on your side."[213]

I shook my head. God on my side. Suddenly life seemed much more manageable. I smiled, sure the blazing flames contained infinitely more power than my pain's energy. "I can see why You would use fire."

Jesus nodded. "He's also like fire in that He's sealed you, like a beacon proclaiming that you are Ours."[214]

It made sense when He explained it that way. At any rate, I knew it wasn't a picture I would easily forget. I stared at the flickering flames and listened once more to the Holy Spirit's voice. This time I could discern Him whispering, "This is the way, walk in it."[215]

"The implications and practical outworkings are more than you can imagine just now," Jesus said.

Then He gently pulled me along to the last painting. Here the mist streamed away, like pennants proclaiming the advent of royalty. I took a step back.

I had seen plenty of paintings involving light, but in this one the artist had literally used light as paint. It was another picture of me, though as a child. I stood in a hallway outside a huge, ornate set of double doors. One hand was poised on the door. Through the slim opening you could just see the King,[216] eagerly looking up.

I was clothed as the daughter of the king. My hair flew about my beaming face. My crown sat askew, skirts crooked. You could tell I was not a staid child, but rather the type to race through the halls, laughingly playing hide-and-seek. I looked as though I had been running when I decided to come and find Him: my Father. [217]

There was no tentativeness to my precipitous entry. No insecurity about my reception. No thought of tidying my appearance before approaching. And there was a familiarity in the act, as though I'd done it hundreds of times before. It seemed to embody coming "boldly before the throne of grace."[218] I'd always understood that phrase as relating to what I did, rather than who I was. But perhaps the doing was simply a natural outflow of the being, of knowing I belonged, knowing I was a desired relationship, rather than a tolerated interruption.

I belonged. The thought took my breath away, speaking to an overwhelming hunger deep in my being. My natural instinct proclaimed that if I belonged in God's presence, it was as a slave, not even daring to look at His majesty, let alone to bask in it. In my wildest dreams I had never seen myself as a favored child allowed to run tamely into the throne room of the Sovereign One.

We stood in silence for a time as I tried to grasp the significance. A Father who loved me and wanted me. Tears formed in my eyes. Someone who could run the universe while I lived out the reality of being His beloved daughter. I didn't have to keep fighting to control everything around me. A knot of tension loosened in my chest.

Jesus touched my shoulder. I turned to Him. "My Father loves you," He said.

I nodded, still overcome by the thought.

"You are not rejected," He said quietly.

The paintings vanished and the previous art collection reappeared. "*This* is who you are," Jesus continued. "Not the rejected one, but the chosen one,[219] the beloved one. You are a priceless work of art created by Us—the One all artists only imitate—a genuine creation of God. You are the only you that exists or will ever exist. You are, in the true sense of the word, unique. You are made in Our image.[220] Not only that, but you were bought with a price: My death.[221] You are valuable to Us."

Me. Valuable. I looked up at Him, finally beginning to believe that He spoke the truth.

Jesus stepped closer, looking down into my eyes and putting His scarred hands on my shoulders. "Do you want to start living out who you are? Do you want to be healed?"

I flinched. I longed to be healed, but I didn't even want to think about how painful it would be to remove my breastplate or dress the wound. Yet . . . I could live like the me in those paintings. Loved. Wanted. He stood there patiently as I weighed my options.

"Yes," I finally croaked out, shaking at the thought.

"Come with Me," He said and clasped my hand. He led me over to a table I hadn't noticed before. Cutting implements, gauze, and a basin sat on the table. Jesus pulled up a stool and seated me on it.

I examined the table, wondering how exactly He would get my breastplate off—I hadn't designed it for easy removal. In fact, I had molded it into shape and allowed the crystal-hard material to solidify after I put it on.

He picked up a scalpel. I clutched the stool as the scalpel came in contact with the hard crystal and braced myself for agony. However, instead of exerting any force on it, He ran it along the sides of my breastplate, as though He were drawing. Then He picked up a small hammer and tapped the front of it. My breastplate promptly split in half and fell to the floor with a loud clatter. The air stabbed at my wound and a foul smell filled the air. Hissing, I tried to remain still.

Jesus pulled the basin close. "This will hurt. I have to wash out the poison that's been collecting in there."

He began to gently dab at my wound with a cloth. Each time He rinsed the cloth, I saw blood and sparkling black flecks. I focused on the black flecks, trying unavailingly to drown out the searing agony. I bit back a scream as the burning intensified.

What am I doing? I'll be defenseless! What if someone else tries to hurt me? Immediately, the portraits of me flitted through my mind. I'm becoming who God made me to be. I took a deep breath, my resolve strengthened. It didn't do anything for the pain that drilled into my consciousness. I needed a distraction, fast.

I looked up at Jesus. "Poison?" I asked through gritted teeth.

"Yes, the bitterness and hatred that have been festering in here. Almost done now," He said. An eternity of moments later He finished. "All right, that looks better."

I looked down, and then wished I hadn't. Dark blood collected in the gaping hole. "It's still bleeding!"

"I know. Just be patient." He picked up a clean cloth and put pressure on the wound to staunch the bleeding. Sweat ran down my face and body as the throbbing ache grew and grew. Then abruptly it lessened, leaving only a whisper of pain behind. I looked down again. The hole was beginning to close up. He slathered some ointment on it and began to bandage it.

"I've laid a slow healing on you," He said.

"Why? Why not heal it completely?"

He held my gaze. "Because it'll keep you close to Us long enough for you to grow. That way your brokenness can be mended, so you won't find yourself back in a similar situation."

"I see." I studied the floor. Perhaps there was something to this idea of my brokenness making me ripe for heartbreak. Jesus had proven He knew me better than I knew myself—but how was I broken?

I squared my shoulders. No time like the present to find out. "How am I broken?"

Jesus smiled and patted my shoulder. "Hang on. We'll get there. First, let's get something for you to wear that befits who you are. You don't need to keep wearing mourning."

I glanced down at my tattered, black rags, then nodded. Maybe new clothes would help me feel more myself. I stood up expectantly, wondering if He would just transform my clothes like Cinderella, or what.

He chuckled. "No, you still have to choose. We won't force you to change."[222] He indicated a newly-appeared seam in the rock face. "Through that door."

THREE

I walked up to the "door" and tentatively put a hand on it, trying to find some sort of knob. After a moment, the door changed: the space between the particles became visible. It was like looking through a curtain of water droplets; each tiny particle hung there like a jewel. Then the particles danced away from the middle, leaving an opening. I slipped through quickly, lest the door re-solidify with me in the way.

On the other side was a windowless changing room. Light, like that of a miniature sun, shone across the top of an elaborate room divider. I caught my breath and blinked in the sudden brightness. Rainbow light sparkled from the divider itself.

Mesmerized, I found myself across the room without any forethought. The lamp was like nothing I'd ever seen. The tiny rainbows reflected from inlaid mother-of-pearl on the divider. I studied it, fascinated by the play of color. Gradually, I realized the inlays depicted various scenes—scenes now familiar to me.

The first one was Creation—culminating with the man and woman made in God's image. I pored over the image, feeling there was more somewhere beyond my comprehension. Finally, I tore my gaze away and examined the other panels: the Fall of man, the birth of Jesus, His death and resurrection, and at the bottom, a picture of me on the day of my rebirth.[223] Each panel engrossed me for what felt like hours, yet I was unable to unravel their mysteries. I glanced back over the whole. And then I understood: this was my story, the story of my rebellion against God, of His rescuing me.

I remembered the painting of me clothed in light. Could this be something similar? I reached up to the lamp. It was! It was actually a dress. I shook it out. The material felt silky beyond belief and warm, like standing in sunlight. Holding it out, I suddenly became aware of how dirty I'd become. My fingernails were black and my skin was still encrusted with dirt and old blood. I wrinkled my nose, unable to recall the last time I'd cared enough to get myself really clean. How could Jesus stand to touch me?

I walked behind the screen and discovered a steaming bath set into the floor. I replaced the dress on the screen, then shucked off my own filthy rags. I dipped a toe in; the water was the perfect temperature. Delicate scents wafted from the soap at the pool's edge. I took a deep breath, reveling in the luxury. When I got in, I tried to shield my bandaged wound from the water, but wetness was unavoidable. Yet when I checked the bandage, it was still dry!

I scrubbed and scrubbed, delighted as the years of grime loosened. From start to finish the water remained crystal clear. Once I had scrubbed and soaked, and scrubbed and soaked some more for good measure, I stood up. The water sheeted off, leaving me dry and my hair tangle-free.

I brushed a finger across the dress. It felt unreal that I could wear something like this. In fact, it felt downright wrong, as though the world had turned upside down. I supposed it had.

Not that long ago I had seen myself as the rejected one, ugly and unworthy. But God had transformed my perspective, opening my eyes to my image-ness and showing me I had been fought for and won, just like the heroine in a fantasy story. Me. All these long years, I had believed the lies and lived in disguise. But now He was rescuing me and giving me back my true identity. He had restored my dignity.[224]

For a moment, I longed to remain in darkness and obscurity. Instead, wrong as it felt, I went with what I knew to be true. With shaking hands, I pulled the gown over my head. It was like wearing running water or sunlight. I felt warm in its glow. Safe. Almost hidden yet simultaneously revealed.

A new glimmer caught my eye. I turned and discovered a full-length mirror. I examined the reflection. This woman did look more like the woman in the portrait. My eyes seemed more lively, almost hopeful. And the gown . . . . No doubt about it: this gown was going to draw attention. Yet it obviously wasn't made by any human. In a way, it proclaimed I'd been touched by God. I smiled at the idea. People could take it up with Him if they thought I wasn't worthy to wear it. God knew that I was unworthy. A sob caught in my throat as I considered His grace.

Someone knocked on the door.

I cleared my throat and smoothed my dress. "Come in," I called, stepping back around the screen.

The door flitted open once more, and Jesus entered. My heart skipped a beat just looking at Him. He regarded me for a moment, then spoke. "Listen, O daughter, consider and give ear: Forget your people and your father's house. The King is enthralled by your beauty; honor Him for He is your lord . . . All glorious is the princess within her chamber; her gown is interwoven with gold."[225]

I blushed. I'd never imagined anyone quoting poetry at me, least of all Jesus.

"Shall we go?" He asked and held out an arm to escort me.

I took it. "Go where?"

He smiled. "To your castle, O princess," He said whimsically.

"My castle? What castle? What about my cocoon?"

He covered my hand with His own. "Cocoons aren't meant to last forever. You don't need it anymore. Besides, we need to continue changing out your lenses."

I tried to slow my racing pulse. I'm not that girl anymore. God will keep me safe now—safer even than I was in my cocoon. Deep breath. I want this. This is good.

Jesus stepped towards the door. Tightening my grip on His arm, I kept pace. As we reached the rock face, the door particles parted, and we stepped out above ground into what appeared to be sunlight. I stopped in my tracks and gawped at the scene before us.

The blazing sunlight came not from the sun, but rather from a domed structure made of the same light as my gown. "This is the place," Jesus said and gently pulled me forward.

Maybe I should pinch myself.

Jesus laughed. "You can pinch yourself if you think that's necessary, but this is no dream. Let's go in." He led me to another outline door. As in the cave, the particles danced open, welcoming us.

A slow smile spread across my face and I shook my head. This was incredible. A brook wound its way about, laughing merrily. Emerald green moss glowed on its banks. Flowers bloomed profusely, giving off a delicate perfume. Huge trees spread their shelter. Everything shone from within, as though ordinary bright colors were not good enough for this place. I spun slowly, wide-eyed as a child, still wondering if it could be real.

The meandering path we followed gradually led towards the middle of the dome. In the center lay a gazebo. Something about it called to my soul. I climbed the steps dazedly, then paused at the top and surveyed this new wonder. The three paintings of me in relation to God floated above the railing. The floor seemed made of glass, full of tiny twirling bubbles, like ice in a pond. I stepped onto it, expecting to feel the chill. Like everything else, the floor defied my imaginings; it felt warm and almost soft. What a strange place! I took another cautious step, still intent on the floor. Then, a flicker of reflected light caught my eye, and I glanced up.

My mouth fell open. Scenes from the stars whirled across the roof, twinkling like fairy lights. The whole thing was beyond comprehension.

I eventually tore my gaze from the ceiling and turned to face Jesus. "Are you sure we've got the right place?" I asked.

He smiled. "Yes, we do. I built it, so I should know."

"Why? Why would you build something like this for me?"

"This place is designed to remind you who you are, to provide a counter to all those lies you so easily believe." He sat down on a bench. "It's also a place where we can regularly spend time together."

"I don't know how I could forget with all this shouting your love for me."

"You can grow accustomed to most things. Just now, because of where you were living, this is quite a change. Someday though, it could become boring, blasé even, if you start hanging on to the place rather than Us."

I nodded. I had never expected to get used to my pain either. "Speaking of my cocoon, are you finally going to tell me how I'm broken?"

"A bit of it," He said. My face fell. "You don't really want a full picture. It would be too overwhelming." He walked over to a nearby telescope and carefully aimed it at some part of the ceiling. He motioned to the telescope. "Come look back before your betrayal."

Nervously, I joined Him, hoping this self-revelation would be less painful. Through the eyepiece, I saw myself walking along a road. I carried a loosely rolled drawing in my hand. When I tried to make it out, the picture changed, becoming plain. Across the top was scrawled, *My Identity*. A fuzzy portrait of me lay underneath. I squinted at it, wondering why it remained unclear.

As I moved through life, I traveled with various people. Each time I changed companions, the portrait flickered and changed. Sometimes the whole thing seemed crystal clear. Other times, entire portions were obscured by grey fog, like static across a television screen. Like a chameleon, I changed, taking on the values of whomever I accompanied.

Finally, my betrayer came into view. I longed to hide my eyes, to cry out against his winsome ways. I watched myself give him my portrait. I let him fill in the missing pieces, opened my heart, and eagerly walked with him mile after mile in ignorant bliss. Eventually he left, but only after he had stabbed my heart through and hurled those last, loud verbal daggers: "I don't want you. No one will ever want you." Before he left, he crumpled the picture and threw it in the dust. I picked it up, smoothed it out, and wept over it.

Jesus put a hand on my shoulder, and I looked up. "Do you see now? You didn't know who you were even before your betrayer came around. You were looking to the wrong people to define you. Who actually knows who you were created to be?"

Tears streamed down my face. "I suppose only my Creator would know," I said shakily and sniffed.

Jesus gave me a handkerchief. "That's right. We're the only One who knows you. Any time you let someone else define you, you're putting them in Our place. They've become your god," He said. "Even in your cocoon, your betrayer remained your god, because you held on to his view of you. You worshipped him by arranging your life around him."

His words pierced my heart, proclaiming their truth. My gaze dropped to the floor as shame rolled over me. I sagged. The very person I had vehemently hated had become my god.

"I still feel awful," I confessed. "Watching the betrayal just made me sick all over again . . . I think the worst part is seeing how naïve I was to trust him, and yet, part of me misses him. I hate being like this."

"Of course you miss him. Your heart is still healing. What do you miss most?"

I ventured to look up at Him. No condemnation filled His eyes, nor did pity, but rather compassion. I sighed. "A hundred ridiculous small things . . . I guess most of all, apart from missing him for himself, I miss feeling wanted and loved."

"Did he know you?" Jesus asked.

"No . . . ."

He raised an eyebrow. "So then did he want or love the real you, or only the picture he created?"

I paused, struck by the realization. I scrubbed at my face. "Ugh! I suppose he was attracted to the person he thought I was."

Jesus nodded. "It sounds like you're saying he couldn't love or reject the real you because his false picture of you got in the way. Is that correct?"

I made a face. "I hadn't thought about it that way before, but that makes sense."

"So what you're really missing is not something he ever gave you or could ever give you?"

I mulled that over and tried to remember my feelings on the subject before my betrayal. "I guess not. If I'm honest with myself, I can see that the relationship only masked my hunger, rather than satisfied it."

"Then who can meet your need for love and acceptance based on your true self? Where are you going to go now?"

I looked down at my gown and around at my extravagant surroundings, lingering on the paintings. Turning to face Jesus squarely, I said, "You alone know me, so You alone can meet that need."

"I'm glad you realize that," He said.

I looked up at Him and discovered that, between one heartbeat and the next, something had changed: I trusted Him.

"Knowing who you are, what does your betrayer's rejection say about him?" Jesus asked.

"What do You mean?"

"What kind of person throws away a da Vinci?"

I smiled a little. "I suppose a philistine, uncaring or ignorant of the object's value."

"Maybe you should take another look at your betrayer now that your view is anchored in Our love and acceptance," He said.

I shook my sweaty palms, then looked into the telescope once more. Jesus stood behind me, hands on my shoulders, His love drowning out my rejection. I realized I felt better. Maybe because that picture wasn't me anymore. Before, it had felt like he was rejecting me. But now that picture was just a poor caricature, not even close enough to be entertaining.

"Focus on your betrayer," Jesus said.

Now I could see his path, far before it intersected my own. I saw the same chameleon-like drawing, the same unceasing search for true love. Funny that love has to be based on truth, yet there's so little care for truth and so much emphasis on love.

I had changed to be acceptable and so had he. He too had been wounded to the core. Eventually, he had discovered an expedient protective mechanism: redrawing others' pictures. I now saw two broken, dissatisfied people creating a broken relationship—one that only highlighted our predicament. I saw that we were each marred in the betrayal; the destruction expanded with the final blow, like a woodcutter's wedge splitting a log.

Compassion for my betrayer flooded my healing heart as I saw the depth of his wounding. I turned to Jesus, "Did he find healing, too?"

"The heart knows its own bitterness, and a stranger does not share its joy,"[226] He replied.

I wrinkled my brow. "The heart knows what? What does that mean?"

"It means I'm not going to answer that question. It's a matter between him and Us."

"All right. I hope he does."

He smiled warmly. "That's the right attitude to have. Now, what about people in general?" He asked and walked with me over to a nearby bench.

I fingered a lock of hair, trying to follow the abrupt subject change. "What about them?"

"What are you going to do? You've been avoiding any real relationships."

"Only to keep from getting my heart broken again," I retorted.

He raised an eyebrow. "And now?"

"Now . . . now, it seems less likely. With You defining my identity, it'll be the real me they're attracted to."

"True, unless they intend to change you."

I sat bolt upright. "*Can* they still change me?"

Jesus shook His head. "Not unless you let them. You'll be fine as long as you hang on to your identity in Us, though it may be difficult. Do you have any ideas about how to avoid a situation like that?"

"Pick my friends carefully,"[227] I replied promptly, then added, "Choose people who don't try to define me. I guess that means they respect Your place in my life—they don't want to be my god."

He nodded. "And they don't want you to be their god either."

"I suppose that limits it to people who know their identity, which, since You said identity can only be seen through Your eyes, limits it to people who know You."

"Right, as far as people in your inner circle.[228] What else? What about your need for love?"

I recalled the aching emptiness and need for belonging my betrayer had seemed to fill. "Well, it would be nice to be loved by others." I glanced up at the portraits of me as God's beloved and smiled. "On the other hand, Your love is so much better than theirs. You're more like my cake, and they're just the icing."

Jesus smiled. "And that's the only way love can happen."

"Really? How so?"

"Only when you don't need the other party in the relationship can you truly love. Then there's no self-interest getting in the way. Since We're completely self-sufficient, We're free to love you. When you're secure in Our love for you, it opens up vistas of possibility. You're free to pass Our love on to others, loving them wholeheartedly. You can be your true self, because you don't need that love and acceptance primarily from them."[229]

I sat in silence for a few moments, digesting this thought. How freeing to have a never-ending source of love and acceptance apart from human relationships! I tried to imagine what such pressure-free interactions would look like. Even if the person rejected me, they still couldn't reject the real me. They'd never fully know the real me—

"And even if they could, whose fault would their rejection be?" Jesus interjected.

I stared at Him blankly for several moments.

"Apart from their culpability in rejecting one of Our creations, it would be Our fault for making you the way We did. So when they reject the person We created you to be, the weight of their rejection falls on Us."

I remembered the first painting of me with my heavy burden. "I like that," I said.

"We can handle it. It isn't heavy for Us. And speaking of weight, if you were going to put Our love and acceptance on one side of a scale and your rejection on the other, which do you think would be heavier?"

I pictured a scale broken down by the immensity of His love and smiled. "Your love and acceptance."

"What if every person in the world rejected you? What then?"

"Still Yours. It's more authentic, because it's based on truth. Plus, there's a lot more of You than them."

"Right. You'll never be more rejected than you are chosen." He reached into His pocket and pulled out a red rose. It emitted a soft glow. Carved on its stem, I saw the word *Beloved.* "You dropped this," He said and handed it to me.

With trembling fingers I took it. The rose felt like a normal plant but somehow seemed more substantial. I wondered how long it would bloom.

He clasped my hand and held my gaze. "Just in case you're tempted to forget how chosen and loved you are."

"Thank You," I whispered.

"Now what would happen if your heart got broken again?"

I looked down at the rose. My wound throbbed as I considered the possibility. "I don't know. I hope that I would use the energy of that pain to grow closer to You. And You could always heal me again, though I would really rather not get my heart re-broken." I looked up at Him, fishing for reassurance that nothing of the sort lay in my future.

"Right," He said, ignoring my unspoken question. "You don't have to fear your interactions with others, as long as you stay grounded in Us. You are made in Our image, though."

"What does that mean?"

"You're created to be in relationship.[230] Your tendency is to 'know' that you're safe, but never risk yourself in relationship.

But isolation makes you less human. As you continue to grasp Our love, you'll be drawn to relationships more and more, because you'll be more and more restored into Our image."

"I think that's something I'll have to take Your word for." I knew He was right, but I was still a little gun-shy. Maybe the more these truths sunk into my core, the less I would have to act contrary to my feelings.

He stood and looked me over, a grin on His face. "It's a start—a good one."

I frowned. "Why do you keep saying 'a start'? Didn't we make more headway than 'a start'?"

"I say 'a start' because it's the beginning of a process. Now that you've changed your visional priorities, the process can continue."

"What process?"

"The process of revelation. The more clearly you see Us, the more clearly you'll see yourself and others. Earlier, you saw yourself as the rejected one and Us as the One who rejected you. You thought We were in league with your betrayer. Now, you can see more clearly, and as you grow, your lenses will get even better."[231]

"I see," I replied, smiling.

He lifted me to my feet, then motioned to the telescope. "You were right about one thing, though." I stepped over to it and looked through. "We did allow your pain."

This time I saw myself teetering on the edge of a vast canyon. Then I stepped off into the depths below. A ledge several feet down halted my fall. My betrayal was the guard rail encircling that little ledge, proclaiming, "This far and no further."[232] Pain was the lifeline He threw down to me, providing a way to regain the ground I had lost, allowing me to live again in the wide open spaces above, rather than the cramped ledge with its terrifying drop.

Gratitude welled up in me for the God who loved me enough to allow pain in my life, instead of rescuing me from pain and allowing far worse to continue. I was awed by the fierceness of His love for me and amazed by the lengths He had gone to and permitted in me. In the breaking of His heart, He had provided a way to deliver me, and in the breaking of mine, He had provided the opportunity for change.

She . . . went after her lovers, but Me she forgot. Therefore I am now going to allure her; I will lead her into the desert and speak tenderly to her. There I will give her back her vineyards and will make the Valley of [Trouble] a door of hope. There she will sing as in the days of her youth, as in the day she came up out of Egypt. ~ Hosea 2:13d–15

EPILOGUE

I replaced my narrative in its box, next to my rose. Many years had passed since that encounter with God. When I had returned to everyday reality, the rose sat on my bedside table. It still glowed, looking as beautiful and perfect as it had all those years ago. The rose and the first telling of my story resided in a wooden box.

I had taken it out one last time. I had other copies of my adventure, but I wanted to savor the original, to remind my heart once more that I was God's beloved. Tomorrow I planned to pass on the rose and the story to my daughter. I had noticed her apathy and a distant, pained look in her eyes. She had already shut everyone out. But perhaps this was just the thing to get past her guard. I had never shown her the rose before.

I pulled out a sheet of stationary and a pen. "My darling Daughter," I wrote. "God asked me to pass this along to you. I know that your wound is too deep and painful to be probed, even by a mother's touch. And so, I pray that you too find healing in the touch of the One who loves you far more than I ever could. I love you!" I signed the note and placed it on top of the box.

I felt a slight pang in giving up the rose. But I knew that she needed it more than I did. Jesus would never have asked me to pass it along otherwise. After all, I didn't really need the rose: years of companionship had seared the knowledge of my belovedness into my soul. Our relationship burned brighter than any rose.

169 Beth Moore, "Video Session 9," *Living Beyond Yourself: Exploring the Fruit of the Spirit,* (Nashville, TN: LifeWay Press, 1998).

170 Listening is the art of creating space for someone to be fully themselves. See Henri Nouwen's book *Reaching Out: The Three Movements of the Spiritual Life,* (Garden City, NY: Image Books, 1986), 95.

171 John 20:24–29; Isaiah 50:6

172 For the sake of readability I've used both the singular and plural pronouns with regards to the Trinity and the Persons therein. When talking about the Trinity, it's almost impossible not to emphasize either the oneness of God or His threeness. Since the American church tends to prioritize God's oneness, I've used the plural pronouns in places to highlight God's essential relational nature. I in no way wish to imply that God is not one (Deut. 6:4–5; 1 Kings 8:60; Isa. 45:5–6, 45:21–22; James 2:19) or to stray into Tritheism (Matt. 28:19–20; 2 Cor. 13:14; Eph. 4:4–6; 1 Pet. 1:2; Jude 20–21; John 1:1–2, 1:9–18, 17:24, 14:26, 16:7; Acts 10:38).

173 Wikipedia is an apt illustration of our tendency to equate consensus with truth. Comedian Stephen Colbert pointed this out in an episode of *The Colbert Report* where he instructed his viewers to "save the elephants" by altering the Wikipedia entry on African Elephants to state their numbers had tripled in the past six months. *The Word: Wikiality,* accessed October 26, 2012, http://www.colbertnation.com/the-colbert-report-videos/72347/july-31-2006/the-word---wikiality

174 John 17:17

175 John 14:6

176 One way God's commitment to holiness and justice is displayed is by His unwillingness to overlook our sin. As the writer of Hebrews says, "without the shedding of blood there is no forgiveness" NIV (Heb. 9:22). Jesus' death provided said blood for our forgiveness while still maintaining God's justice (Rom. 3:25–26).

177 Jesus' incarnation and death on the cross is the quintessential display of God's love. John 3:16; 1 John 4:9–10

178 For an excellent treatment on wrestling with God, see Dr. Dan B. Allender & Dr. Tremper Longman, "Chapter Three: Stunned into Silence: The Liberating Insult of Grace" in *Bold Love* (Colorado Springs: NavPress, 1993), especially 76–80.

179 Rom. 8:28

180 Ps. 119:24

181 Isa. 52:14; Matt. 26:47–28:10; John 20:21–31

182 Matt. 26:64–66 (see Dan. 7:13–14); John 1:1–3, 1:14, 1:18, 8:57–59 (see Exod. 3:14); Rom. 9:5; Phil. 2:5–11; Col. 1:15–20; Titus 2:13; Heb. 1:8; 2 Pet. 1:1

183 Col. 1:17; Heb. 1:3

184 John 1:1–3, 1:14

185 1 John 1:5; James 1:13

186 e.g., Rom. 5:3–5; James 1:2–4

187 1 John 4:8; We see this exemplified within the relational nature of the Trinity. C.S. Lewis, *The Problem of Pain,* Macmillan Paperbacks Edition (New York: Macmillan, 1962), 29.

188 Lewis, *The Problem of Pain,* 46.

189 John 14:8–10

190 As God is the only transcendent being, He is the only one with a third-person perspective on the nature of reality, a complete view of the truth (both spatially and temporally). See C.S. Lewis' bit on how the Fall alienated us from our true selves by causing us to create a false third-person perspective based on our understanding of how we appear to others in *Perelandra: A Novel* (New York: Scribner Classics, 1996), 116–18.

191 Eph. 1:4–6

192 Luke 2:1–20

193 Gen. 3; Matt. 4:8–10; Eph. 6:11–12; 1 John 5:19

194 John 8:34; Rom. 6:16–18

195 Heb. 2:14–18

196 Matt. 16:21; Luke 24:25–27; Rom. 5:6–11, 8:1–4; 1 John 4:10

197 Heb. 12:2

198 Luke 24:1–12

199 Ps. 139:13

200 Chuck Missler, "Whence Our 'Reality?'," *Personal Update NewsJournal* (December 2003), accessed October 26, 2012, http://www.khouse.org/articles/2003/498/

201 Luke 15; "Lostness" connotes all the pain of distance from God, the sense of purposelessness and helplessness. In my case, it was accompanied by despair.

202 Ps. 10:4, 14:1

203 Gen. 3:1–7; Prov. 14:12

204 Isa. 61:10; Gal. 3:27

205 John 14:26, 16:13

206 Acts 2:1–4; 1 Cor. 6:19

207 1 Cor. 6:19

208 Eph. 4:30; 1 Thess. 5:19

209 Matt. 23:37; Ps. 81:8–12

210 Acts 1:8; 2 Cor. 12:7–10; Gal. 2:20, 5:22–25; Phil. 4:13

211 Prov. 17:3; Ps. 66:10

212 John 16:8–11; Rom. 8:1–17

213 Rom. 8:28–32, 7:21–25

214 Eph. 1:13–14, 4:30

215 Isa. 30:20–21; John 14:26, 16:13

216 Ps. 10:16, 29:10, 47:7

217 Rom. 8:14–17; Gal. 4:4–7; 1 John 3:1–3

218 Heb. 4:16 NKJV

219 Isa. 41:9; Eph. 1:4–6

220 Gen. 1:26–27

221 1 Cor. 6:20

222 Matt. 23:37; Ps. 81:8–12

223 John 3:3–8

224 For more information on dignity, see Beth Moore's book *So Long, Insecurity: You've Been a Bad Friend to Us* (Carol Stream, IL: Tyndale House Publishers, 2010), 145–160.

225 Ps. 45:10–11, 45:13

226 Prov. 14:10 (NASB)

227 Prov. 13:20

228 1 Cor. 5:9–11; Matt. 28:19–20; Mark 2:17; 1 Pet. 3:15–16

229 Lewis, *The Problem of Pain,* 50.

230 Gen. 1:26–27, 2:18–25; Eccles. 4:9–12; 1 Cor. 12:12–27; Gal. 6:2

231 John 8:31–36; As Anselm puts it, "I seek not, O Lord, to search out Thy depth, but I desire in some measure to understand Thy truth, which my heart believeth and loveth. Nor do I seek to understand that I may believe, but I believe that I may understand. For this too I believe, that unless I first believe, I shall not understand." Clement Charles Julian Webb, *The Devotions of Saint Anselm, Archbishop of Canterbury* (London: Methuen, 1903), Proslogion: Chapter 1, accessed October 26, 2012, http://www.ccel.org/ccel/anselm/devotions.txt/. See also Millard J.Erickson, "Contemporary Issues in Christological Method: An Alternative Approach," in *Christian Theology,* 2nd ed. (Grand Rapids, MI: Baker Book House, 1998), 689–691.

232 Lewis, *The Problem of Pain,* 93.

Freedom's Paradox

ONE

This is love for God: to obey his commands. And his commands are not burdensome. ~ 1 John 5:3

"Impossible!" I slammed the phone down and began pacing. Today marked the third day of my fruitless fight to break through bureaucratic red tape.

"'Because that's the law,'" I mimicked bitterly. I knew the poor woman on the other end of the line was just doing her job, but that didn't make me feel any better.

"Rules!" I threw up my hands in disgust and continued my vigorous pacing. If only all these stupid rules would disappear, the world would be a much better place. I'd been hemmed in with unwarranted rules my whole life. That's why I became my own boss, for crying out loud! And yet, here I was again, trapped by regulations.

There's no way all these rules are really necessary. *For the good of the many.* Ha! More like the inconvenience of most. No wonder so many people cheat the system. I slowed my pacing. Could I find a loophole or another way to slide in under the radar?

I snorted. "Not if that officious cow has anything to say about it," I muttered, then blushed as my mother's strictures came to mind: *Do unto others as you would have them do to you;*[233] *Pretty is as pretty does.*

My anger slowly drained away, leaving ample room for guilt. Stupid rules. Without rules, guilt would disappear. Although, according to my pastor, God's law was engraved on our consciences and written laws were only a reflection of His higher Law.[234] Maybe I'd always be fighting rules and guilt.

I closed my eyes. That woman *is* a person—a person who's just trying to do her job. And I had been testy and downright rude to her. I pushed the guilt away. It wasn't my fault. I was on edge from the hassle of regulations. I needed a break.

I checked the clock. Quitting time, or at least dinner time. Monday would be soon enough to take another run at the red tape.

I found myself careening down a freeway, about to smash headlong into an enormous concrete barrier. Trapped in yet another replay of a recurrent nightmare, I fought to awaken. The dream varied: sometimes I was driving, sometimes I was the passenger. I always awoke, drenched in cold sweat, right before impact. In each dream, I fought to change the timeline. If I could prevent the crash or at least figure out what to do differently the next time, maybe I could stop having this nightmare.

There was the barrier, mere feet away, moving closer and closer, rising up to swallow everything else in view. Sweat poured down my face. Terror—or maybe it was just repetition—etched the scene in my brain: the barrier, larger than life, loomed against a backdrop of barren grey clouds. The smell of hot pavement filled my nostrils. I thought my heart might force its way out of my chest. "Help me!" I cried aloud, able to speak for once.

Time slowed, then stopped. The car froze, inches from the barrier. I looked around. What new horror was my tortured mind about to produce? In the distance, I saw a man walking beside the barrier, coming toward me. I squinted at him, but he was still too far away for a good look.

I realized I should at least attempt escape from my current predicament. With shaking hands, I unbuckled my seatbelt. The door opened, which surprised me (my car dreams always involved problems with the door). I tumbled out of the car and looked around dazedly.

Other drivers and vehicles were still frozen. Yet the man was walking.

I edged closer to my car, then closed my eyes and pinched myself. Despite the pain, I failed to awaken. My eyes flew open. What now? Maybe I could simply avoid him until I woke up.

He's walking now, so try not to look suspicious—no need to make him rush. Right. I turned and tried to walk back along the barrier.

It didn't matter how quickly I moved, I remained directly beside my car. It reminded me of walking the wrong way on a moving sidewalk. I started to run, certain the man must be someone terrible since I couldn't escape him. It didn't help. He continued to advance, and I remained stuck, running in place by my frozen car.

If I couldn't escape, I'd need my strength to fight. I stopped running and began waiting. It seemed to take forever, though it's hard to tell time when time is standing still.

As he walked, I studied him. His dark brown hair curled a bit, and he had a swarthy complexion. I watched his demeanor, looking for clues to his character. His stride was confident but not arrogant. He walked purposefully but not hurriedly. Laugh lines creased his face, though it was currently in repose. He seemed deep in thought. He doesn't really look like a bad guy—but the worst ones never do.

Finally, when he was about ten feet away, he caught my gaze and smiled. I was hooked immediately. His eyes sliced right through my desperate facade of confidence to the heart of my terror. I knew he could tell that I longed to escape. His smile warmed my heart right down to the places cold with dread. It reassured me that he was not coming to do harm.

"Hello. You said you needed help?" he asked, still smiling, as though I were a friend he'd run into at the store.

I nodded, speechless and off-balance.

"So what did you need?"

"W-w-well, I was about to crash," I managed to squeak out.

"Oh really?"

"This is my car," I said, pointing to it. I couldn't even squeeze between it and the barrier. I wondered if the man was blind, dense, or mocking me.

"I've seen you come here quite a few times lately. You always leave right before impact."

At first I was puzzled, then remembered how often I found myself in this dream. "Do you mean when I wake up?"

He nodded.

"Then why didn't I wake up this time?"

"I stopped your dream."

I started. "Who are you?"

He brushed that aside. "Why do you think you keep having this dream? Are you afraid of concrete barriers or of crashing?"

"Both, actually," I said, reminded of the last time I had been stuck in a long stretch of road construction: I had had a panic attack. Squishing myself against the door hadn't been far enough away to escape the barrier.

"Why do you think they bother you so much?"

"I don't know! If I knew, maybe they wouldn't bother me. Why do you keep asking me questions?" I shot back.

"Perhaps it's because I enjoy watching you think, among other reasons," he said lightly. "Maybe you're having this dream so often because there's something you need to learn."

He walked over to the barrier and opened a small door. I could have sworn it wasn't there a second earlier.

"Maybe you just need to look at this from another perspective." He gestured for me to follow, then ducked through. I stared at it for a moment. There was no help for it. I couldn't stay here. What if time resumed? I took a deep breath, then walked forward.

I emerged on the other side of the barrier. The man stood to one side of the doorway, waiting for me. I turned to look back at my car, but the opening had vanished.

Here I could see that the barrier partitioned off a strip of pavement about the width of a lane. Opposite the barrier lay rolling grasslands turned a late-summer brown. Other than the freeway, the land seemed void of human incursion. In one direction, the road stretched on and on into the distance. To the other, it curved. This side of the barrier felt like another world entirely.

"Now what?" I asked.

"Now, we observe." He pointed back the way he'd come. "Let's walk down a little farther this direction."

Once around the curve, we came upon a construction worker, complete with hard hat and reflective vest. He too stood frozen in time. In one hand he held a measuring device and in the other a notebook. His pen had fallen to the ground.

"Watch," the strange man said.

Time moved forward again. The construction worker reached down to pick up his pen. Suddenly, there was a horrific crash as something smashed into the barrier. I shrieked and jumped at least a foot. Brakes squealed, followed by more sounds of collision. The construction worker paled and began running back to his parked pickup truck. I stood, petrified.

The barrier remained solid. For the first time in my life I was thankful to be near a concrete barrier. Abruptly, time stopped once more, then rewound, ending with the construction worker again poised in the act of measuring.

Wild-eyed, I looked around. All appeared as before: frozen. My pounding heart slowed. I glared at the man shakily. "All right, so concrete barriers can be a good thing if you're on the right side of them. So what? This doesn't help me! I'm not a construction worker."

"Why is this concrete barrier here?"

I sighed. "To protect construction workers and to prevent any construction debris from flying into cars."

"Right. It's a place of safety, just like my Law."

"Your law?" I asked, watching him warily, trying to figure out who he was. I remembered he hadn't answered my earlier question. I tensed. Had I been wrong about that smile?

"My Law shows you the way of freedom and acts as a barrier to protect you from the consequences of sin," he continued and flashed that warming smile at me again, as though he could sense my unease.

I took a step back. "Wait, wait, wait. Who are you?"

"Don't you recognize me?"

I stared a little more, and then it dawned on me. He's Jesus. But why is He here? I mentally catalogued all my recent sins: none too heinous in the list. I'd even been attending church regularly. Granted, I often nodded off a bit during the sermon, but I was fully engaged during the rest of the service. I worshipped and such. I was passionate about God.

"You're Jesus."

"Yes," He said, His smile still intact.

"Why are You here?" I asked. I felt like a kid caught with her hand in the cookie jar.

"Because you're stuck, and you asked for help. Because I[235] love you."

"Um, thanks."

I had yet to feel particularly helped. It was nice that this instance of my nightmare had been resolved, but the fear lurked, waiting to snake its tentacles around my heart at some unseasonable moment.

"So You were saying? Your Law?"

"My Law is a barrier to create safety, so people can walk freely—"

"Wait just a minute! You can't connect freedom and restrictions like that. Don't You know that rules decrease freedom?"

How in heaven's name could Jesus be so far behind the times?

"Oh really?" He said.

"Well yes, of course," I said, trying to soften my tone. "We put people in jail because it restricts their freedom. We fight against oppression because people have the right to be free."

"So you're saying that more restrictions mean less freedom, that the two are inversely proportional?"

I nodded. "Exactly."

Jesus quirked an eyebrow at me. "Would you be willing to test that theory?"

"Uh, sure."

He snapped His fingers, and we began to soar into the air.

"What is going on?" I demanded, attempting to keep my voice steady despite the fear coursing through my body.

"I just lessened your restrictions," He said, His hands clasped behind His head.

My teeth started chattering—even my aggravation wasn't enough to keep me warm this high up. I clenched them. "How so?"

"Gravity. It was keeping you down. You're much freer this way."

"Wait! What about oxygen? Will I get high enough that I can't breathe?"

"Probably."

"I can't survive without air!"

"Hmm, in that case, perhaps I will add a small restriction. I'll keep us from going up quite that high."

I heaved a sigh of relief. "Thank You."

"You're welcome. Now perhaps we can continue our discussion."

I nodded, still shivering.

"You look cold. Would you like a coat?" He asked and produced one out of thin air.

I took it. I had never considered gravity an asset in getting dressed, but it is. Grappling with the coat caused me to gyrate about wildly. In the end, I only managed to get into it by hanging on to Jesus' proffered arm. He didn't seem to be affected by gravity, or by the lack thereof.

"Thank You, again," I mumbled, thoroughly humbled—or perhaps humiliated—by this point. Though to be fair, He hadn't been cruel or indifferent as He exposed my foolishness. In fact, I had seen compassion on His face. I suppose it was mostly my pride which smarted so badly.

"So do you feel more free?" He asked kindly.

"Not so far."

He began pacing through the air. "Perhaps you haven't fully explored your lack of restrictions. Just think of all the things you can do now that you couldn't before. You can fly anywhere you want."

"Only if I had a method of propulsion," I said. "And how would I go anywhere? And then what would I do when I arrived? Live my life with an anchor tied around my waist?"

He stopped in front of me. "So, would you agree that this particular restriction is not depriving you of freedom?"

"Yes!" I said, hoping that my emphatic reply would convince Him to reinstate my personal gravity. Every rule has an exception.

Jesus smiled. "Mhm. I can see we need to continue this conversation, but I know you'd be more comfortable on the ground. Let's see," He looked around, and we began a slow descent. "This looks like an ideal place," He said as He floated us to the edge of a large pond.

The pond seemed virtually untouched by human hands, which is to say that grass and weeds had overgrown everything. A slight breeze ruffled the water's surface, stirring up the moist smells of algae and fish. The sky had cleared and the sun reflected blindingly off the murky water.

I sank down onto a nearby rock, barely resisting the urge to kiss the solid ground.

Jesus settled Himself across from me. "So what's keeping you from believing that freedom is not the absence of restrictions?"

Other than the fact that most of the time, it isn't? Maybe it was all the pointless restrictions I'd endured, simply because they were the whims of the authority figures in my life: it isn't ladylike to chew gum, always wear shoes, girls shouldn't run, and on and on. How many times had someone used "because I said so" as justification for a dumb rule?

"I don't like people telling me what to do," I said, "particularly when I don't know why I ought to obey."

"It's an emotional objection then? Not a cognitive one?"

"Well, it's both. For instance, look at restrictions that dehumanize people—women and children are sold into slavery, and corrupt officials kill their people for petty reasons. The world is full of brutal examples. How can You say that restrictions don't limit freedom?"

"I can't. I didn't," He said. For a moment His eyes were distant and pained. I suddenly realized that if He was omniscient, He was far more aware of those horrors than I. And if He was all-good and loving, then it must cause Him unimaginable pain to let them endure.

His eyes cleared, and He turned to look at me once more. "All restrictions don't increase freedom any more than all restrictions decrease freedom." He gave me a half-smile. "I'm not the one arguing for restrictions and freedom in inverse proportions."

"Then I'm confused. What are You suggesting?"

"I was merely responding to your objection that I can't link freedom and restrictions. You were arguing for freedom as the absence of restrictions. Freedom is not nearly that simple, as you've discovered."[236]

"I have?"

"Well, can you really argue that freedom equals a lack of all restrictions?"

"I suppose not *all*," I said, thinking that I could have argued for the absence of most.

"Think about a traffic light. If it's always green in all four directions, what do you get?"

I grimaced. "An accident, at worst. Really slow traffic at best."

"So are people more likely to get to their destination with or without both red and green traffic lights?"

"With," I said, forced to agree despite myself. Next time I had to remember not to begin my argument with a universal statement.

"Okay, so You've convinced me that freedom is not the absence of all restrictions. I'll even give You that they can be useful—occasionally."

"Then let's go back to the emotional level. Why don't you like to be restricted?"

"Bad experiences, probably. Too many people who restricted me right into a ditch—or maybe a concrete barrier," I said with a shaky smile.

He put a gentle hand on my knee. "It sounds like it comes down to a trust issue. You don't want just any old restrictions—you want the right ones: those that will help you, that will increase your freedom to experience the things you really want. Yet you don't trust anyone but yourself to decide which restrictions fall into that category. Is that what you're saying?"

"Right. Who else is going to know what makes me happy? I can run my own life better than anyone else."

"Can you? How do you know which restrictions fulfill that category? How do you even know that you've ever been happy?"

I cocked my head to the side. Never been happy? "I suppose by trial and error, though I can also learn from other people's mistakes. And doesn't everyone know what happiness is?"

"Don't you think people spend a lot of time chasing it? As if they couldn't pin it down, like a half-remembered scent."

"Maybe. But just because it's hard to get doesn't mean you shouldn't look."

"Do you think it's easier to find water in a desert or at a spring?"

"I would generally go with a spring," I said. Why were we suddenly talking about water?

"So if people are trying to find happiness in a desert when there's a spring available, is all their hard work worth it?"

"I've never thought about it. If happiness were readily available elsewhere, I suppose their efforts could be categorized as—"

"Foolish? Heartbreaking?" He said, His voice full of sorrow and anger.

I leaned forward. "Where is the spring?"

He shook His head and smiled. "Let's start at the beginning: What is happiness?"

I wracked my brain. Why are the most basic of ideas often the hardest to define? "A feeling . . . when all seems as it should be . . . like when your spirits lift, because the day was grey and now the sun is shining . . . . Or when you have a sudden, blissful moment of perfect understanding with someone you love . . . . Moments when you want to sing and dance or be still because everything is so beautiful and perfect . . . . It's hard to explain. How would You define it?"

"I would say happiness[237] comes in those moments when you're in line with the way We designed the world to work. It's the sense of being the person you were created to be, in the circumstances you were created to thrive in."[238]

"I've never thought about it that way."

"I know," He said dryly.

"No wonder it's elusive. Even if I could get myself where I needed to be, there's no way I could make everything and everyone else cooperate. Is happiness even possible?" I asked.

"Of course it is. Though as you've alluded to, it is less common in this broken world and impossible to attain if it's the goal."

"What? Impossible if it's the goal? I'm not sure I agree with that. I've been happy. I mean, that's what got me involved with church in the first place."

"Is it?" He asked. His gaze sliced through me once again, laying bare my motives so that I could examine them myself.

I had begun my spiritual journey out of a hunger for significance. I had stayed in church because I'd thought it made me happy. But had it really? The more I thought about it, the more I kept coming back to guilt. Attending church gave me a bone to throw at my gnawing sense of guilt whenever it raised its wolfish head.

"I'm not saying that being in My Body[239] can't make you happy," He said gently. "We created you to be in relationships.[240] As you experience healthy relationships within the Church, happiness is a byproduct. But is that really why you go to church?"

I looked down at the ground. "I suppose not. I guess I've been going because it makes me feel less guilty . . . though I did enjoy my friends . . . ."

"Just keep that in mind," He said, asking me to do the thing I least desired to do at that moment.

I nodded, then, determined to move the conversation along, I asked, "So what did You mean when You said happiness is impossible if it's the goal?"

"Once happiness becomes an end in itself, you've divorced it from Us."

"Okay . . . ." What was I missing?

"If happiness is a byproduct of living the way We designed you to be, and We designed you first and foremost to be in a right relationship with Us,[241] why do you think it's possible to find happiness elsewhere? How do you expect to act in line with the design specifications when you refuse to talk to the Designer or read the manual?"

"I see what You mean—but still, some people catch hold of happiness in bits; why else would they work so hard to find it?"

Jesus pointed to the dancing shadows on my rock. "For some, the 'bits' they catch are only the shadow, not happiness itself. Like Plato's shadows,[242] these bits only emphasize their longing for the substance.[243] Others seek it because of the moments when everything in them cries out in despair, 'This is not the way things ought to be!' Happiness apart from Us is all in glimmers and counterfeits, rather than substance. Full happiness is yet to come, revealed in the day when We set all to rights."[244]

"So what do happiness and freedom have to do with each other?" I asked.

"What do freedom and restrictions have to do with one another?"

"Some restrictions can free you," I began, like a bored student parroting back a set of half-grasped words. Then understanding came in a blinding flash. I sat stock-still, amazed. "You're talking about things like music lessons or physical training, aren't You? If you restrict yourself by practicing or training, it actually opens up new possibilities. It creates freedom to do things you wouldn't otherwise be able to accomplish."[245]

"Yes!"

"But then not all restrictions free you," I added, thinking back to injustices, like slavery, which were often within the realm of legality.

"Right. Think about physical training. Suppose a person trained to fly like a bird, using only his body. He could spend his life strengthening his muscles and studying birds, but would those restrictions help him achieve his goal?"

"No." I snickered, then realized I'd done things that were likely just as foolish.

"And would his life be fulfilling, or would it be wasted?"

"Wasted."

"Do you see that this person is less himself? The wrong restrictions dehumanize you. So, as you were saying, not all of them are freeing—"

I ground my teeth. "And now, I suppose, we're back to how to determine which ones are freeing and which will suck the life out of you." I didn't want to talk about it!

Jesus smiled at me. "There are fish in this pond."

I blinked at Him a few times, then decided to just go with it. "Yes, yes there are," I said, noting the many ripples disturbing the water's surface. The fish were in a feeding frenzy.

"Do you suppose the fish know they need water?" He asked, idly slipping His fingers into the pond.

"I have no idea."

He stood up and held out a hand. "Let's go find out."

I gulped. "Um, okay, sure." I took His hand.

I began to shrivel and shrink. It was an unpleasant sensation, like being squished into a box much too small. Then all at once, I was a fish, out of water. It was exceedingly uncomfortable.

I flopped about, my gills gasping for water until Jesus unceremoniously plopped me into the pond. I gulped deep breaths of water. Much better! What in the world was all that near-suffocation about? I swam a bit and was delighted to discover how well my new fins and tail worked.

Jesus dove in after me, now a fish Himself. "So what do you think?"

"If I'm going to be a fish, I prefer to be a fish *in* the water rather than out," I said primly.

"Why's that?"

"Fish are not designed to breathe air!" I slashed a fin downward, trying to emphasize my point, but mostly just flailing.

"So?"

"They can't function well without water. In fact, to the best of my knowledge, the vast majority of fish can't survive outside it."

"Aha, I see you've found another freedom-enhancing restriction."

I didn't have anything to say to that. I floated there, my mouth opening and closing repeatedly as I cast about for a suitable reply. None came to mind. My only hope was that I just looked fishy, not ridiculous.

Jesus waited a few moments, then asked, "Shall we go find a fish to chat with?"

I tried to nod, and off we swam with Him leading the way. Here, flecks of something glimmered in the sunlight and the water was comfortably warm. Though it was murky, I found that I could see clearly enough. In fact, near the surface a plethora of bugs lingered. I thought hungrily of dinner, then brought myself up short. I may have looked like a fish, but I refused to eat like one.

The farther down we went, the gloomier and chillier it became. After a bit, we found a large fish swimming purposefully along with an air of self-importance.

"Excuse me, sir, could you spare a moment?" Jesus asked.

The fish looked us over and apparently decided we were worthy of his attention. "I suppose so. You are not denizens of our fair country. You must be from the other side," he said, as though uttering a shrewd pronouncement.

I wished I'd had a fish-sized monocle to hand—or flipper?—him. It would have perfectly completed the picture of his pomposity. I stifled giggles lest I offend his self-importance.

"You're right, we aren't from around here. Would you tell us about your country?" Jesus asked pleasantly.

The fish bobbed up and down in the water. "Of course. It is always wise to familiarize oneself with the locality one is visiting. Our country is a delightful place, almost magnetic. Obviously, you must be aware of this fact since you, too, have been drawn here. Food is plentiful and so are neighbors. There are plenty of the right sorts of fish who make their homes here." He seemed to swell ever so slightly. "I, myself, am a fish of some standing in the community and can recommend a hostelry, if you so desire."

"Actually, we were wondering if you could tell us more about your country. Where are its borders?"

The fish stared at Jesus for a moment, as though trying to ascertain if his intelligence was being insulted. Apparently he decided that we must be applying to his magnificent wisdom, or perhaps were merely impaired in some way. In any event, he answered the question kindly. "The borders are, of course, the murk and the standing stones."

"And what exactly is the murk?"

"The murk is part of the shallows, where the world is smaller."

"Where the shallow water is?"

"Water? What is that?" he asked.

"Water. The liquid medium we're moving through. Separate from the air."

The fish's eyes bulged out even more. "You've been talking to those frogs, haven't you? Well, I've no time to waste on nonsense. I should have pegged you for *that* sort of fish immediately!" And with that, he harrumphed away, muttering something about troublemakers.

"I think that should be enough. Would you like to stay here, or shall we find somewhere warmer to talk?" Jesus asked me.

"I think I'm ready to be a human again, preferably one on dry land," I said, thinking longingly of sunshine. The water was mostly dark now and getting cold as the sun continued to sink.

"Okay, let's go somewhere more comfortable."

Jesus swam toward a pile of large rocks in the middle of the lake. I wondered if these were said standing stones. He headed for a small tunnel in their midst, and I hurried after Him. The tunnel abruptly darkened, then I found myself standing, once more human, in a narrow hallway with Him. He opened a door in front of us and invited me in.

TWO

We entered a cozy, old-fashioned kitchen. A huge cast iron sink stood against one wall. Above it, a picture window looked out onto the grounds. Weeping willows, benches set in shady groves, and little stone walkways throughout the flower gardens all gave it a feel of elegance.

On the adjacent wall, a fire burned merrily in a cavernous stone fireplace. Immediately conscious of my freezing extremities, I walked over to the fire and held my hands out. Nearby stood a small wooden table set with dinner. Something smelled delicious. I inhaled deeply, and my stomach growled, startling me. Had I ever felt so hungry in a dream?

"Shall we?" Jesus asked and pulled out a chair for me.

I walked over and sat down. I lifted the covers off the dishes and discovered steaming soup and bread. As I ate, I felt refreshed, as though I had just consumed a full night's sleep. We ate in comfortable silence while I tried to sort through my time as a fish.

Whatever this was—dream, vision, or something else—the fish was probably imaginary, but he still raised an interesting question. Could any creature really understand its own environment? The very nature of environment seemed to preclude comprehension on some level. One could take a step back and try to examine other points of view, like when people traveled abroad to gain a clearer view of their own culture.

I settled my chin in my hand. Yet if there was no comparison, like the frogs spreading "nonsense" about air . . . . I supposed only a creature able to experience another medium could tell the fish about their own environment. Even then, the fish couldn't really comprehend the realities.

What did my "water" look like? Things that would have been ever so much more concrete if I were at a higher vantage point—like happiness and love and right. Intangibles that were perhaps only intangible because I couldn't fully apprehend them.

"You're right," Jesus said. "It does take someone who's outside the environment to comprehend what's inside and communicate its nature."

"Are You saying that I can't determine which restrictions are actually freeing . . . because I'm stuck in my own environment?" I asked, as the realization hit me.

"Yes!" He exclaimed.

I sat there, turning the idea over and over in my mind to see if it could be true. After some thought, I realized the pieces had been there all along. The idea fit, like a key clicking into a lock.

Then I wriggled in my chair and shook my head. No, that can't be right. If it were, I'd be trapped, left at someone else's mercy—helpless. There has to be another way.

Jesus put a hand on my arm. "We've crashed back into your emotional obstruction, haven't we?

I glared at Him. I hated being so transparent. But even more, I hated that I could reject truth just because I didn't like it. Where has all my objectivity gone?

"What objectivity?" Jesus asked.

"The objectivity I've fought to maintain! The only way to identify truth . . . ." I put a hand to my now aching head. Was the independence I'd wrested out of those bad experiences an illusion? Or had I lost it somehow along the way?

He caught my gaze. "Love, We're the only One who can have a third-person perspective on reality.[246] You're stuck in your medium."

"Why? What gives You the right to tell me what to do?" I wailed, half defiant, half anguished. Then, belatedly recalling I was questioning God, I braced myself for His wrath.

Jesus paused, looking at me, allowing me to feel the crushing weight of His presence. He didn't need to say anything.

I found myself face down on the floor without any forethought. My heart beat as though it would escape my chest. I struggled to draw breath, and I wondered if I would last much longer like this. Then, by degrees, the awesome weight lessened. Gradually, I caught my breath and slowed my racing pulse. I stayed put on the floor, though. It seemed the wisest course to appease the terrible anger I imagined He must be feeling.

He gently raised me to my feet and pulled my downcast gaze back to His own. I was shocked to still see compassion in that look. I had expected to be incinerated by His wrath at my impudence. I guess it really is God's kindness that leads us to repentance.[247]

"What gives Us the right to tell you what to do? Ours is the right of the potter. Does the clay have the right to demand anything of him?[248] Ours is the right of the Creator. Can Hamlet say to Shakespeare, 'How do you know what I was made to do?' " His voice was all the more terrible for its quiet gentleness.

"I retract my objection," I said stiffly, feeling doomed to slavery to this deity I had so lightly gotten involved with.

He held out His nail-scarred hands.[249] "These, too, give Us the right. Love gives Us the right. We have bound you to Us with cords of human kindness.[250] Listen. Listen to Me. This is the answer to your emotional obstruction. You fear losing your independence. You fight to maintain a semblance of control lest someone enslave you. We created you.[251] You are known through and through.[252] And you are loved,"[253] He said, His eyes declaring His love even more emphatically than His words.

I wanted to believe Him, but I'd been told that far too many times, at least the part about being known and loved. But maybe God was different, trustworthy. It doesn't matter—I refuse to trust anyone that deeply again. I choked back tears and shook my head.

"If you see through everything, you'll see nothing at all,"[254] Jesus said quietly.

"What?"

"Look out this window," He said. "It's designed to be transparent so that you can see what's on the other side. What do you see?"

I walked over to the sink. "I see stars, the moon coming up, the grass and trees. There's a bench in that little grove over there."

Jesus moved to stand beside me. "All right, now suppose you argue that the bench is not really there, or at least has some ulterior motive for manifesting itself. Therefore, you discount it."

I gasped as the bench vanished into thin air.

"Now, let's say something similar with regard to the trees, the grass, and all the other plants. They're revealing themselves under false pretenses." They too disappeared, leaving only barren earth. "While we're at it, let's throw out all other matter and energy. Now what do you see?"

"Nothing," I replied, gazing thoughtfully at emptiness where moments before had been life and beauty.

"To see through everything is to see nothing at all," He repeated and led me back to the table. "I'm not saying that motives aren't important. They matter. But this is a case where you'll be blind if you discount everything based on past experience. If you dismiss the existence of truth, you're going to throw away much more than you've bargained for. We've already proven Our love."[255]

I looked down at the table. So had others, supposedly. I remembered the succession of gifts and remorse dished out to "prove love." One person in particular had that sort of manipulation down to an art form.

"No, that's masking selfishness, not proving love. Even true tokens of love only express love, rather than prove it. You've got to stop using him as your measuring stick. Besides, that relationship wasn't real love anyway."

My eyes flew to His face. "What? How do You know?"

"Because a love relationship involves both parties giving up freedom—he demanded all the sacrifice come from your end. Besides, true love is not based on need."

"But, but, we were in love," I said loudly, trying to drown out the whisper of doubt He had awakened in me.

He shook His head and put a gentle hand on my arm. "You were in infatuation."

I jerked away. "Infatuation doesn't feel like that!"

"Oh really? Then how does it feel?"

I frowned, wishing I could stamp my foot like a child. "I don't know. Less . . . substantial."

"How do you know you were in love?"

"Well, when you're in love, you want to stay with that person forever. You love everything about them, and being with them is the best feeling in the world. That's how I felt."

"What about when your feelings change?"

I glared at Him. "Isn't the nature of love that it lasts?[256] Isn't it 'forever' if it's the real thing?"

"Did you feel loving even on days when you were tired or irritated?"

"Maybe not always," I admitted. "But relationships ebb and flow. The predominant emotion is what really matters."

"'Love is not love, Which alters when it alteration finds, Or bends with the remover to remove: O no! it is an ever-fixed mark,'"[257] He said. "How do you suppose it stays fixed?"

I stared at Him blankly. Love had come rather suddenly for me and refused to leave, no matter how hard I'd tried to get rid of it. The other person involved had fallen out of love as abruptly as he had begun it. Sadly, these wildly different perspectives left me no nearer to an understanding of love, and so I remained silent.

"It is fixed because one chooses it to be so. Love is not a pilotless ship to be blown about by the winds of circumstance. Love chooses to restrict one's own freedom in preference to another out of abundance, from needs already met. Infatuation, on the other hand, is characterized by need.[258] One is attracted to someone based on perceived characteristics that promise to fulfill some need. And so, whoever has the greatest need ends up making the most sacrifices."

I looked down at the table. He couldn't be right. I tried to envision love like He'd described. Sudden longing stole my breath. To have that kind of love . . . it'd be amazing. Maybe there was something to it. Switching the label on my feelings explained more than it didn't. Cold comfort. Why couldn't I have kept my little illusions? How much more of this could I take?

I clenched my teeth, then met Jesus' gaze. "All right. I guess I can see Your point."

"Do you also see how this understanding of love can break through your emotional objection?"

"Yes . . . ," I said, my head still spinning. "If love is as You say, I can know that You love me because You've taken the first step . . . You've already sacrificed for me by becoming human[259] and dying on my behalf."[260]

He nodded. "It also means that you can trust Us to take care of your best interests, because We don't require you to fulfill Our needs."

"Wait, I thought You demand obedience because it glorifies You. Because You need us to acknowledge Your glory."

"No!" Jesus said, looking me straight in the eye. "It's because We love you. It's in your best interest to obey so that you're in line with the way We designed the world to work. It's in your best interest to worship Us so that you won't end up worshipping something that will ruin you. No one else can handle the pressure of being worshipped. Nothing else can satisfy. So, no, it's not to feed Our ego.[261] We're still God, whether you choose to worship and obey or not."

I leaned back in my chair and studied the fireplace stones, wishing I could call for a timeout. So many people—myself included—viewed God's Law as an unwanted interference, if not outright meddling. Seeing God's commands as an expression of His love was just plain strange.

I thought back over my dream. I rubbed my forehead. How many more of my foundational notions was Jesus planning to shake up today? Truth. Happiness. Love. I snorted. Just a few small items.

I supposed ignorance was part of swimming about in all those intangibles. The reasonable part of me knew that talking to Jesus was bound to be a learning experience. If anyone was a frog, it was Him. By definition, He was both God[262] and man:[263]the highest vantage point coupled with the ability to communicate clearly to us fishes.

I swallowed hard. *Us* fishes? I guess it was pointless to argue that I wasn't a fish. Much as I hated to admit it, this encounter with God had forced me face-to-face with my own ignorance. I wish I'd paid more attention in church; it might have at least cushioned the blow of all these new ideas.

THREE

"That's a good idea. Let's talk about church," Jesus said.

I returned my attention to Him, uneasy at His all-too-innocent tone. "What about church?"

"Let's start with last Sunday."

"Okay . . . ," I said, trying to remember what had happened.

"Why don't I jog your memory?" He said and pulled what appeared to be a remote control out of His pocket. He pressed a button, and a large image appeared suspended in the air directly in front of us. He pressed another button, and a video began to play, as though we were watching a movie without the bother of a television.

I recognized the scene immediately and went hot, then cold all over. I had been drinking coffee during Sunday school. I set the cup on the table in front of me but decided it sat perilously close to the edge. I moved it closer to the table's center, then released it just in time to collide with the person next to me. She had been gesturing to emphasize a point and knocked the cup over. Coffee spilled onto both of us, though she got most of it. My face crimson with mortification, I mumbled an apology and began mopping up, wishing the floor would swallow me right then and there.

Jesus mercifully flicked the screen off. He turned to me. "How are you doing?"

My stomach roiled. "All right," I said, knowing I really should be. My eyes traced the mortar between the stones. It was such a small thing. No murder or anything of the sort committed. Yet . . . . Why hadn't I been more careful?

After my beverage fiasco, I had vowed never to bring drinks to class again. I considered switching classes (or at least sitting in the back from now on) and wished I could stop being such a careless person. Rather than assuaging my guilt, these thoughts served only to intensify its weight. I wondered if I ought to apologize once more to the woman, or maybe send her a nice note or a new sweater.

Jesus touched my arm. "So is this the sort of behavior you're trying to cancel out by attending church?"

"No. Yes. Maybe." I closed my eyes for a moment and tried to sort through my conflicting thoughts. "Maybe it wasn't very loving of me to put my drink in such a precarious place. I wasn't looking out for her interests above my own,"[264] I said, feeling the familiar tightening in my chest as guilt ensconced itself.

"Maybe you just don't understand guilt," Jesus said.

I sighed. Now guilt. Great. I prefer to continue shoving it to the edges of my consciousness, thank you very much.

Jesus patted my hand. "That's only because you're confused."

"All right, but can we please get this over with?"

"Then let's start at the beginning: What is 'guilt'?"

I tried to ignore the knot in my stomach and view guilt objectively. "When you feel bad because you've done something you shouldn't have, or you haven't done something you should have."

He shook His head. "That's *feeling* guilty. What is 'guilt'?"

"Um, well, I suppose those guilty feelings are precipitated by doing something wrong, so guilt is when you've done something wrong."

"Such as? How do you know what fits that category?"

I rearranged my silverware and tried to think what overarching criteria one could use to determine a moral code. I had been dragged through multiple ethics by various authority figures. In the end, it all seemed to come down to whatever they wanted. For a while I had abandoned any sort of broad standards, but I found it untenable. Thus I'd landed on "the greater good."

But did it still work? I wasn't sure anymore. How could any limited human perspective recognize what was best for society? Even if we had a general idea for a specific timeframe, we couldn't really know how any ethic would play out long-term or even how it would work on an individual level.

Plus, what about rights? No one had the right to impose a particular set of standards on anyone else. Suddenly, I remembered Jesus' discussion of rights. God had the right—He alone had the knowledge and rights of the Creator. He alone had a third-person perspective on reality. He alone was capable of and justified in determining right and wrong.

I smiled ruefully. "I guess wrongdoing is anything contrary to Your Law."

Jesus beamed at me. "Right! Being guilty is breaking Our Law."[265] He pulled a silver balance scale out of a cupboard and set it on the table. One side was labeled *bad* and the other *good.*

"Now, what about church? Are you trying to use it as a 'good work' to balance out your misdeeds?"

I fingered the tablecloth. "Maybe? I'm not sure. I know that's not my avowed reason for attending church, but that seems to be what You found in my heart. Actually, I think it's to get rid of *feeling* guilty rather than actual guilt."

"Let's examine the idea to see if removing guilt has anything to do with getting rid of your guilty feelings." He gave me a square of blank white paper and a pen. "Write down something you feel guilty about."

I wrote down a white lie I'd told and handed Him back the paper. He placed it on the scale. Surprisingly, that side dropped as though the paper were significantly heavy.[266]

He handed me another square. "Now let's see if 'going to church' can counterbalance your lie."

I obediently wrote it down and put it on the good side of the scale. The scale didn't budge.[267]

"Suppose you could do enough good actions out of right motives to balance the scale"[268]—Jesus put a finger on the good side, perfectly balancing the scale—"What would happen to your bad deeds?"

I stared at the scale in consternation. The same number of good actions and right motives as my bad ones? Might as well call the thing impossible and be done with it. I groaned. "Well, supposing I did, somehow, balance out the scale, my bad deeds would be gone."

He waved a hand towards my lie. "The scale is balanced, but are your bad deeds gone?"

"Well, no . . . ."

"How many good deeds would it take to make them disappear permanently?"

"I guess—I guess it doesn't matter. I guess they would still be there no matter how many good things I did . . . ."

"It sounds like getting rid of guilt is more complicated than just balancing out your bad thoughts and actions. You need to truly eliminate them."

I thought of all the things I'd already tried in vain: apologies, penance, going to church, blaming myself, blaming others, denial—what other options were there?

Jesus reached into His pocket and removed a lightly used Bible: mine. "Remember, we're talking about getting rid of guilt, not guilty feelings. Read Genesis 3:11–13," He said and passed me my Bible.

I found the passage, recognizing it as part of the fall of Adam and Eve: " 'And [God] said, "Who told you that you were naked? Have you eaten from the tree that I commanded you not to eat from?" The man said, "The woman you put here with me–she gave me some fruit from the tree, and I ate it." Then the LORD God said to the woman, "What is this you have done?" The woman said, "The serpent deceived me, and I ate." ' "

"How did Adam and Eve get rid of their guilt?" Jesus asked.

I reread it, thinking I must have missed something. "I don't think they did. It seems like they each just blamed their actions on someone else."

"You're right. They tried to move their bad stuff onto someone else's scale. Now look at David. He had just committed adultery with Bathsheba, Uriah's wife, and murdered Uriah.[269] Read Psalm 51:3–4."

I flipped forward, then read, " 'For I know my transgressions, and my sin is ever before me. Against you, you only have

I sinned and done what is evil in your sight, so that you are proved right when you speak and justified when you judge.'"

"Now, what's David doing with his sin?" He asked.

I shrugged. "Nothing. He just confessed its existence."

Jesus tapped my Bible. "It's much more than that."

I read over the passage once more, without enlightenment. I looked up at Jesus. "Okay, then what's David doing with his sin?"

"He's taking ownership. He's not blaming anyone here, nor giving a mere shamefaced acknowledgment of his guilt."

I stiffened. "How is that helpful? I know I'm guilty too."

"Read verses 1, 2 and 7."

My eyes flickered up the page. "'Have mercy on me, O God, according to your unfailing love; according to your great compassion blot out my transgressions. Wash away all my iniquity and cleanse me from my sin. . . . Cleanse me with hyssop, and I will be clean; wash me, and I will be whiter than snow.'"

Suddenly I recalled how I'd begun my relationship with God in the first place. It hadn't been mere acknowledgement of sin that had rescued me, any more than Adam's and Eve's assent had rescued them. Grace had bridged the gap—grace I'd left neglected in a dusty corner of my heart. It was Jesus' blood sprinkled on me that had rescued me.[270]

I looked up at Him, once more feeling the weight of His mercy and grace. "It's never changed, has it? I still need You to cleanse me, to blot out any record of my sin."

He put a comforting hand on my own and held my gaze. "Correct. All those things you listed are things you've tried. You see, Adam and Eve had the right idea in one way: guilt has to go onto someone's scale. I died in your place.[271] I took the penalty for your sins on Myself.[272] Your sins were written on My record and My perfect record became yours.[273] It is My blood that cleanses you."[274]

I remembered when I had prayed for that exact thing. I'd been sick of my life, desperate to find meaning somewhere, to make sense of senselessness. When my friend Ginny invited me to church, I figured I had nothing to lose. So, I began attending. The people were different, more at peace somehow. In the end, I'd come around: I too had prayed for Jesus to "save me from my sins."

"Would you like to see what your record looks like now?" Jesus asked.

Sweat broke out across my body. Did I? It probably looked awful. I hadn't kept up my end of the bargain. I couldn't count the number of times I'd broken His Law since that first prayer. But Jesus wouldn't have asked if He didn't want to show it to me for some reason. "Y-y-yes?"

He reached into a nearby cabinet and took out a pile of paper squares. I cringed a little; it was a hefty stack. To my surprise, He piled them onto the good side. He touched my lie with the scar on His hand and the paper disappeared in a puff of smoke. Now the bad side stood glaringly empty. The good side clanked down.

I started, looking back and forth from scale to scale. "Really? How can that be?"

"Because this is *My* record that has been applied to your balance. My righteousness fills your scale's good side. I died for you before you were even born. I didn't just die for the sins you committed from the day of your birth until your salvation. I paid for all of them: past, present, and future."[275]

I looked down at the table, guilt still gnawing away at my middle. My hands balled into fists. If this was my record, my feelings made no sense. Bits of guilt littered my past, anchored to my soul in some inexplicable way, weighing me down. Most of the time I could pretend they didn't exist—though even this pretense was exhausting at times. Would I have to live with guilt forever?

I looked back to Jesus pleadingly. "Why do I still feel so guilty then?"

He gently unclenched my fists. "You've got a few different things in that mix of feelings."

"Such as?"

"Well, let's take a closer look." He stood and helped me up. I followed Him over to the stove where a large empty pot sat. He held out a hand, palm up. "Will you give Me some of your guilty feelings?"

I looked at it. How exactly am I supposed to obey? Spit in His hand or something?

He laughed. "No, just close your eyes and reach into your heart. Then pass some of the feelings over to Me."

I closed my eyes and found myself in a room of wall-to-wall grey metal filing drawers. In one hand I held a square plastic container and in the other a ladle. I walked around, examining the labels on the drawers: *Happiness, Excitement, Anger, Jealousy, Confusion,* and on and on. Finally, I found an oversized drawer labeled *Guilt.* I pulled it open. Inside lay a misty, greenish-grey goo; looking at it turned my stomach. I ladled some into the container and hastily closed the lid and drawer.

When I opened my eyes, the container of guilt remained in my hands. I gave it to Jesus.

"Thanks," He said and carefully poured the gelatinous mixture into the pot, then turned on the heat. "Sometimes heat is quite useful in bringing things to the surface."

After stirring for a bit, He rummaged around in a nearby drawer and pulled out four petri dishes. He turned off the heat and gave my guilty feelings a final stir. Then He deftly filled the dishes. As He did, the liquid fluctuated, developing different consistencies and colors in each dish. "Now to examine these," He said cheerfully.

I stared at them, much as one might eye a rabid bear, and gulped. "How do we do that?"

"A microscope projector should work nicely," He said and waved back at the table. Our supper dishes were gone and in their place stood the projector. He walked over to it and inserted a petri dish containing a thin, spring-green liquid. Then He turned the projector on, casting the image onto a nearby wall. "Have a seat," He offered.

I sat on the edge of my seat and clasped my hands tightly in my lap.

The image showed a winding dirt road that stretched away into the distance. Jesus stood on the road, facing toward me. I, on the other hand, had turned my back on Him and ventured off the path. Vine tendrils crept up my legs. A glowing wasp buzzed in front of me, flashing off and on like a lightning bug.

"What kind of crazy bug is that?"

He chuckled. "It's not a bug at all. It's a representation of My Spirit."

"How does that work?"

"He's alerting you that you're setting out on your own, blazing your own trail away from the protection of Our Law. You're also creating distance between us."

I looked back at the image, noting the obvious physical and emotional distance. "So He's kind of like the warning light on my car. But why a wasp?"

"Because if you don't pay attention to the warning light, His conviction can get a whole lot sharper."

"So that's why I feel guilty? Because He's convicting me?"

"Sometimes. Before you traded records with Me, He showed you your sin and guiltiness.[276] He opened your eyes to the true state of your balance. Now that you have My record, He continues to convict you of your sin. Even though it's been paid for, you still need to confess your sin—to say the same thing about it as We do."[277]

I frowned. "Why?"

"Because We love you; conviction is love-based.[278] What happens if you just continue in your sin?"

I immediately recalled a particularly uncomfortable time I had ignored my guilt and persisted in sinning. Eventually, I didn't even want to pray or go to church. It made me feel guiltier, and I wasn't ready to stop sinning. My heart had hardened more and more towards God until the fallout had become unbearable and forced me back to Him. I made a face. "The distance between us gets wider."[279]

"That's right. What happens to your consequences?"

"They get worse," I said ruefully.

"Yes. Therefore, this is conviction. Good guilty feelings that lead you to repentance."[280]

Good guilt . . . *good* guilt. I rolled the idea 'round in my mind. I'd never even considered such a thing.

Jesus leaned forward. "Guilty feelings are like any other emotion—We created you to have them for a purpose. They can still be twisted and misused, but somewhere, among the wreckage, the true thing exists."

I snorted. All guilt still seemed like wreckage to me. "How do I—How can I differentiate between good guilty feelings and bad guilty feelings? And how do I get rid of them?"

"Good questions. Here, let's make a chart." He opened a door and pulled out a large chalkboard. "Why do you think you're being convicted in this portrayal?"

I glanced back at the image. "For striking off on my own, away from the path."

"Right, so then the focus of My Spirit's conviction is on your behavior—"

"Wait. Is it always on my behavior? Don't thoughts and motives matter? I mean, my pastor just preached on how You clashed with the Pharisees over that very thing."[281]

He nodded. "Yes. Absolutely. Thoughts and motives do matter.[282] I'm including them under the umbrella of *behavior,* as contrasted with *identity.* Before you traded records with Me, My Spirit convicted you that your wrongdoings displayed your sinful heart.[283] If you recall, when We saved you, We gave you a new heart.[284] Your core identity changed.[285] So now when He convicts you, it's to provide the opportunity for you to repent: to get back on the path, following Our Law, and to lessen the distance between us."[286]

"I see, I think. Conviction is love-based because it saves me from getting further entangled in sin and then having more dire consequences. But why does it feel so bad? Why does it make me so tired?"

"Because you're not supposed to be able to just ignore conviction. If it was an enjoyable emotion, you wouldn't pay as close attention to it. And the effort of ignoring conviction can take a lot of energy. But actually, conviction energizes you to do what's right when you work with it."

"It energizes me? How?"

He gave me a piercing look. "Would you have the strength to make things right without it?"

The question stopped me in my tracks. He was right. Feeling guilty had goaded me into changing my ways, sometimes almost against my will. Sometimes I'd found the energy to apologize and fix things just to get rid of those feelings. In fact, fear of guilty feelings had acted as a preventative measure at times.

"Hmm. I see what You mean . . . . So it's kind of like the current in a river: if you swim with it, you get farther than you could alone, but if you fight it, you'll end up exhausted just trying to stay in one place. Is that right?"

He smiled. "That's a good way of looking at it. However, true conviction is motivated by fear of Us,[287] not by fear of guilty feelings."

"Fear of You?"

"A healthy understanding of who We are and who you are. Think of it like reverence. When, through Our Word, you grasp who We are—that We created everything and are present everywhere, all the time—proper fear follows naturally."[288]

As He spoke, I recalled my own blinding experience with the weight of His deity. I could easily see how that would motivate one to keep His Law. After all, I had just found myself prostrate from said fear.

"And what do you think is the end result of My Spirit's conviction?" Jesus asked.

"I get back on the path?"

"Right. The end result is freedom. Rather than being all tangled up in sin, you're able to walk freely.[289] And once you've dealt with your sin, conviction goes away."

"Dealt with it?"

"Confessed it to Us, turned away from your sin, and done your part to restore any other sin-damaged relationships."[290]

"But—but, sometimes I still feel guilty, even after I've done that."

"We'll get to those feelings. For now, here's a summary of conviction."[291] He tapped the blackboard and a list appeared:

Conviction
Focuses on behavior
Causes you to repent and restore relationships
Energizes you to do right
Motive: Fear of God
End Result: Freedom
Expression of Our love

"Now, let's move on to the next one." He selected a dish of shadowy liquid and put it in the microscope. This liquid seemed to be only half-present.

Now the projector displayed an image of the silver balance scale. The good side remained weighed down by Jesus' righteous acts. The bad side, however, was no longer empty. Instead, it held two translucent stacks of paper. Several large weights, also translucent, sat on top of one stack.

"What are those?" I asked.

"Why don't you take a closer look?"

I walked over to the wall and peered at the image. I still couldn't make it out.

"Would you like some help?"

"Please."

He moved to stand next to me, then reached into the image. He pulled out the two stacks and set them on the table for me to examine. I looked back up at the image. The translucent stacks had disappeared. I brushed a hand against the wall; it remained solid. My eyes went from the table to the wall and back again.

"So what are they?" Jesus prompted.

I sat back down at the table and turned my attention to the mysterious stacks. They had stayed translucent, but looked substantial, as though they really sat on the table. I poked one of the weights. It gave like a partially-deflated ball. The label on this weight read: *consequence: loss of relationship*. I grimaced. Just looking at the stacks had reminded me of the guilty feelings that remained eternally entwined about my heart.

I glanced hurriedly through the papers under the weights. My stomach began to churn, and I wished I hadn't eaten dinner. My hands shook as I re-stacked the first pile of weights and papers. I looked up at Jesus. "These look like some of my past sins."

"Just the ones you think are too evil for Us to forgive or where you feel the consequences are too big for Us to handle."

I squirmed in my seat. Those sins began to parade through my mind, flaunting their enormity. It was no wonder they were sticking around.

"Why are they so insubstantial?" I asked.

"Because you're no longer guilty." He put a hand in front of the stack, blocking it from view. "Your sins are paid for. You just feel guilty. Do you really think it's possible for your sin to be greater than My blood?"

I lowered my eyes. Put that way I couldn't say "yes," even though I felt it deep in my soul.

"You've got some unbelief and pride here," He continued.

My head snapped up. "What? Pride seems like the last thing it could be. I feel horrible about my sin, not proud."

"Your fear is born from a belief that your sin, its consequences, and by implication, you yourself, are more powerful than Us. Pride is arguing that you know more than We do. You think somehow We don't know the depth of your sin. Those are lies," He said firmly.

How ironic that my quest to get rid of my guilty feelings had uncovered new sin. I sighed. "So what do I do about it?"

"How do you get rid of any sin?"

"Um . . . ."

He pointed to my Bible. "Why don't you read 1 John 1:9."

I grabbed it and found the place. " 'If we confess our sins, He is faithful and righteous to forgive us our sins and to cleanse us from all unrighteousness.' "[292]

"We've dealt with your sin, remember?" He held up a scarred hand. "We're faithful to wash you clean. You've already confessed all these sins."

"I know. But—"

"No, no 'but.' Don't leave room for unbelief. Here," He picked up my Bible, and without even looking, opened it up to the middle and handed it back. "Read Psalm 103:8–12."

" 'The LORD is compassionate and gracious, slow to anger, abounding in love. He will not always accuse, nor will he harbor his anger forever; he does not treat us as our sins deserve or repay us according to our iniquities. For as high as the heavens are above the earth, so great is his love for those who fear him; as far as the east is from the west, so far has he removed our transgressions from us.' "

"How far away are your sins?"

" 'As far as the east is from the west,' " I recited.

"And how far is that?"

"It's—it's—well, I guess it's impossibly far. East can never become west."

"Right. Now read Romans 8:1–2."

I awkwardly flipped around and found the passage. " 'Therefore, there is now no condemnation for those who are in Christ Jesus, because through Christ Jesus the law of the Spirit of life set me free from the law of sin and death.'" I looked up at Him. "That's so hard to wrap my mind around. It feels impossible when I look at these specific sins."

Jesus held my gaze. "All things are possible with Us.[293] When I died, I bought up all your sin and all its consequences.[294] There's nothing left—just these shadows that you keep hanging onto. Change your focus: stop fearing your sin and its consequences, and instead, fear Us. Come live in the light of truth. Confess your sin of hanging onto these, and move on."

I stared at my sins and tried to imagine them gone. Impossible task. Jesus put His hand on my shoulder. I tore my gaze away from the stack and looked up at Him, desperately trying to focus instead on the immensity of my God and His love for me.

"Jesus . . . I'm sorry that I doubted You. Please forgive me for . . . for my unbelief and pride. Help me to believe. Fill my eyes with Your vastness so that I can fear You instead. Thank You for getting rid of these sins. Thank You for rescuing me."

"Of course, My darling. We love to give you good things," He said, smiling tenderly at me. "Now was that so bad?"

"What?"

"Confession. You normally dread bringing your sin to Us."

"Hmm. You're right. I don't usually like confession, but this time seemed different." I thought about it. This confession hadn't been so bad, maybe because I was less afraid of the consequences. It had felt like a natural outflow of our conversation, an outpouring of my heart's cry. I wasn't worried that I'd be in trouble if I admitted my sin.

"You're starting to grasp that We love you. Sin is what gets you in trouble, not confession. Confession is the road out of trouble."

"That makes confession seem a whole lot less scary . . . it's almost joyful," I said, surprised by the revelation.

"And it's always available," He reminded me. "Now that we've taken care of that stack," He touched His scars to the first stack of papers with its weights. They too went up in a puff of smoke. "Take a look at stack number two."

I scooted my chair closer and examined it. If confession could banish it forever, I wanted to figure out my stack and get rid of it. Why were these separate? I flipped through them, chewing my lower lip. There had to be a common denominator, but I wasn't seeing it. I turned to Jesus. "These just seem to be regular sins. How are they any different?"

He tapped the stack. "These are sins committed after your salvation, whenever you were relying on yourself."

"Okay . . . "

"These are the sins that you think you can handle on your own by balancing them out."

I thumbed through the papers again. They were all pretty mild sins, especially compared with the previous stack. "I guess I've learned that I can't get rid of them that way anyhow. Please take them," I begged.

He reached over and touched these too. As with the first, they flamed into nothingness. A huge weight lifted from my soul. "Wow, those daily, 'small' sins can really add up!"

He raised an eyebrow. "You do know they were already gone."

"Y-yes, I guess it's just the first time I've really understood what that means."

"What's next?" I asked, squaring my shoulders.

Jesus selected a third dish. Inside glistened a deep black liquid, like sunlight hitting wet tar. I backed into my chair. Jesus inserted the dish into the microscope, and I apprehensively looked at the projection.

I stood there, clothed in a bulky fur parka, wrapped over with a quantity of veils. Thick fur mittens covered my hands. My eyes, the only feature clearly visible, were ringed with beads of sweat. I looked dreadfully uncomfortable.

I squinted at the image. "Why am I all covered up? Is something wrong with me?"

"Shame would like you to believe that there is."

"Shame? Aren't shame and guilt the same thing?"

He shook His head. "No, shame just likes to stay camouflaged with conviction, but it's a counterfeit. Even though people often use shame and feeling guilty synonymously, they have different characteristics."[295]

"Really? How are they different?"

"Why don't you take a look at Genesis 3:7–8."

I found the verse and read, " 'Then the eyes of both of them were opened, and they realized they were naked; so they sewed fig leaves together and made coverings for themselves. Then the man and his wife heard the sound of the LORD God as he was walking in the garden in the cool of the day, and they hid from the LORD God among the trees of the garden.' "

"This is right after Adam and Eve had broken Our Law for the first time. What did shame cause them to do?"

My eyes flicked back to the passage. "Well, they cover their nakedness with fig leaves and hide from You. Is that what You mean?"

He nodded, then asked, "Why did they hide?"

I hunted through the passage and alighted on verse 10: " '[Adam] answered, "I heard you in the garden, and I was afraid because I was naked; so I hid." ' " I turned back to Him. "Fear. They hid because they were afraid."

"And is that consistent with your experience?"

"I suppose so. Fear of being exposed and rejected causes me to hide as best I can."

"Notice that the fear in shame motivates you to stay hidden, to remain in the dark. Now, look at why Adam was afraid."

I glanced down at my Bible. "Because he was naked—wait, why didn't he just say it was because he'd eaten from the tree?"

"Partly because in his shame, he no longer saw himself as complete.[296] Shame argues that the action is an indicator of one's self, of one's character. Remember Sunday? Rather than reacting to the spilled coffee as a simple accident, you jumped to seeing yourself as a careless person." He smiled. "Would you have moved the coffee in the first place if you really were a careless person?"

"I suppose not."

He put a hand on my arm. "Shame creates layer upon layer of lies about you, hiding your identity. Shame argues you're naked. But you are far from naked. You are clothed with the glory of Our image[297] and with Me.[298] Your core identity has changed,[299] but shame conceals your image-ness and identity, just as Adam and Eve covered themselves with fig leaves. It uses fear to keep you in bondage. Fear of exposure leads you to hide and to exhaust yourself trying to prove the lie wrong. Remaining in darkness keeps you in bondage. Eventually, you can begin to believe the lies. You believe you can only act in line with who shame says you are."

"And conviction opens my eyes to my true state," I mused. "I guess they are different."

He nodded. "Shame doesn't just lie about who you are, though; it also creates a rift in your soul."

My eyes widened. "A rift in my soul? How? What do You mean?"

"Take physical nakedness. Can you fully examine yourself?"

"Um, if I have a mirror I can."

"Suppose you wanted to view your soul. We created you to use Us as your mirror. You're made in Our image. Shame, however, uses how you think someone else sees you to judge your identity. You create your own observer, your own third-person perspective. You split into both the observed and the observer."[300]

I frowned thoughtfully. "I've never looked at it that way. Shame really messes me up, doesn't it?"

"Yes, and sadly, shame doesn't just lie about your identity and injure your soul, it also damages your relationships. It engenders isolation: you're driven to hide from Us, rather than being driven back to Us. Adam and Eve didn't run to Us with their sin, they ran away. You also become isolated from other people, just like in your Sunday school class."

I recalled my longing to be swallowed alive by the floor and my intention to sit in the back of class or to switch classes. My only goal had been escape. Just the thought of discussing my embarrassment with anyone, even God, had caused my face to heat.

"I see what You're saying. By the end of the day, I was more alone than when I'd begun . . . . It's such a different way of looking at the same thing."

Jesus smiled. "Truth often is. In the moment of your shame, you became isolated from Us and from the people around you. Conviction is concerned with how you've injured the other person, versus how they see you. Conviction motivates you to restore the relationship. Shame, on the other hand, flees from the exposure of relationships, through outright hiding or through defensive anger and denial. Look at how you handled your shame on Sunday. You apologized, but then you started coming up with ways to change her perspective of you or to avoid her."

"You're right . . . ." I thought back over similar experiences. "I guess I tend to hide, but I've also used defensive anger to mask my shame," I admitted.

"So, that's one way to tell if what you're feeling is shame or conviction."

I gave Him a questioning look.

"You'll know a tree by its fruit.[301] Ask yourself if the fruit of your emotion is closer relationships or isolation."

"That makes sense." My mouth twisted. "At least there's some way of telling shame and guilt apart, even if I'd rather not deal with either."

He smiled. "Yes, there is. Let's expand our list." He again tapped the chalkboard. A second column appeared.

Conviction	***Shame***
Focuses on behavior	*Focuses on identity*
Causes you to repent &restore relationships	*Causes you to hide/ isolate*
Energizes you to do right	*Exhausts you*
Motive: Fear of God	*Motive: Fear of exposure*
End Result: Freedom	*End Result: Bondage*
Expression of Our love	

I looked at the tarry container and swallowed hard. "So what do I do with shame once I've recognized it? How can I get rid of it? It seems like it would just stick around until I change."

"What environment does shame thrive in?"

I thought back over my own experiences of shame and the picture of my parka-clad figure. "Darkness. Hiding."[302]

"Right. If shame hides your identity, what's the antidote for that?"

"The truth? Or exposure of some kind?"

"Both. You need exposure to the truth, not just any exposure." Jesus smiled. "Where are you going to gain access to the truth?"

I smiled back at Him. "From You. I suppose I need to bring my shame to You too. Then You can strip away the lies and get rid of shame."

"Right. Getting rid of shame is something that can only happen in the context of relationships.[303] So how do you feel about the coffee spill now?"

I ran my hand back and forth across the table top. How did I feel? "I feel better about being careless. I guess I'm not really a careless person. But I still feel horrible about spilling coffee on her. Maybe I wasn't being loving."

Jesus touched my arm, His eyes full of compassion. "Let's take a look at our last dish." This one seemed to be filled with a liquid that shifted consistency and hue every few seconds. He placed it in the microscope.

I took a deep breath, then turned my attention to the projection.

This scenario showed my balance scale once more. However, this time the bad side was filled with colored papers of various hues and sizes. Next to the scale sat an enormous book, a veritable tome. It seemed to be broken up into sections, delineated by different colored pages. *Laws* was emblazoned on the front.

"What in the world are these?" I asked, pointing to the papers on my scale's full bad side.

"False guilt."

I wrinkled my brow. "Come again?"

"False guilt from failing to follow someone else's law or from stealing someone else's guilt."

I stared at Him, unenlightened.

"Think about the Pharisees," He said. "I know you've heard some of what your pastor said about them."

"They thought they were extra good because they went above and beyond the Mosaic Law."[304]

He nodded. "You see that particularly in their regulations about the Sabbath. They had numerous rules about what constituted a 'burden' or 'work.'"

I raised an eyebrow. "Such as?"

"Such as whether you put something in a beggar's hand or whether you held your hand out for them to take the thing.[305] Or whether you inadvertently 'carried' a needle in your clothing."[306] His eyes flashed. "By elevating their own perceptions of how things ought to be, they created a system of laws that made a heavy load for people to bear.[307] They put those laws into the same category as Our Law. People can twist parts of the truth into a power play . . . This is why you fear truth and why you see it as a constraint, rather than something that sets you free. Sadly, in your experience it was often used like a club to bludgeon you into submission."

I walked over to the image and studied it. I pictured those papers turning into the links of a chain.

Jesus joined me. "Or such as you elevating the coffee spill into equality with Our Law," He added.

I turned to Him. "It could have been sin, if I had been maliciously putting it in her way. Right?"

"Yes. But were you?"

"No."

"And by taking all the responsibility for the spill on yourself, did you do her any favors?"

"Well . . . it might have helped her save face."

He waved that aside. "Did she learn anything, such as to pay attention to where she was gesturing?"

I stared at Him. "No, I guess not."

"Right. You short-circuit other people's growth when you take their guilt upon yourself. As we've discussed, this was an accident, with no malicious intent on either side."

I took a deep breath, feeling suddenly freer.

"See, true conviction has a purpose, but it's getting lost in all these lies. Conviction keeps you from being imprisoned in your sin by forcing you to come to Us for salvation. It also lets you know when you're on the wrong side of Our Law and liable to smash into consequences." He looked at me out of the corner of His eye and smirked. "Yet another freedom-enhancing restriction."

I chuckled. "But what about other situations like the coffee spill? How can I tell when I'm following Your Law and when I'm hanging on to something else?"

"Our Law is an extension of Our character.[308] No arbitrary rules—they're all anchored in who We are, which never changes.[309] You have Our Word," He said and gestured to my Bible. "Use it. Learn Our Law and come to know Us better. Walk with Me and I'll walk with you."

"You'll walk with me?" I said. Somehow my concept of "religion" consisted of an occasional check-in to verify compliance. Unless I did something truly heinous, I'd be left alone.

Jesus took a step closer. "Forever," He said. "We're talking about a relationship, not merely a system of rules."

My eyes flicked towards the full scale with its tome, then back to Jesus. "I think I get it."

"That's why it matters what you follow and how you follow it."

"*How* you follow?"

"Remember the Pharisees? They were supposedly following Our Law. They had just gotten so focused on the externals—on the actions involved—that they ripped the heart out of Our Law.[310] Our Law is designed to be used in the context of a relationship with Us. You can't divorce it from love.[311] On the other hand, we're not talking about infatuation. You can't follow Our Law out of pure passion for Us. That will fade and dissipate in the shifting winds of circumstance."[312]

I slowly walked back to my chair. I sat down and stared into the crackling fire. A log fell and sent sparks flying up the chimney.

How and what had I been following? Not Jesus. He was so much more than the God I "knew." I chewed my lip. So, some of the time I'd been like the Pharisees, following a what—a set of regulations.

But what about my love for God? Switch the labels? I guess deep down, I'd wanted what I could get from God. And that infatuation had blinded me to the more He is and the more I could have with Him. Perhaps it had been glimmers of Him I'd been chasing all along.

Jesus sat back down.

"I think I'm starting to understand," I murmured, awed that God would take time to demolish my false preconceptions Himself. "A love relationship, not rules or infatuation alone."

He gave me a broad smile and covered my hand with His. "Exactly. Love requires both knowledge and passion. Knowledge alone is anti-relational. 'Love' that's not anchored in knowledge turns out to be infatuation. But put knowledge and passion together and you begin something amazing. The more you come to know Us through Our Word, the more your capacity for love increases. Those feelings of passion then prompt the quest for more relational knowledge, and on and on."[313] He stood up, then gestured towards the door. "Now, let's look at one more thing."

I raised my eyebrows and followed Him out the door. We had returned to my car; the concrete barrier stretched into the distance.

"Why do you think they bother you so much?" He asked once more, indicating the barrier.

The answer came in a flash. "Because they represent rules apart from a relationship," I said excitedly.

He beamed at me. "Yes! To you, concrete barriers are the epitome of faceless rules. You've been so terrified of being turned into a robot and losing your freedom that you've avoided rules." He put both hands on my shoulders and looked me in the eye. "But, darling, if you are a fish, jumping out of the water in protest is not a productive way to assert your freedom."

I smiled. "Right—freedom is not the absence of restrictions."

"It's the presence of the right ones," He finished, pointing to Himself. "So what do you think? Do you want to walk with Us along Our Law? Or would you rather keep smashing into it?" He asked and quirked a smile at me.

I thought for a moment, though the answer seemed obvious. Part of me still longed to control my own destiny. Then I remembered myself, a poor gasping fish out of water. When had I ever controlled my own destiny? I was afraid someone would take advantage of me, but Jesus had proven His love. He'd already restricted His freedom for me. Was I willing to do the same? And then I realized I'd been hooked from the beginning of this crazy dream. Jesus Himself had drawn me, and I never wanted to leave Him.

I turned to Him, then smiled and put my hand in His. "I'll walk with You, wherever that may be."

JOURNAL 11/16

Today marks four months since I saw Jesus. My business is going well. That's not to say it's making more profits. However, I'm handling all those regulations better. I even joined a small business advocacy group to work towards changing the rules and simplifying the red tape.

In fact, as I've learned about the rules, some of them are actually freedom-enhancing restrictions. I wonder if I'll always categorize things in terms of freedom . . . .

Anyway, I think I'm finally beginning to grasp the freedom found in confession and following God's Law. It's so strange . . . I spent my whole life in bondage to rules, either through rebellion or guilt. Yet now that I'm starting to embrace God's Law, I'm finding more and more freedom, not to mention more happiness. It's so paradoxical.

Church has been going better too. I've started trying to live out some of these concepts there and I've gotten involved with a group of like-minded folks. Being in relationship with them has really helped me. I figure I need that kind of openness to make sure shame stays in check.

I haven't had that crazy car nightmare anymore. In fact, seeing concrete barriers has become sort of relaxing, like having someone you love share an inside joke or a smile across a crowded room. They're a tangible reminder of this adventure I'm on with God.

I found this verse this morning in my time with God. I hope I never forget it. In some ways it's already engraved on my soul.

I will walk about in freedom for I have sought out your precepts.
~ Psalm 119:45

233 Matt. 7:12

234 Rom. 2:14–15

235 For the sake of readability I've used both the singular and plural pronouns with regards to the Trinity and the Persons therein. When talking about the Trinity, it's almost impossible not to emphasize either the oneness of God or His threeness. Since the American church tends to prioritize God's oneness, I've used the plural pronouns in places to highlight God's essential relational nature. I in no way wish to imply that God is not one (Deut. 6:4 5; 1 Kings 8:60; Isa. 45:5–6, 45:21–22; James 2:19) or to stray into Tritheism (Matt. 28:19–20; 2 Cor. 13:14; Eph. 4:4–6; 1 Pet. 1:2; Jude 20–21; John 1:1–2, 1:9–18, 17:24, 14:26, 16:7; Acts 10:38).

236 Dr. Timothy J. Keller, "Absolutism: Don't we all have to find truth for ourselves?" (Sermon, Redeemer Presbyterian Church, New York, NY, October 8, 2006).

237 Other authors have used various terms to describe this concept (e.g., "joy").

238 Ultimately, the circumstance God created us to thrive in is a right relationship with Him (Isa. 43:7, 43:10; Ps. 16:11; Isa. 55:1–3; Acts 17:24–31). C. S. Lewis compares it to a car being designed to run on gasoline. We're designed to run on God, and it is impossible to find happiness apart from Him. See *Mere Christianity* (San Francisco: HarperSanFrancisco, 2001), 50. We're also designed to be in a community of healthy relationships as a reflection of God's Trinitarian nature (Gen. 1:26–27, 2:20–25; Heb. 10:24–25). Finally, we're designed and gifted to fulfill certain functions (e.g., to be a "hand" or "eye," etc., [1 Cor. 12:12–27]) and to do the good works God has prepared for us (Eph. 2:10). We can experience happiness as we have these right circumstances. True, full happiness will come once our sin and brokenness are out of the way (i.e., when we are glorified and the presence of sin is removed). Only then will we be able to have perfect relationships.

239 1 Cor. 12:12–27; Eph. 1:22–23, 5:23; Col. 1:18, 1:24

240 Gen. 1:26–27, 2:18–25; Eccles. 4:9–12; 1 Cor. 12:12–27; Gal. 6:2

241 Isa. 43:7, 43:10; Ps. 16:11; Isa. 55:1–3; Acts 17:24–31. As Blaise Pascal put it: "What else does this craving, and this helplessness, proclaim but that there was once in man a true happiness, of which all that now remains is the empty print and trace? This he tries in vain to fill with everything around him, seeking in things that are not there the help he cannot find in those that are, though none can help, since this infinite abyss can be filled only with an infinite and immutable object; in other words by God himself." *Pensèes,* trans. W.F. Trotter (Grand Rapids, MI: Christian Classics Ethereal Library, 1944), Section VII: Morality and Doctrine: 425, accessed October 26, 2012, http://www.ccel.org/ccel/pascal/pensees.txt/. We also see God's intentional relationality towards humanity in His creation of man as an image-bearer (Gen. 1:26–27) and His continual seeking out of man, despite our sinful rebellion (Gen. 3:8–9; Luke 19:10; Rom. 5:6–8; 1 Tim. 2:5).

242 Plato, *The Republic of Plato*, 2nd ed., trans. Benjamin Jowett (Oxford: Clarendon press, 1881), 208–212.

243 C. S. Lewis describes himself as a great example of this. He talks about it in his book *Surprised by Joy* (New York: Harcourt Brace Jovanovich, 1955).

244 Rev. 21:1–5a, 22:1–5; 2 Pet. 3:13

245 Keller, "Absolutism."

246 A third-person perspective entails having a complete view of the entire story, such as that had by the author, rather than by one of the characters. God alone is transcendent, completely *other* than everything else. As Creator, He is outside of all else (Heb. 1:10–12; Gen. 1:1; Col. 1:16). As sovereign, He has a full knowledge of what He planned (Job 42:1–2; Isa. 40:22–28, 46:9–10; Jer. 29:11; Dan. 4:35; Eph. 2:10) and a full view of time (Ps. 90:2–4; 2 Pet. 3:8; Isa. 46:9–10).

247 Rom. 2:4

248 Isa. 29:16

249 John 19:16–24, 20:24–29

250 Hosea 11:4

251 Gen. 1:26–27, 2

252 Ps. 139:1–16

253 John 3:16; Rom. 5:8, 8:38–39; 1 John 4:9–10

254 C. S. Lewis, *The Abolition of Man, or, Reflections on Education with Special Reference to the Teaching of English in the Upper Forms of Schools* (San Francisco: HarperSanFrancisco, 2001), 81. See also Keller, "Absolutism."

255 Rom. 5:8; 1 John 4:9–10

256 1 Cor. 13:7–8

257 William Shakespeare, "Sonnet CXVI," *The Works of Shakespeare* (Roslyn, New York: Black's Readers Service Company, 1937), 1263.

258 See C. S. Lewis, *The Problem of Pain*, Macmillan Paperbacks Edition (NY: Macmillan, 1962), 50.

259 John 1:1–3, 1:14; Heb. 2:14–18

260 John 19:16–37; Rom. 3:22–26, 5:6–11

261 Job 41:11; Acts 17:24–25; "Feeding an ego" implies need and insecurity. God is inherently relational within the Trinity. His relational needs are already met (John 17:5, 17:24; See also Lewis, *Problem of Pain*, 29).

262 Matt. 26:64–66 (see Dan. 7:13–14); John 1:1–3, 1:14, 1:18, 8:57–59 (see Exod. 3:14); Rom. 9:5; Phil. 2:5–11; Col. 1:15–20; Titus 2:13; Heb. 1:8; 2 Pet. 1:1

263 Luke 2:7, 2:20, 24:36–43; John 1:14

264 Phil. 2:3–4.

265 Gal. 3:10; James 2:10–11; Rom. 5:16

266 James 2:10–11; John 8:44; Eph. 4:25

267 Isa. 64:6

268 Ps. 24:3–4

269 Ps. 51 *Superscription*; see also 2 Sam. 11–12, especially 12:13.

270 Exod. 12:21–27; John 1:29

271 Rom. 6:23

272 Ibid.; 1 Tim. 2:3–6; Heb. 9:28; 1 Pet. 2:24

273 Rom. 5:19; 1 Cor. 1:30; 2 Cor. 5:21; Phil. 3:9; Col. 2:13–14

274 Rom. 3:20–26; Heb. 9:22

275 John 19:30; Heb. 1:3, 7:27, 9:25–28

276 John 16:8–11

277 Matt. 6:12; 1 John 1:9

278 Heb. 12:5–6; Rev. 3:19

279 Isa. 59:1–2; Eph. 4:30

280 2 Cor. 7:10

281 e.g., Matt. 15:1–20, 23:1–39 (especially vs. 23–28)

282 One has only to read the Sermon on the Mount to see that God cares about our thoughts and motives (Matt. 5–7). See also 1 Sam. 16:7.

283 John 16:8

284 Ezek. 36:26–27

285 John 1:12–13; 2 Cor. 5:17; Eph. 2:1–7; Col. 2:13

286 e.g., Acts 3:19; F. F. Bruce, *The Acts of the Apostles: The Greek Text with Introduction and Commentary,* 3rd ed. (Grand Rapids, MI: Wm. B. Eerdmans Publishing Company, 1990), 129.

287 Exod. 20:18–20; 2 Cor. 7:1

288 e.g., Exod. 20:18–20; Deut. 4:10

289 Rom. 6:16; Heb. 12:1

290 e.g., Matt. 5:23–24

291 Various authors have use different terms to discuss this same concept.

292 NASB

293 Luke 1:37; Matt. 19:26; Gen. 18:14

294 Ps. 130:7; Joel 2:25; See also Beth Moore's Bible study *Stepping Up: A Journey Through The Psalms of Ascent* (Nashville, TN: Lifeway Press, 2007), 128–129

295 For an in-depth treatment on the difference, read *Shame and Guilt* by June Price Tangney and Ronda L. Dearing (New York: Guilford Press, 2002).

296 There are a variety of views on this matter. Given the complexity of human motives, it seems likely that more than one is true. For a more thorough treatment of this particular aspect, see Marcus Dods, *The Expositor's Bible: Genesis, Vol. 1* (New York: A. C. Armstrong & Son, 1903), 23–26.

297 Gen. 1:26–27; Ps. 8:5; Prov. 31:25. For more information on dignity/glory, see Beth Moore's book *So Long, Insecurity: You've Been a Bad Friend to Us* (Carol Stream, IL: Tyndale House Publishers, 2010), 145–160.

298 Gal. 3:27

299 John 1:12–13; 2 Cor. 5:17; Eph. 2:1–7; Col. 2:13

300 Tangney and Dearing, *Shame and Guilt,* 25.

301 John 7:17–20

302 John 3:19–21

303 Yet another reason God calls us to confess our sins to one another (e.g., James 5:16; Prov. 28:13).

304 Luke 18:9–14; The Pharisees dedicated their lives to fulfilling the Scribal Law (Mishnah), which is much more involved than the Law of Moses (Torah) (William Barclay, *The Gospel Of Matthew Vol. 2* [Philadelphia: The Westminster Press, 1975], 282–283.).

305 Jacob Neusner, *The Mishnah: A New Translation* (New Haven: Yale University Press, 1988), 179.

306 Ibid.

307 Matt. 23:4

308 e.g., Matt. 5:48; Ps. 19:7–8; Mark 10:18; 1 John 2:29; Rom. 7:12; Ps. 25:8–10

309 Ps. 102:27; Heb. 13:8

310 Matt. 23:1–28, see especially verses 23–24

311 Matt. 22:35–40

312 Matt. 13:20–22

313 Phil. 1:9–11; Eph. 3:16–19

The Abyss

ONE

"Be appalled at this, O heavens, and shudder with great horror," declares the LORD. "My people have committed two sins: They have forsaken me, the spring of living water, and have dug their own cisterns, broken cisterns that cannot hold water." ~ *Jeremiah 2:12–13*

Have you ever stared at yourself in the mirror, trying to see past mere appearances and glimpse your true self? On this particular day, that's what I was doing: attempting to view my soul.

They say the eyes are windows to the soul, and through them I peered, hunting for something. I hardly knew what I was looking for. The eyes that stared back at me were dull and shadowed; pain and longing drowned out everything else.

They should have been happy eyes.

Today I had completed a major project at work, maintaining my reputation as a "miracle worker" and earning a verbal and financial pat on the back. I should have been feeling happy, fulfilled . . . satisfied. But, like so many times before, all the pieces were in place, yet nothing ever satisfied. Not the next job. Not the next pay raise. Not the next relationship. Nothing ever filled the longing.

Normally, when I felt this restless and dissatisfied, I ignored it. I pushed my feelings aside as unwarranted or temporary. Lately, I had blamed it on work stress, but my feelings tonight seemed to mock that idea. I had a whole weekend before I could throw myself into my next project. Friends had congratulated me and suggested a celebratory night on the town. I declined, pleading exhaustion. Really though, the hollowness of my victory had snuffed out any desire to celebrate.

Instead, I decided to enjoy a quiet evening at home. I had earned a night off, even from friends. I ordered take-out from my favorite restaurant, but dinner didn't help, nor did my nightly chocolate. Even my favorite television show failed to quiet my restlessness. Partway through I switched it off, disgusted with my inability to relax. I prowled around my apartment, wondering what I could try next. Eventually, I ended up in front of my full-length mirror.

I had been telling myself for nearly a year that everything would get better once I finished this project. But it hadn't. The accolades had been satisfying on one level. However, they failed to touch my deep-down longing and emptiness.

Thus, I found myself soul-searching. I grimaced at my reflection. What did I really want? I'd thought I was "following my heart" when I took this job. But my heart was still empty. Was I really that fickle? I stared and stared, mystified. Somewhere along the way, I'd lost myself and now my own heart was a stranger.

Unbidden, the thought came: Maybe I should pray.

A shiver ran through me. Though I had been raised in the Christian church and came to a genuine faith in Jesus, I hadn't prayed in ages. I'd just been too busy for God. "I'm not rebelling or anything like that. I'm going to go back to church as soon as things calm down," I said aloud, trying to soothe my gnawing sense of guilt. "God knows that I'm busy. I'm sure He won't hold it against me."

Despite my justifications, my unease at the idea of praying lingered . . . yet something made me think it was my best course of action.

I shook my head in disgust. "Listen to me talking to myself. Pull it together!" I sternly told my reflection.

My aching emptiness remained. So did the urge to pray.

Distraction. That's what I need. I wandered over to the kitchen, absent-mindedly getting a glass of water. I downed it, attempting to wash away my turmoil. The more I tried to avoid thinking about praying, the more I couldn't think of anything but. Once more I found myself in front of the mirror. At this rate I would be miserable all weekend. Just get it over with!

"God, um, I know it's been a while . . . but uh . . . I need some help . . . I don't even know what's wrong. What *is* wrong with my heart?" Absurdly, I started to cry. Was God even still listening for me? Maybe He'd forgotten me.

Suddenly, I became aware of someone in my apartment. Not another human: God Himself. I froze, goose bumps prickling. And then I heard it—a voice. Not audible, but echoing through my heart. *Are you sure you want to know?*

Did I? A knot of cold spread from my middle. What if I discovered something horrible? I was trapped. Without knowing the problem, I'd never be able to move on. My dissatisfaction would never leave. I was already miserable without reason. What did I have to lose?

I cleared my throat. "Y-y-yes, I think I do."

Abruptly, my reflection wavered. The mirror appeared to be melting, faster and faster, until it looked like a rushing waterfall of liquid silver. I slowly brushed a fingertip across it, then pushed. My fingers passed through the liquid and discovered empty space on the other side.

Something drew me on. I made an effort to still my trembling hands, then stepped through.

I found myself in a dim, rocky expanse, so huge I couldn't see its ends. Rock walls extended up beyond sight, as though I were in an enormous cavern. Most caves have some variation in coloring, but this place was a uniform, dismal grey. Light came from somewhere far above. Whatever the source, it was a dreary, cloudy-day sort of light that only emphasized the cheerlessness here.

Several feet in front of me gaped a giant abyss. In places, the sheer drop was almost perfectly smooth. In others, however, something had eaten away at the sides irregularly and the abyss yawned about a half-mile to a mile wide. In those spots, the rocky descent was gradual and left a ledge at the bottom before dropping off.

"Hello? Hellooooo? Where am I?"

No answer. I still felt God's presence, but evidently He was leaving the exploration up to me. "I thought You were going to show me why I'm so dissatisfied," I muttered. Still no answer. "Fine! Be that way." I suddenly remembered all the times of fruitless prayer in my youth. Why had I expected anything different?

I turned back to my mirror. The silver waterfall glinted invitingly. I put a hand up to it once more, but the surface was as hard as stone.

Okay, stay calm. Think it through. Either I can wait here to see if this is a dream or a hallucination, or I can work on leaving.

Once more I surveyed my surroundings, this time searching for another mirror or some other likely route of escape. No luck. I could see narrow footpaths worn into the sloping sides of the abyss—paths fit only for mountain goats. No need to tempt fate by trying one of those.

"Very well then, if that's how You're going to be, I'll find my own way out," I told God. I turned to my left and began walking along the rim of the abyss.

After about twenty minutes, I came to a section that had been roped off. I paused eagerly at this sign of life. Perhaps there was someone nearby who could give me directions. A trail marker stood to one side, and a narrow, rope-railed path wound down to the precipitous bottom rim. The sign read *Death by Chocolate*. The gulf was narrower here. I studied the trail doubtfully, trying to decide if it was passable. Near the bottom gleamed something silver and familiar looking. I squinted at it, then recognized it as the wrapping on my favorite candy.

Craving swept over me. I had never experienced such a loss of reason in the face of desire.[314] Before I even realized it, I hurtled down the trail, barely able to keep my footing. Breathless, I reached the bottom. Mountains of candy surrounded me, piled so high they spilled over the edge. I knew I shouldn't touch it, but I soon found myself rationalizing. One wouldn't be missed.

I looked all around in case someone was nearby to witness my trespass. For a moment I considered God's presence but decided since He had brought me here, He could simply deal with it. Maybe He was giving me some kind of strange vacation. Who knew? I ate one candy, then another and another, until the sugar rush began to make me feel woozy. I sat down on a partially exposed boulder, my hand resting on the cold stone.

Suddenly, I stood in a school playground. Kindergarten children ran wildly from one play area to the next, clambering around like little monkeys. Where was I? I reached out a sticky hand to steady myself on the nearby jungle gym. My hand passed right through it, and I almost fell over. Evidently, I wasn't really here, or else here wasn't real. Maybe I had lost my marbles.

Watch.

I started, then looked around warily.

A group of children surrounded a little girl wearing a blue dress and began throwing kickballs at her. All at once, I recognized the scene. I was the girl getting pelted and jeered. I watched myself cry helplessly, hurt and angry, unable to escape.

Eventually a teacher put a stop to their torture. Then she handed me a tissue and smiled kindly at me. "Don't mind them. They won't always be this difficult. Here, would you like a treat?" She reached into her pocket and withdrew a piece of candy. My child self nibbled on it. I remembered how it had made me feel a little better.

Then the scene vanished, and I sat once more in the abyss, my chocolate-covered fingers clutching the boulder. I felt awful, disoriented as to when and where I ought to be. I groaned and tried to block out the memory I had just relived. Kindergarten was the first in a long line of bad school experiences for me; I preferred not to think about school at all.

In fact, I determined not to think of it anymore, and instead returned my attention to getting home as soon as possible. I started back up the wall, no longer tempted by the candy. My laborious ascent took forever—especially compared to my mad dash down. Midway up, I glanced around once more, but there was still no one in sight.

When at last I reached the top, I picked up the pace. "Definitely not a vacation spot," I muttered to myself. The candy section ended before long, and I breathed a sigh of relief.

However, another roped-off section abutted it: *Le Entrée*. Probably food related. My stomach rebelled at the thought of more food. I thought about going down to look for a way out or a guide, but discarded the idea at once. It wasn't worth the risk when I could simply yell.

"Hellooоooo? Anyone down there?"

I waited for a minute or two, but all I could hear was my own echo. So I pressed on. This time I carefully avoided the path and kept my eyes on the rim ahead of me. At first my disgust for food carried me forward, but the farther into the section I got, the more the temptation to look grew. Thankfully, the section came to an end before my willpower gave out.

As I looked down the length of the rim, I could see roped-off areas stretching on and on, one after the other. Finding a way out might be a lot harder than I'd thought.

I glanced at the next trail sign: *The Book Nook*. It would be so nice to sit down and lose myself in a good novel—No! I don't have time for that. The gap was much larger here. I imagined how many books must be waiting in the wide space below the rim. Work had kept me too busy to even glance at a good novel in ages. There was probably even a comfy chair down there, so perhaps I could avoid a flashback. I could rest rock-free.

I peeked over the edge. A large, inviting, leather chair sat amidst mountains of books. I forced myself not to run down the abyss' side. My heart pounded with longing and the effort of waiting. Once seated, I reached for the nearest book, just to look at it: *Pride & Prejudice* by Jane Austen. Exactly what I was in the mood for. I'll just read a chapter or two while I rest.

Hours later, I finished it, then began another book. I fleetingly considered returning to the upper rim, but decided to finish one more chapter . . . then one more book. In between books, I flipped to the front of one, idly wondering whose they were. My own name was inscribed in the front. The book slid from my cold fingers and thumped to the ground.

Where am I? How do I get home?

I sat there, trying to slow my shallow breathing. I could still sense God's presence. Maybe He'd brought my books here?

Gradually, the sight of all my books soothed my jangled nerves. It couldn't be such an awful place if these were here. My heart rate calmed. As my muscles loosened, they began to ache. I'd definitely been sitting for too long. I stood up and stretched. Maybe I'd pick one more book. I could just read the good parts version. After all, I ought to read at least part of one to purge the last bits of my terror. I can't think clearly when I'm this upset. Later would be soon enough to formulate a plan. I'd better make it a good one. I walked over to examine the various stacks.

I noticed worn copies of my favorite novels here and there in the piles. This one had gotten me through my most recent breakup. Another volume had kept me company through countless nights of insomnia. Right after my family moved, the characters from this childhood favorite had been my only friends. I ran my hand over my books fondly. They were beloved old friends.

My stomach growled and exhaustion gnawed at my bones. How long had I been down here? Judging by the pile of discarded books near my chair, it must have been hours, maybe even days. What if I was late for work? I'd better go. I looked around lingeringly, wishing I could somehow bring the tranquility of my books with me.

I hunted among the stacks for the perfect last book. My foot slipped a bit, and I glanced down to see what I'd caught it on. I was right on the brink of the abyss. My vision greyed as I discovered there was no visible bottom. I flung myself away from it, landing hard on the rocky ground and scraping my hands.

Memories began to play once more, a kaleidoscope of brokenness . . . wounds soothed and numbed in the arms of a good novel. Nausea swept over me, and my knees felt weak. On and on the memories beat at me, aggravating old wounds. I thought the agony would never end. This time when the memories subsided I was sweaty and shaking, barely able to keep the sobs contained. My only thought was escape.

On legs of jelly, I climbed back to the top and continued walking. This time I took the precaution of walking far from the edge, lest my eyes entice me to descend. I kept them fixed on the ground and tried to while away the time by imagining my favorite movies. It was too bad this place was so horrible. It had some of my favorite things and I wished I could indulge myself safely. Maybe it was an example of God's twisted sense of humor?

The following trail was entitled *Romance Novel Ravine*. I shuddered a little. I'd been both pleasantly surprised and a little disappointed by the lack of steamy romances in my book stacks. It had been years since I'd picked one up. They aroused frustrating sexual tension in me. I always felt fascinated in the beginning and somehow soiled and full of sickly guilt afterwards. When I heard them called "emotional pornography," I could understand why.[315] Hence I had, with difficulty, given them up. Work had gradually taken up most of my free time anyway.

Work . . . I hope I'm not missing anything important. Thinking about work distracted me enough to get past Romance Novel Ravine. I continued on.

Another sign caught my eye. *The 5–9*—work. Those of us who lived there called it that since it required so much overtime, the downside of being a salaried employee. Here the abyss gaped close to a mile across. I wondered what would happen if I went down. Would the abyss show an accurate picture of what was happening in the office right now? Had my secretary been managing things all right without me?

I took a step closer, and then another. But what if the memories were even worse since the abyss was so wide? I paused and weighed my options. Realistically speaking, I felt unequal to leaving. I had to know. I had to go down. But a part of me rebelled. Fear kept me from going forward. Desire prevented me from continuing along the rim. I stood there for what felt like an eternity, locked in place by my ambivalence.

Finally, I gave up. It was impossible. I needed help. God was the last person I wanted to talk to, but I didn't have anywhere else to turn . . . .

"God, please help me," I whispered.

Strength flooded my limbs. One agonizing, slow step at a time I moved past the cherished section.

And then I reached Lover's Leap. Piece of cake. There was no way I wanted to go down there. The latest in my long string of boyfriends was not someone I wanted to see right now.

Then again . . . . I had been stuck here for ages, alone. And then I recalled all the times I'd found solace in the arms of some man, and all the times my heart had been broken as a result. I clearly didn't want to relive those memories. One more step, I coached myself. Now another. I forced myself to continue on, despite the almost inescapable pull to look, just once. The longer it went on, the more miserable I became. I longed to go home and pretend this had all been a terrible nightmare . . . maybe it was.

I thought about raging aloud to God, but refrained. I didn't want to interact with Him at all. So I assiduously ignored Him. I examined the next trailhead eagerly. Anything to get my mind off my ex-boyfriends and my current predicament.

Oh no! You've got to be kidding me! God's section? He has His own section? I could go down there and . . . and what? Yell at Him? Tell Him how much I hate this? Listen to a lecture? Give Him the satisfaction of watching me beg for a way out? I wasn't sure what exactly would happen if I followed the path, but I didn't want to find out. I kept walking.

Farther on, I came to a section roped off with construction tape. It had a sign, but lacked a trail. The sign proclaimed it under construction until I reached my perfect weight. A second construction site followed, this one awaiting a certain amount in my bank account. I discovered more and more of these sections, some frivolous—the new dress I saw yesterday—and others less so: *Mr. Right.* The abyss absolutely yawned at his section. I shrank away from the pain contained in that wide, wide place. Thankfully, it too was trail-less. I had a feeling the memories here would have been far worse.

As I reviewed the under-construction trails, I realized they were all things I wanted. Maybe this was the key. Maybe my emptiness was as simple as that: lack. Is that what God was trying to show me?

After passing Mr. Right's section, I came to something different. The tape proclaimed it was still under construction, despite a winding path. I looked around for a sign, but none was apparent. I peeked over the rim.

At the bottom, near the edge, stood a round table covered in a dingy, white tablecloth. I cautiously picked my way down. The table had been set for three. An elaborate floral arrangement sat in the center, but the flowers had withered and died, littering the table with dried petals. A thick layer of dust coated everything. I picked up one of the place cards and blew on it, then dropped it like a hot coal. It was for my mother. I cautiously dusted off the other cards at the table. They were my dad's and mine. A wave of sadness engulfed me, and I sank onto a nearby rock.

Memories tore through my mind, showcasing my parents' absence. The pain stole my breath. Why had I come down here? I was an adult and didn't need parents anymore. Why did I still crave their presence and approval? It was an ache deep in my soul, a raw searing pain I told myself I barely noticed anymore. I knew I was part of a generation of dysfunctional families, linked by the common thread of our unmet needs. Absentee fathers lost in their own addictions, whether they be success or drink. Emotionally bankrupt mothers with nothing to give. Our pain rang across the land. So why couldn't I move on? Other people seemed to adjust, to grow accustomed and get on with life.

"Why did You bring me here? Take me somewhere else! You want to see me beg? I'm begging!" I sobbed towards the ceiling. "Please, please, please. I can't take this anymore. Help me!"

A dislodged rock clattered to the ground. Startled, I whipped around to the path. A tall man with dark hair was climbing down it. Scars disfigured his face and hands.

I dashed tears from my eyes and tried to regain my composure. I hoped he hadn't seen my little breakdown. Maybe God was actually answering my prayer.

He reached the bottom and smiled at me. Strangely, I felt at ease, as though I'd known him forever.

"Hello, do you know how to get out of here?"

"This way," the man said and gestured back up the path.

"Thank God! I've been trying to find someone who could get me out of here for ages!" I smiled up at him winsomely, wondering if I could wheedle my way into using a shortcut, even if it wasn't generally open to the public. "Who are you? Some kind of tour guide?"

"Something like that."

I stared at him for a moment, then realized who He must be. All the hope drained out of me. "You're Jesus, aren't You?"[316]

"Yes," He answered.

"Why are You here?"

"You asked for help."

I looked at the ground unseeingly. I had asked for help. But this wasn't what I wanted. I want to get out of here!

I glanced back at Jesus. He stood there quietly, watching me and waiting.

I bit my lip. Why won't He say something? Typical, so typical. I guess it was up to me to drive the conversation.

"Where am I? What is this place?"

"This abyss is a representation of your heart," Jesus answered.

Blood pounded in my ears. My heart? No wonder I felt so empty! How could He have made me so poorly? And how could He have the gall to come here of all places?

I took a step towards Him. "Why in the world does my heart have a giant crack in it? Whose great idea was that?"

He didn't even flinch. "Let's walk back up and get a bird's-eye view."

"Fine. Whatever You think is best." I smiled a sickly sweet smile and ground my teeth in frustration. I was tired and hungry. I wanted to go home, not get some lecture from a God I barely knew and presently wanted nothing to do with.

Jesus turned and walked back up to the abyss' rim. I dragged myself along, forcing my aching legs and burning lungs to keep going. Once there, He led me to a door in the cave wall. It opened onto yet another climb: stairs this time. At the top, we entered a narrow room carved out of the solid rock. It was completely bare, save for the floor-to-ceiling window at one end. I walked over to it and looked out. The room sat directly over the abyss. It was like we were in the top box at a stadium. Too bad I didn't want to see the view. Too bad Someone had to wreck my heart.

From here, I could see the abyss' ends, though they were miles apart. At least it didn't go on forever. The central gap, however, was a completely different story. It may not have been infinitely wide or long, but my hunch was that it was bottomless.

Jesus moved to stand by me. I took a step away.

"Here's how your abyss used to look," He said. Abruptly, it shrank down to the central gap.

I licked my lips. "How far down does it go?"

"Why don't we take a closer look?"

"I would rather not."

"If you don't see enough to understand what you've seen, you won't be any better off than you were before."

He sounds like a fortune cookie.

The thought caught me off balance, piercing my rage and dissipating a little of my fury. My sense of humor reasserted itself, and I considered responding in kind, maybe throwing out some line from a kung fu movie. But I was still angry with Him, so I squelched my levity.

"Are You crazy? Do You really think that's safe?"

"I won't let any harm come to you,"[317] He said and held out a hand.

Strangely, a part of me wanted to go with Him. I hesitated, then slowly put my hand in His. The window vanished, and He jumped into the abyss, pulling me with Him.

TWO

I screamed and closed my eyes, bracing myself for the inevitable impact. None came. I opened my eyes, one at a time. I felt like I had been transported into *Alice in Wonderland*.[318] We fell and fell and fell.

As we continued to fall without any ill effects, my terror ebbed, and I began to look around. The grey rock walls were smooth as glass and the space around us completely empty. We almost seemed to hang motionless between the stark walls. Only the rush of air betrayed our terrific plunge through the endless void. I glanced down, hopeful the abyss wouldn't last forever, yet fearful we would crash into the bottom. I could see the walls going down and down, sloping inward as the distance warped my perspective, until they were lost in gloom. My intuition appeared to be well-founded; there was no visible bottom.

No need to panic yet. Just because it looked this bad in the past, didn't mean it had stayed so. I turned to Jesus. "If this is what my abyss looked like before, how does it look now?"

"Like this," Jesus said.

The walls down here remained glossy and gaping. But now we were surrounded by falling objects: candy, books, clothes, etc. I pictured the overflowing piles stacked along the bottom rim. "I suppose all these things must have fallen off as new things were added."

"Actually, you put them down here."

"What? Why?"

"To fill up this crack."

I glanced down—still no bottom. "But if it's bottomless, how can those things fill it up?"

"They can't."

"Then it's hopeless . . . unless . . . unless I can somehow get rid of it another way?"

"You have to understand the nature of your abyss before you can start trying to get rid of it."

"Well, what is it?"

"It's a manifestation of your hunger for Us."[319]

"Then how did it change so much? I've had You in my life for quite some time. Why is it still here? It should have gotten smaller, not larger!"

"Let's observe."

Immediately, we were above the abyss. Jesus had restored it to the central gap with its smooth walls. He gently floated us back into the small room, and the window reappeared behind us. In our absence, two stone chairs had grown out of the floor in front of the window. Happily, the chairs had cushions. I dropped into one, still feeling drained.

A blast tore through the cavern. Bits of rock sprayed everywhere, gouging chunks out of those smooth, glassy walls. The explosions continued, and huge portions of the walls crumbled.

"What's happening?" I yelled and jumped out of my chair to get a better view.

"Your abyss is getting blown up," He yelled back.

I held my breath as the carnage continued. I couldn't make myself look away. Eventually, the explosions stopped. The injuries of a lifetime had been compressed into the space of 15 minutes. I sat back down, my emotions scraped raw.

"What were those explosions?"

"Experiences that wounded you. They're imprinted in the stones themselves. You saw some of them."

I recalled how I'd been transported back to relive various painful memories. Humph! "Imprinted!" I raged internally. So nice and neat. Just a fancy impersonal way to minimize my agony. I decided I would rather not discuss those carved-out wounds lest I lose my tenuous grip on my emotions.

"All right then, so if this abyss is a manifestation of my hunger for You, what are all those trails?"

"You mean your addictions?"

"Whoa, whoa, whoa. Wait just a minute. Don't You think 'addiction' is a little too strong? I mean, I could quit any of those things. I'm not addicted. Besides, addictions are things like alcohol or drugs, not chocolate or relationships. I'm not that bad of a person."

"Addictions aren't only for the 'unspiritual.'[320] And you're right. You could change addictions, but that doesn't address your heart," Jesus said.

"What do You mean?"

"Think of it like this: Imagine you're trapped in a cage. It has some nice wallpaper—say, pictures of your favorite foods. After a while, you want out. You're fed up with the cage. So you repaper it with photos of exercise equipment. Are you free?"

"No, but who would be crazy enough to equate changing wallpaper with escaping?"

He sighed. "Lots of people—they mistakenly believe the wallpaper is the problem, rather than the cage. And so they trade wallpapers, continuing to cover over the same cage. Food addicts become exercise addicts. Alcoholics become workaholics. Smokers become overeaters. The wallpaper is more attractive, but they're no closer to freedom . . . I noticed that you have several trails completed and more under construction. Is your abyss filled?"

"Obviously not."

"Alcoholics are simply trying to medicate a heart problem with alcohol.[321] How is that any different from your attempts to fill your emptiness with chocolate?"

The man was ruthless. I didn't have a snappy comeback—mainly because I'd never thought of my passions in that light. "Everyone has vices. It's just life. Mine aren't nearly as bad as some people's. There are some seriously hard-core addicts out there." I thought about suggesting He bother one of them instead.

"That's not the point. It's about the state of your heart. If you don't deal with your underlying heart problem, there's nothing to keep you from ending up a 'hard-core addict.' "

"Me? I don't think so!"

"You're already teetering on the brink," He said quietly.

"How so?"

"Your soul is needing more and more to be pacified.[322] Look at tonight: even that 'amazing business deal' couldn't satisfy. A couple years ago, it would have soothed your emptiness for a time."

I squirmed, trying to escape His relentless gaze. He's right. I hated to find myself agreeing, but there it was: truth I couldn't escape. Maybe I didn't want to know my own heart after all.

"That doesn't necessarily mean I'm going to become a hard-core addict though."

His eyes bored into me. "You've developed a tolerance to all your 'vices.' I know you keep telling yourself that it'll only take 'one more,' but does 'one more' ever really satisfy?"

I recalled the countless times I had read one more chapter, eaten one more chocolate, or attained one more milestone of success. They all rang hollow. In the moment, I felt like one more might help, and for a short time I usually felt better . . . but it never lasted.

"Of course it doesn't last. It's not supposed to. You're not using those things the way We designed. You wouldn't be surprised if your kitchen knives went dull after cutting down a tree, would you? The continual lusting after 'one more' is screaming that whatever you're trying isn't working."

"Hmm . . . Maybe . . . ."

"Your 'vices' are not comforts. They're false friends. They entangle and lull your heart so that you're never able to find true satisfaction. Their empty promises of fulfillment hold you captive."

I simply listened. I didn't exactly disagree on a cognitive level, but I certainly rebelled on an emotional one. False friends? He was plainly determined to see them as the enemy. But who is He to decide whether or not they help?

"You asked," He said.

"I asked?"

"You asked to know what was really wrong."

"I'm sure I would have figured it out eventually."

"I don't think so."

"Why not? It's me we're talking about here—not a voyage to an unknown planet, not the exploration of someone else. Me. I think I know myself better than anyone."

"But you don't. Sin has estranged you from yourself."

"Come again?"

"How do you know yourself?" He asked.

"I suppose I pay attention to myself—to my thoughts, feelings, and actions. Sometimes I ask other people how they view me, or try to guess how they view me based on their manner."

"You're right. Apart from Us, you really only have those two options: to look at yourself through your own eyes or to use another person as a mirror. However, sin in your life prevents you from seeing yourself clearly. Even when you try to use someone else as a mirror, you're still limited by your flawed understanding of them. Only We have a true third-person perspective.[323] Only We created you and know you through and through."[324]

I crossed my arms. "How could I not see myself clearly?"

"Because you're viewing yourself through a haze of mistaken beliefs and brokenness. Those things distort the reality of who you are. Try as you may, you'll never be able to gain a full perspective."[325]

"Are You sure?"

"Yes. For instance, you don't remember every detail of every event in your life, do you? Do you know how each event has shaped your character?"

"I guess not." The more I thought about it, the more I could see His point. "Let's just say that You're right. I still think it's a relatively small number of vices. I'm not sure I would consider myself an addict."

He looked at me pointedly. "Have you explored every trail?"

"Well, no."

"What about the other side? There are lots of trails over there, places for things like TV, shopping, computer time, approval, being needed, competency. Shall I go on?"

I paled. There were more on the other side?

"Not to mention all your unfinished trails."

"Now wait just a minute! The unfinished ones aren't addictions. There's nothing in them to fill my emptiness with."

"Oh really? What about this one?" Abruptly, we stood in front of the trail set aside for when I reached my perfect weight. "What happens if you never get this thin?"

"Nothing. Absolutely nothing."

"You're exactly right—nothing happens. This part of you remains empty. By earmarking it thus, you've almost certainly doomed yourself from the start. And it's all for the sake of lies."

I had been about to protest that I might one day get around to losing weight. But that last sentence arrested my attention. "Lies? What kind of lies?"

"That We did a poor job of making you. That you don't have enough worth just as you are. That others will like you more if you look different."

"I don't know if I would go that far. All people have value, no matter their physical appearance."[326]

He took a step towards me. "You can parrot that truth. You can even relax your standards for everyone but yourself. Deep down, though, part of you is convinced that you will be more valuable if you attain this 'perfect' number. You've bought into the lie that physical appearance determines some portion of worth. If you weren't convinced, this trail wouldn't exist."[327]

"Fine," I grumbled, eager to change the subject.

"Even if you completed this trail, would it satisfy you? Have any of your other trails satisfied?"

"No," I admitted quietly.

"These earmarks for things and people are still taking your time and energy."

Maybe He was right. I recalled all the energy I'd exhausted in trying to obtain my unmet desires and in the work of waiting. They spoke for themselves, drowning out any objections I might have made. "Wait. Things *and* people? I know I've got places for people, but really, can people be addictions?"

"Well, what are relationships for?"

"I've never thought about it—to help each other out, I guess."

"Let's go look at your table."

"Do we have to?"

"It's a good place to begin. There's a reason We start you out with parent-child relationships—they can teach you about the nature of relationships in general."

I stepped back. "Can't we just talk about it up here?"

"C'mon. I'll be with you the whole time," He said with a smile.

"All right. Fine."

Jesus held out an arm to escort me, and I took it. He raised His foot to take a step. The ground rushed by underneath us and halted at the table.

"What do you see here?" He asked and covered my hand with His own. Maybe He knew how much I tried to avoid this place, to deny its existence even to myself.

I shrugged bitterly. "Nothing very unusual: unmet needs. People who couldn't be bothered to show up."

"May I show you something else?" He asked, watching me intently.

I nodded.

He reached down, moved the place card for my father, and lifted the tablecloth. Underneath, engraved in the table, was another name: *Abba God.*

I gasped. How in the world did God's name get on my table? It pierced my bitterness, somehow laying bare all the anguish underneath. I tried to smother it, to steady my breathing and pay attention.

"You see, everyone has 'daddy issues' and 'mommy issues' and 'spouse issues' because these are a special class of relationships. They're analogies designed to teach you about Us."[328] He gestured to the table. "They can give you a glimpse of what it's like for Us to sit here. Sadly, most people don't use those relationships for that; they rely on humans instead and are left with unmet needs."

I looked at Him blankly.

He produced a hollow, metal cylinder and held it up. "No human can fully satisfy those needs. No human can fill the cylinder. Some fathers are more like a diamond trying to fill it. Even if you have a truly excellent father, he's still just a sunburst. Earthly fathers can't fill the daddy-void in your heart. That's not what they're designed to do. They're designed to help you transition to knowing your heavenly Father,"[329] He said, compassion writ across His features.

Tears trickled down my cheeks. "But what if they're more like an obstruction? Or what if they aren't around at all?"

He put a hand on my shoulder. "My Father is father to the fatherless.[330] Just because your earthly father has failed, it doesn't mean that you shouldn't trust your heavenly Father. It's the nature of polyhedrons to be unable to fill a cylinder. Every earthly father will fail to fill your daddy-shaped void, no matter how good he is."

I stood there, sobbing uncontrollably as I looked at the engraved name on my table. I desperately longed for things to be different somehow—for my void to have been filled in one way or another, for this agony never to have existed. But the past remained obdurate, and I remained trapped in my pain.

"Keeping it open, hoping they will one day decide to change, isn't helping you. Nor is leaving it empty going to punish them," He said gently, and enfolded me in a comforting hug.

"I know," I choked out, clutching Him.

"Your father is merely saving the Daddy void in your heart for My Father so that you can find true fulfillment in being a child of God. A place card is only valuable while the person is absent. Once they sit in their seat, it's no longer needed. Even if your father is absent, your father-needs can still be met."

"But what if I don't know what it's like to have a father? What if I can't make the transition?" I wailed into His chest.

He held me in silence while I wept. After a while, my sobs subsided. Tenderly, He raised my gaze to His own. "Listen to Me. It's true that your father gave you a flawed picture of what a father should be like. It's also true that your beliefs about fatherhood need to change. But you don't have to be stuck with those lies.

"I came so that you could see the truth: what My Father and your Father is really like.[331] I've eased the transition in a way no human ever could, because I alone have seen the Father.[332] Use Me to see the Father. Don't use your father's failure as an excuse to stay away. Don't condemn yourself to living without a father."

I took a step back, sniffled and wiped my eyes. Tears reformed when I saw my table, so I turned my attention to the abyss. It was all so overwhelming.

"Do you see now how you're using people as addictions?"

I took a deep breath and massaged my temples. "What?"

"You're using people like they're things, instead of being in relationships. People can't fill your heart any more than chocolate or money can."

"What am I supposed to do? I can't stop working or eating or being in relationships!"

"I'm not suggesting that you should. Some of your addictions are sinful by nature; you need to permanently get rid of those. And with others, a fast may be helpful to break your dependence on them. However, with most it's less about the 'what' and more about the 'how.' "

I shook my head. "The 'how'?"

"How you're using those things and people."

"How am I using them?"

"You're worshipping them, aren't you?"

I frowned. "Worshipping them? Is that even possible?"

"Come see." Jesus turned and began climbing back up to the rim.

Not more walking! I stumbled forward, feeling incapable of doing much more. Once we reached the rim, He headed to the cave wall. It took forever to get there. Finally, He led me to a silver button set directly in the rock face. It reminded me of an elevator button. He pressed it, and immediately a large, door-shaped section of the wall swung inward.

We stepped through.

Sunlight dazzled my eyes. Color, scent, and sound sang around me. It's as though I've been dead and come alive again.

We stood in a glade. It felt like late spring—the plants bursting with color and the air perfumed with the earthy smell of growing things. Sun-dappled tree shadows lay all around us.

"Where are we?" I asked.

"In a forest, watching this tree," Jesus answered, pointing at a cypress sapling some 15 feet in front of us.

"Watching a tree? Why are we watching a tree?"

"To learn about worship and addictions. Now watch."

Time began to speed up. The sun moved back and forth across the sky, faster and faster until it was just a blur. Dutifully, I watched the tree.

Rains watered it. The sun warmed and fed it. Winds tore at it, but it remained rooted. Seasons passed, then years. The tree grew and grew, its branches stretching towards the sky, eventually covering us in shade. The trunk thickened until a mighty cypress stood before us.

Time began to slow, then resumed its normal pace.

"What now?" I asked.

"Shhh. Just keep watching."

I soon heard rustling footsteps approaching. A middle-aged man appeared out of the underbrush. He had broad shoulders and muscular arms. A bushy beard covered his face, and he carried an axe and a long cord. Apparently, he couldn't see us. He seemed distracted and hurried, worry furrowing his brow. The man looked the tree up and down, then wrapped the cord around the cypress' trunk. It seemed to meet some criteria, because he nodded decisively, and then began to chop it down.

In the space between one blink and the next, the job was completed: the wood was neatly chopped, and the last load appeared to be in a nearby wagon. Only the stump remained. The glade felt barren and empty without the giant tree.

"Now what?"

"We wait," Jesus said.

I sighed. Waiting had never been one of my strong points.

Jesus sped up time again. The woodcutter returned. I wasn't sure how much time had passed. He seemed much happier now, almost lighthearted. When he reached the stump, he threw his arms around it and kissed it. Then he took out a hammer and chisel and began to carve it. Time continued to move forward in spurts. One moment, his project had just begun. The next he looked to be about a quarter of the way done.

When finished, he surveyed his work with a smile. The tree trunk had been transformed into a tree sprite. Leaves wreathed the figure's head and dripped down to form a garment. The eyes and mouth were open wide, as though the figure was staring intently at the person in front of it and speaking. I was surprised at the beauty this rough woodcutter had discovered in the tree stump.

The woodcutter bowed low to the figure and his lips moved soundlessly. A short time later he left.

"What was he saying?" I asked Jesus.

He looked at me, His eyes clouded. " 'Save me; you are my god.' "[333]

"Wait! How can that tree save anyone? What did he do with the rest of the wood?" That wood must have done something truly magical to be confused with a deity.

"Nothing yet. Once it's seasoned, he'll use it for firewood; he'll cook meals and keep warm with it."

"Then why in the world does he think it can save him?"

"Maybe you should ask him that."

The man appeared again, this time carrying a bucket of something that he poured out onto the ground in front of the carved stump, then he bowed down again.

"Sir?" I called out.

The woodcutter jumped up and whirled, grabbing his axe and taking up a defensive posture in front of the wooden tree sprite.

He eyed me warily. "Who're you?"

"We're not here to hurt you or your tree," I began.

"We?" He scanned the area around me.

I half-turned, momentarily sick with dread that Jesus had left me here all alone. He was still right beside me.

"Why doesn't he see You?" I asked Him.

"He's been ignoring Us for so long that he can't even recognize the truth anymore,"[334] Jesus said.

"What should I do?"

"Ask him your question."

I turned back to the woodcutter. He was watching me, as though it was anyone's guess what I would do next.

"Ma'am, are you all right?" the woodcutter asked. "It ain't safe to be out in these here woods alone."

I smiled reassuringly. "I'm fine."

"How'd you get out here, if you don't mind me asking?"

"Umm . . . ." I considered for a moment, running through various scenarios, before discarding them all as unworkable. In the end, I opted for the truth, or at least part of it. "I'm not exactly sure."

He took a step back.

"That's beside the point, though," I added hastily, trying to distract him. "What's that behind you?"

"My god," he said reverently.

"But it's a tree stump. How can it be a god?"

He shrugged. "Who knows the ways of the gods?"

"How do you know it's a god then?"

"'Cause it saved me once. I figure I owe it my worship now."

"I'm curious—how did it save you?"

He scratched his beard, then glanced up at the late afternoon sun. "I suppose I can take time to tell you. If nothing else, I owe it to my god." He crossed the clearing and sat down on the ground.

I glanced at Jesus inquiringly. He nodded, then walked over to the woodcutter and sat down too. I followed. My legs almost buckled as I gingerly lowered myself to the ground. All that standing around made me stiffer than the tree.

"I make a living selling wood—firewood, furniture, and woodcarvings. Last year business was terrible, all year. Nothing I did helped. I even tried praying to the one I thought was God, but he never did come through."

I looked over at Jesus involuntarily, and He nodded. So the woodcutter had cried out to God, and for some unfathomable reason God hadn't answered.

"A 'no' is still an answer," Jesus said softly. "So is an unguided tour of your heart."

I flushed as I remembered my earlier belief that God hadn't really answered my prayer and had instead forasaken me, despite bringing me through the mirror.

"Then what happened?" I prompted, eager to abandon my current train of thought.

"Times got leaner and leaner 'til finally there weren't any more food left—nothing to give to my children." He stared off into the distance, worry etching his face once more.

"We ate boiled tree roots and the like, just to stay alive. After a while, my youngest daughter got real sick. I didn't expect her to live—she had nothing left to fight with . . . We didn't know what to do. I tried to pray, but God refused to listen. One night, I fell asleep sitting up with her and had a dream. In it, a voice told me to 'harness the strength of the forest.'"

"Did you see this tree in your dream or something?"

"No, but I measured a goodly number of the trees in this forest, and this here cypress is the largest I found. I figured taking it'd be the best way to get the forest's strength."

"So what happened to your daughter?"

He smiled. "She got well—right as rain now."

"How do you know this tree healed her?"

"How else would she have gotten well? I had the dream. Then I cut down the tree, and not a day later, she began to mend."

"Okay, but what about your business? You must have something pretty concrete in that area, or you wouldn't expect this tree to save you."

He shrugged. "It's still slow but better than it was."

"Is it as good as normal for this time of year?"

"Not yet. But it's just a matter of time. If I keep worshipping my god, just you wait—business will pick right on up."

"But didn't you make your god? Weren't you just protecting it? How can it change circumstances?"

"Now you listen here—you're meddling in things that don't concern you. Who can tell the gods how they ought to act?"

"That doesn't answer my question, though. I'm not trying to meddle; I just want to understand."

"That's what I been telling you—there's no understanding the ways of a god," he said darkly.

I pointed to the stump. "But I still don't see how this can be a god. It grew here because of a seed and the rain and the sun. It didn't create itself."

"I can't help it if you're a little crazy, lady."

"Me? Crazy? You're the one worshipping a block of wood!"

The man stood up and raised his axe threateningly. "I think you'd better move along. Now."

Jesus rose to His feet as well, and then helped me up. Silently, we walked back into the forest.

"I just don't get it," I confessed as we walked. "I don't understand how he can believe the tree will help him. Why didn't You fix his problem? Then he wouldn't be confused. He would know the tree can't help him."

"We did heal his daughter. We're still taking care of him and his family."

"But why didn't You do it right when he asked? Why haven't You fixed his business?"

"Because even if We fixed his immediate problems, it wouldn't fix his heart. He'll never be saved until he truly turns to Us, instead of trying to manipulate Us. Discomfort is a useful tool. It rips the veil off your longing and forces you to confront reality."

I raised my eyebrows. Discomfort? Useful?

He held my gaze. "Would you have reached out to Us tonight without it?"

I thought about it, trying to worm my way out of agreeing. "No, I suppose not," I finally answered, then quickly changed the subject. "I still don't see what worship and addictions have to do with each other, or even with me. I've never made an idol in my life."

"He feeds on ashes, a deluded heart misleads him; he cannot save himself, or say, 'Is not this thing in my right hand a lie?' "[335] Jesus murmured.

"What?"

"Why did the woodcutter start worshipping that tree?"

"Umm . . . because he didn't think You were doing anything about his misery. So he looked for something else to save him."

Jesus nodded. "And how did he worship his 'god'?"

"He bowed down?"

"What else did he do for it?

"Well, I suppose he began by fashioning it, then he bowed down."

"And?"

I replayed the scene in my mind. "He poured that bucket of liquid in front of the tree. Was that worship?"

"Yes. He offered wine to the tree—wine that he bought with his meager increase in business."

"Are You serious? You mean he didn't use it to buy food for his children?"

"No. He's still hoping to control his god with that offering, to force his god to increase his business even more."

My eyes flew to His face and I stumbled. Jesus grabbed my elbow and steadied me.

"Did you notice anything else?" He asked.

"He protected his god, or was going to, until he realized I wasn't going to hurt it."

"He also took time and energy to make several trips out to it," Jesus noted.

"Okay, so what's this supposed to show me about worship?"

"Well, what do you think worship is?"

"Arranging things around whatever you're worshipping? Changing your life for it?"

He halted. "A heart attitude of lifting something up, proclaiming its worth as displayed by a change in every facet of your life.[336] Notice too, he expected the tree to rescue him."

"Okay, so the woodcutter began running his life around the tree and asking it to save him. What's that got to do with me? Or even with addictions for that matter?"

Suddenly, the stone door appeared in front of us, still open.

"Good questions," Jesus said, and then walked through the door.

I threw up my hands. Why couldn't He just give me a straight answer? Then, fearing to be left behind, I hurried through the door after Him.

THREE

This time it opened into my apartment. It seemed so prosaic in comparison with the forest that I felt thrown off-balance. In fact, were it not for the presence of Jesus and a copy of myself, I would have shrugged off the whole adventure as a bad dream.

"Now what?"

"Now we're watching your memory to discover what the woodcutter's tree has to do with you."

I sighed heavily, then watched myself prowl around my apartment, my emptiness screaming.

The room began to grow transparent and dissipate, tattering like fog in a strong wind. Once more, we stood on the edge of my gloomy abyss. I continued to watch myself as I ran down the trails, unable to control my own hunger or to escape my emptiness.

"Do you see the connection yet?" Jesus asked.

All at once something clicked. In an instant of direct revelation, the scales fell from my eyes.[337] I'm exactly like the woodcutter. I thought God didn't come through earlier in my life, so I shunted Him to the background . . . Jesus was right. I was arranging my whole life around these things, even the things I didn't have.[338] I was trying to use them to fill God's place in my life.

I thought back over the past week, full of work and my quest for competence and approval. Sprinkled in, I saw other addictions, other idols. Food. TV. Chocolate. Other "stress reducers." Shame overwhelmed me. Do I do anything but worship my addictions?

Jesus reached out to hold my hand. "Now you're starting to understand."

I gazed across the abyss, wishing I could escape the knowledge that pressed in. The roped-off sections stretched on and on, filling the space. How could my heart be so full of addictions, yet so empty? How in the world could I change things? I guess the first step was to get rid of my addictions. I had to stop loving them or using them, whichever it was. I remembered racing down the sides of the abyss in my haste to obtain chocolate. Could I stop? I felt like I didn't even have a choice.

"How do I get rid of my addictions then?" I asked Jesus.

"Wrong question. That's a trap."

"A trap? Isn't getting rid of sin the whole purpose of the Christian life? Wasn't the point of this little excursion through the mirror to open my eyes to my slavery to addictions?"

"Here, remember the cylinder?" He pulled it out of His pocket. "Let's use this to represent your empty heart. Like a vacuum, your heart is always hungering to be filled." Suddenly I could feel a disturbance in the air; suction was coming from the cylinder. Bits of dust flew up towards it. "Let's use clay to represent your addictions." A lump of clay appeared in the cylinder and the surrounding air quieted. He handed me the cylinder. "Now, try to remove the clay."

I tugged on it, but the vacuum was stronger. Then I handed the cylinder back. "I can't."

"If you spend all your time trying to remove your addictions, you'll exhaust yourself fruitlessly."

"So what should I do?"

"Why do you think the woodcutter believed the tree could rescue him?"

"I understand his rationale—that You didn't appear to help and the tree did—but it still seems kind of ridiculous to me."

"You're outside of his culture so it's easier for you to recognize his bondage. What started the process though?"

"He didn't believe You were helping. So he looked for help elsewhere."

"Right, his deluded heart misled him. The woodcutter began by disbelieving the truth, and that left him open to believing a lie. Where do you think you went wrong?"

I thought back to my frantic search for something, anything to fill my emptiness. "Probably the same place—by not believing You were enough. If I believed You could fill me, I wouldn't have been hunting elsewhere."

He smiled at me. "Good observation. Addictions begin in unbelief and are anchored with lies."

"Lies? What lies?"

"That your addictions can satisfy and We can't. That We don't know your needs. That We won't meet your needs. That emptiness is part of life and ought to be tolerated or ignored—"

I motioned for Him to stop. The current list was plenty. "How in the world am I supposed to see these lies?"

"Ask for revelation, like you did tonight. We'll show you what's really going on in your heart."[339]

"Okay, so suppose I finally figure out all the lies—then what?"

He shook His head. "No, it's not a step-by-step process. You don't discern all the lies and then move on. *As* you recognize the lies, you replace them with the truth."[340]

"Why not get rid of all the lies first, and then figure out the truth?"

"Because it's impossible to believe nothing. You can be ignorant, or you can believe or disbelieve something, but you can't believe nothing."[341]

"Huh?"

He held up the clay-filled cylinder again. "Suppose this represents your capacity to believe. Let's use the clay to represent your false belief, or lie. If you can't leave the space empty, how do you remove the clay?"

"Push it out with something else?"

"Does it matter what you replace it with?"

I tapped my chin. "I could just change it out with another lie, couldn't I?"

"Yes—like changing your wallpaper." He removed a lump of clay from His pocket and pushed it into the cylinder. The first lump fell out, but the cylinder remained full of clay.

"So I need to exchange it for the truth."

"Does it matter which truth?" Jesus asked.

"What do You mean?"

"Can the truth 'the sky looks blue' counter the lie 'God doesn't work on my behalf'?"

"No."

"What about this half-truth: 'God works on my behalf, except in these certain situations'?"

As He spoke, He took a metal star out of His pocket, like one from a child's shape-sorting box. He inserted it into the cylinder. A star-shaped chunk of clay fell from the cylinder to the ground.

"No. I suppose those 'certain situations' remain unaffected. It didn't completely clean out the lie."

"Right. You need to believe a truth that's big enough to counteract the full lie. What sort of truth would do the job?"

"That You do work on my behalf in all situations?"

In answer, He pulled out a solid metal cylinder and pushed it into the hollow cylinder. It was almost the same size and required some effort to shove in. However, it did scrape out all the remaining clay.

My mouth fell open. "Is it always going to be that hard?"

"Change takes work. But it's beyond your ability to do on your own,[342] so it doesn't matter. You have to use Our strength, regardless of the effort involved. It isn't too hard for Us."[343]

"So what sorts of truths do I need to begin to believe?"

"You are no longer a slave to sin.[344] You have been bought with My blood.[345] You have been made new.[346] Just like the prodigal son, your addictions portray you as less than who you are. You are not a pig keeper who is forced to choose between scavenging and starvation.[347] Rather, you are a child of God.[348]

You have a loving Father who is rich beyond your wildest dreams and who longs to bless you."[349]

"It's the same way with getting rid of my addictions, isn't it? I need to replace them with something."

"Yes! Instead of trying to fight against the vacuum in your heart, what do you think you should fill it with?"

"Well, if my abyss is a manifestation of my hunger for You, I suppose I should fill it with You, right?"

He beamed at me. "That's right."

"How exactly do I do that though? I had You in my life before. How do I know it'll be any different this time?" I asked, remembering the years of emptiness and distance.

"You used Us before, and banished our relationship into the background."

"Used You? How?"

"You cordoned off a little section of your heart for Us, as though We were just another addiction to throw at your emptiness. Like the woodcutter, you tried to manipulate Us into blessing you. You focused on what you could gain from Us. That's significantly different from having a love relationship with Us. You don't simply need what We can give you. You need Us. Don't run after food. I am the bread of life.[350] Don't hunt for Mr. Right. You are My betrothed.[351] Don't keep your father-void open. My Father is your Father."[352]

I stared at Him for a moment. Use God as an addiction? I'd never even thought of it that way. He did have His own little section though, just like my other addictions. I guess I had wanted His blessings more than Him.[353] The blood drained from my face as a thought rang through my mind: I'd been treating God like a whore![354]

"Jesus, I'm so sorry. Can You forgive me?" Maybe He doesn't even want me anymore. I wasn't sure I would if our positions were reversed.

"I died before you were born. I've already paid for all your sins: past, present, and future.[355] We forgive you. We still love you. We still want you. We wouldn't have come today if We didn't."[356]

I hugged Him, then asked, "How do I do things differently this time?"

"The same way you grow any relationship. Your need for Us is relational by its very nature."

"Looking at my abyss, I don't think I know how to do that." I blushed. "I've always tried to use people to fill my heart."

"There's still time to learn. Spend time with Us, get to know Us—not for what We can give you, but simply for the sake of Our relationship. In a lot of ways, the outward actions aren't all that different from what you've been doing. It's your heart attitude that needs to change."

"I know I haven't spent much time with You lately. I've been too busy, I guess."

"Not 'too busy.' Busy with the wrong things. All these counterfeits are stealing your time and worship energy. Once you stop worshipping them, you'll have more available. It's not about finding more time or energy, but rather redirecting what you've already got."[357]

"How does that work?'

Jesus smiled. "Like this."

At once we were in the rocky upper room. In the center of the room stood a large table with a miniature landscape on top. I walked over to get a closer look. At one end of the table a mountain range rose up out of the ground. There, small streams coalesced until a vast river tumbled into the valley. I bent down to examine it more closely, then gasped. It was real!

The river rippled and sparkled, as though basking in the light of an unseen sun. Tiny branches and other flotsam rushed along, the river carrying them effortlessly forward. Trees lined the river banks, their leaves blowing in a phantom wind, and wildflowers dotted the meadows. A herd of tiny cows munched complacently on miniscule blades of grass. I could even faintly hear their lowing. Rabbits, birds, and various other small animals completed the pastoral scene. The pleasant scent of growing things wafted up.

I circled the table, wondering if the river ran off the edge. Instead the water ceased to exist, or perhaps continued its merry way into some space I couldn't see.

It's like we're viewing a valley from the mountain's vantage point.

"Look at the river. What do you see?" Jesus asked.

"It's running pretty fast. And it's huge compared to those cows."

"How much force do you suppose it has?"

I examined the branches being carried rapidly downstream, trying to guess their size relative to the river.

"I'm not sure. Quite a lot though."

"Look at the river further downstream." He put both hands above the landscape, and somehow shifted it. The mountains and early portion of the river slid back into nothingness. As they disappeared, another leg of the river came into view.

This leg was vastly different. As it rushed downstream, it began to diverge into smaller streams. At first it was one small desertion, and then another, and another, until at last the mighty river had branched out, like fingers grasping at the land. Some of the streams slowed to a trickle, mired in the marshy wetlands the river's dispersal had created. Gradually, the smell changed from the vibrant perfume of life to a swampy miasma.

"Do you see the main branch?" Jesus asked.

I tried to trace the river through the profusion of splits. There it was, discernible only by its continued course rather than by a size difference. "Yes, I see it."

"How much force does it have now?"

"Not much."

"When you spread out your worship energy so widely, not much is left over to push you along in your relationship with Us."

"I see . . . . I understand the metaphor. But I still don't see how exactly I can get rid of the smaller streams."

"Remember, it's about the 'how.' Think about how you're using them. Dig out the main channel—start by expanding your relationship with Us so that your addictions are less of a temptation. Arrange your life around Us. As you do that, you may have to dam up your distributaries—cease them entirely if they're sinful and take breaks from the rest."

I remembered my headlong rush into the waiting arms of my addictions. "I don't think I can."

"You're right. Sin is an incurable disease from the human perspective,"[358] Jesus said. "Apart from Us and My death and resurrection, you are without recourse, doomed to a life of slavery to your appetites and emptiness. However, We didn't leave you trapped thus.[359] I came to give you freedom.[360] You can have that freedom through the power of My Spirit. Self-control is fruit of My Spirit."[361]

"Then what do I do?"

"Where's your treasure?" He asked.

"Treasure? I don't have treasure." I smiled a little, picturing a pirate's cache.

He chuckled. "Sure you do. You have things like time, energy, and money. Watch where you spend those. That'll show you where your heart is. Conversely, part of changing your heart is moving your treasure.[362] So keep investing those things in a relationship with Us, and your desires will follow suit."

"But how do I do that?"

"Darling, you're looking for a shortcut, but there isn't one. Relationships are organic things—they grow at their own pace."

"But even with plants you can encourage them to grow! Isn't there something I can do? Some spiritual equivalent to fertilizer?"

"Imagine you were starting a new relationship. How would you get to know the other person?"

I frowned at the river. "I'd try to get in extra time with them and pay attention to the things they say. I'd also watch how they handled various situations."

"So spend time sitting in Our presence. Pray. Read Our Word, the Bible. Practice relationships in the Church."

"*The* Church?"

"My Body."[363]

"Why?"

"A relationship with Us is designed to be lived out on both an individual and a communal level."[364]

My heart sank. "But why? Why can't I just work on my relationship with You on my own?"

"Well, what are relationships for?"

"To help me understand what it's like for You to fill that role."

"You'll experience Our love in tangible ways through relationships with members of My Body.[365] Plus you need help seeing the truth."

"I thought You said You would help me see the truth," I said and shoved my hands in my pockets.

"We will, but a lot of the time We use the Church.[366] When you share your true self with others, they can help point out the lies you're believing.[367] The truth then gives you a clearer view of Us. You can also help each other grow more into My image."[368]

"Really? I'm not sure I can help anyone grow right now."

He smiled. "Think of it like a bunch of rough stones getting shaken around together. You naturally end up rubbing up against each other."

I rolled my eyes. "Well that sounds fun."

"It's supposed to be uncomfortable. If you were always comfortable, you'd never change. This way, you can rub the rough edges off each other."

"Won't it hurt? I don't think I can handle much more," I said, thinking of my poor battered heart, already riddled with wounds.

"Sometimes. The Church is full of sinful people. But healing also happens in the context of relationships.[369] If you stay isolated, separated from Us and My Body, you'll stay wounded."

I made a face. "So I guess I have to find some kind of community of Your people."

"Yes. And finally and most importantly, ask."

"Ask? Ask what?"

"Ask for filling.[370] When you ask, We always answer,"[371] Jesus said and led me over to the window. He gestured to my gaping abyss. "What are you going to do about this?"

As I surveyed it, the pain of my wounds and emptiness swelled. "I don't know. It shouldn't be here in the first place!"

He put a gentle hand on my shoulder. "I know it's hard to walk through that pain. But you would still have an abyss without your injuries. Don't get bogged down in your pain."[372]

All at once we stood in front of my table again. I averted my eyes from that horrible place.

"What are you going to do with this?"

"What should I do with it?"

He swung me around to face Him. "I offer you this invitation: Dine with Us.[373] Remove the place cards and let Us sit there."

I looked back at the place cards. Moving them seemed to embody giving up on finding satisfaction in anything or anyone else but God. Maybe, if I could just move these dearest and most painful hopes, everything else would be easier. Mr. Right's place flashed through my mind. Maybe they wouldn't all be easier, but most should be. Yet, I just couldn't do it. Part of me longed to be done with the whole thing, to be free from the weight of this pain. And yet, part of me couldn't bear to lose this small token of my parents.

"I don't think I can, and I—I only half want to," I said in a low voice. "But I want to desire You more than them."

"Would you like help?" He asked.

"I don't have to do it alone?"

"No."

I put a hand on His arm. "Help me," I begged.

Tenderly, He placed a hand over my own. All at once desire for Him flooded my heart. Together, we removed the place cards, dead flowers, and dingy tablecloth, exposing the engraved names on the table. He pulled out a chair opposite to His own, and I saw that my own name had been engraved into the table too. This was where I belonged—with God. After we sat down, the table and chairs floated out into the center of the abyss and hung there, suspended in empty air.

As we talked, a liquid light, so intense it had mass, buoyed up our table. It was a yellow and green and blue that rippled and sparkled, like sunlight in deep water. The abyss began to fill up, slowly at first, then faster and faster.

I stared in wonder at my previously unsightly abyss. It didn't even matter that no sunlight found its way in. Jesus filled it with light and beauty. All those rocky disfigurements looked amazing with His light lapping in and about them. Tears filled my eyes. I think those "disfigurements" might actually be my favorite things about myself.

As I watched, I groped towards an understanding of this glimpse into truer reality. Maybe my emptiness was actually an opportunity for wholeness. Perhaps my greatest weaknesses and sufferings could become doorways to joy.[374]

Jesus smiled tenderly. "It's a beginning."

I found myself lying on the bathroom floor in front of my mirror. What had just happened? A dream? Hallucination? Vision? Did it matter? Something seemed different on the inside. My heart felt lighter than it had in ages—maybe ever.

What did Jesus mean when He said it was a beginning?

As I lay there, I realized every bone in my body ached. I ached in places I didn't know I could ache. I groaned, then rolled over and attempted to rise. Finally, by dint of holding on to the counter and pulling, I managed to get up. With a pounding heart, I turned and faced the mirror.

It looked solid enough. However, the reflection that stared back at me was disheveled and covered in rock dust. My appearance, coupled with my screaming muscles, gave mute testimony to the reality of my experience.

I hobbled out to the couch and gingerly lowered myself onto it. My phone lay on the nearby end table. I checked it, wondering how long I'd been gone. No messages, and it was only 11:00 p.m. on Friday night! "That can't be right!" I felt like I had been gone for a lifetime.

"Friday night . . . hmm . . . how am I supposed to find some of Your people?" I asked God. I could still sense His Spirit with me.

Immediately I recalled how Jessica, an acquaintance from work, had periodically invited me to visit her church.

"I guess that answers that question," I said, relieved I had somewhere to start.

A beginning . . . I glanced over at my chocolate stash. The pull to indulge myself was still there. I sighed. Time to dam up my distributaries. I bagged up my chocolate and staggered over to the trash can. "Goodbye, old friend," I said, then threw it away. How long would it take my distributaries to dry up? Would I ever stop wanting them? Still, the task seemed less daunting, now that my abyss had been filled.

I brightened. As long as I kept spending time with God and worshipping Him, it would be a lot easier to give up all the things I loved. Maybe the reality is that God doesn't pry my fingers off all those things I "love." Maybe, as I fell more in love with Him, my addictions would be less of a draw. In fact, the more I thought about Him, the more that made sense. My desire for them had already paled a bit. I could see how giving up my addictions could become less of a hardship and more of a joy—a joy to make room for more of Him in my life.

I smiled. He's right. It is just a beginning. But it's a good one.

Do not get drunk on wine, which leads to debauchery. Instead, be filled with the Spirit. ~ Ephesians 5:18

"Come, all you who are thirsty, come to the waters; and you who have no money, come, buy and eat! Come, buy wine and milk without money and without cost. Why spend money on what is not bread, and your labor on what does not satisfy? Listen, listen to me, and eat what is good, and your soul will delight in the richest of fare. Give ear and come to me; hear me, that your soul may live." ~ Isaiah 55:1–3a

314 If food addiction is an issue in your life, there are lots of great resources available. One resource that has been helpful for me is Dee Brestin's book *A Woman of Moderation: Breaking the Chains of Poor Eating Habits* (Colorado Springs: David C. Cook, 2007). See also http://www.settingcaptivesfree.com.

315 If sexual addiction of any variety is an issue in your life, some great starting resources are http://www.xxxchurch.com and http://www.settingcaptivesfree.com. Both these sites have lists of other available resources.

316 For the sake of readability I've used both the singular and plural pronouns with regards to the Trinity and the Persons therein. When talking about the Trinity, it's almost impossible not to emphasize either the oneness of God or His threeness. Since the American church tends to prioritize God's oneness, I've used the plural pronouns in places to highlight God's essential relational nature. I in no way wish to imply that God is not one (Deut. 6:4–5; 1 Kings 8:60; Isa. 45:5–6, 45:21–22; James 2:19) or to stray into Tritheism (Matt. 28:19–20; 2 Cor. 13:14; Eph. 4:4–6; 1 Pet. 1:2; Jude 20–21; John 1:1–2, 1:9–18, 17:24, 14:26, 16:7; Acts 10:38).

317 Ps. 121; Rom. 8:28

318 Lewis Carroll, *Alice's Adventures in Wonderland and Through the Looking-glass* (Racine, WI: Western, 1970), 10.

319 Eccles. 3:11; Acts 17:24–31. As Blaise Pascal put it: "What else does this craving, and this helplessness, proclaim but that there was once in man a true happiness, of which all that now remains is the empty print and trace? This he tries in vain to fill with everything around him, seeking in things that are not there the help he cannot find in those that are, though none can help, since this infinite abyss can be filled only with an infinite and immutable object; in other words by God himself." *Pensèes*, trans. W.F. Trotter (Grand Rapids, MI: Christian Classics Ethereal Library, 1944), Section VII: Morality and Doctrine: 425, accessed October 26, 2012, http://www.ccel.org/ccel/pascal/pensees.txt/.

320 Gal. 6:1

321 Addictions have physical, mental, emotional, and spiritual components. When breaking them, it's important to address all these areas. For example, I found my thyroid issues and candida overgrowth played a significant part in my sugar addiction. As I was renewing my mind with Scripture and working through my use of food as an emotional crutch, I also treated the physical side of my addiction. For an overview of how addiction affects each of these areas, see Gerald May's book *Addiction & Grace: Love and Spirituality in the Healing of Addictions* (New York: HarperOne, 2006).

322 "Tolerance" is a mark of addiction. We grow accustomed to current levels of input and require a higher level to achieve the same stimulation as we initially experienced. See May, *Addiction & Grace*, 25–26; Eph. 4:19

323 A third-person perspective entails having a complete view of the entire story, such as that had by the author, rather than by one of the characters. God alone is transcendent, completely *other* than everything else. As Creator, He is outside of all else (Heb. 1:10–12; Gen. 1:1; Col. 1:16). As sovereign, He has a full knowledge of what He planned (Job 42:1–2; Isa. 46:9–10; Jer. 29:11; Dan. 4:35; Eph. 2:10) and a full view of time (Ps. 90:2–4; 2 Pet. 3:8; Isa. 46:9–10).

324 Ps. 139:1–16

325 Ps. 139:23–24; 1 Chron. 28:9; Heb. 4:12–13; See C. S. Lewis' bit on how the Fall alienated us from our true selves by causing us to create a false third-person perspective based on our understanding of how we appear to others in *Perelandra: A Novel* (New York: Scribner Classics, 1996), 116–118.

326 The value of humans is grounded in our being image-bearers. Gen. 1:26–27; 9:6

327 For resources related to this subject, see Constance Rhodes's book, *Life Inside the "Thin" Cage: A Personal Look into the Hidden World of the Chronic Dieter* (Colorado Springs: Shaw Books, 2003).

328 For verses where God compares Himself to a husband/betrothed see the book of Hosea, as well as 2 Cor. 11:2; Eph. 5:22–32. For verses where God compares Himself to a mother, see Isa. 49:15–16, 66:12–13. For verses where God compares Himself to a father, see Ps. 103:13–14; Matt. 6:32, 7:7–11; Heb. 12:5–10; Gal. 4:4–7; 1 John 3:1.

329 e.g., Heb. 12:5–10

330 Ps. 68:5

331 John 20:17

332 Luke 10:21–22; John 14:8–9, 1:14, 1:18

333 Isa. 44:17; 44:14–20

334 e.g., Zech. 7:11–12

335 Isa. 44:20

336 To a certain degree, there's the already-not yet tension. True worship will spread to engulf the entirety of one's life, even though it begins with only part. e.g., Rom. 12:1; 1 Cor. 10:31

337 e.g., 1 Cor. 2:11–14; Rom. 10:17

338 Eph. 5:5; Ezek. 14:3; 1 John 5:21

339 Ps. 139:23–24; Jer. 17:9–10; 1 Sam. 16:7

340 Rom. 12:2; John 17:17; Sanctification (growing in Christlikeness) is a lifelong process (2 Cor. 3:18; 1 John 1:8; Phil. 1:6). For example, Jesus instructs daily confession (Matt. 6:11–12). Additionally, sometimes we can't discern further lies until after we've begun to change in response to the truth we know (John 8:31–36). One very practical way I've found to immerse myself in the truth is to keep verse cards around. Beth Moore introduced me to this concept in her Bible study *Breaking Free,* updated ed. (Nashville, TN: LifeWay Press, 2009),

211. I keep two 3"x5" spiral bound index card notebooks in my house (one in my bathroom and one in a prominent place where I'm working). I write down whatever lie I'm struggling with (e.g., *Lie: Continuing in sin is okay—God will forgive me.*), the truth (e.g., *Truth: God may let me follow my sin to its logical end.*), and then related verses (e.g., *Ps. 81:8–12*). When I walk by them, I read the card and flip it to the next card.

341 We are already immersed in our worldview from a very young age. A worldview is similar to the foundation and framework on a house. All other beliefs are affected by these base beliefs. The moment we come into contact with a piece of information, we automatically begin classifying it, and hanging it in an appropriate place, relative to our foundational beliefs. Therefore, the reality is that we can never be 100% neutral. For more information on worldviews, see "Chapter 1: A World of Difference: Introduction" in James Sire's book *The Universe Next Door,* fifth ed. (Downers Grove, IL: InterVarsity Press, 2009).

342 God reveals spiritual truths to us by means of His Spirit (1 Cor. 2:11–14; John 14:26, 16:13; Rom. 10:13–14)

343 Jer. 32:27; Matt. 19:26

344 John 8:31–36; Rom. 6:6–7

345 1 Cor. 6:20; Rev. 5:9

346 2 Cor. 5:17

347 Luke 15:11–32

348 John 1:12–13; Eph. 1:4–6; 1 John 3:1

349 Matt. 7:7–11; 1 Cor. 2:9–10

350 John 6:35

351 2 Cor. 11:2; Eph. 5:31–32

352 John 1:12–13; Rom. 8:15–16

353 Timothy Keller, *The Prodigal God: Recovering the Heart of the Christian Faith,* paperback ed. (New York: Riverhead Books, 2008), 41-43.

354 Matt. 16:4; Deut. 31:16; Judg. 2:17; Hosea 1:2, 4:12–13

355 John 19:30; Heb. 1:3, 7:27, 9:25–28

356 Ps. 18:19

357 e.g., Rev. 2:4–5

358 Isa. 64:6; Rom. 3:23, 6:23; Eph. 2:1–3; For an in-depth explanation of the addictions-as-disease view, see Edward T. Welch, "Chapter 2: Sin, Sickness, or Both?" In *Addictions: A Banquet in the Grave: Finding Hope in the Power of the Gospel* (Phillipsburg, NJ: P & R Pub., 2001).

359 Rom. 5:6–8, 6:22–23; John 8:34–36

360 Gal. 5:1

361 Gal. 5:22–23

362 Matt. 6:19–21

363 1 Cor. 12:27

364 Heb. 10:24–25; 1 Cor. 12:7, 12:12–27 ; 1 Pet. 2:5; Luke 5:16; Heb. 12:1

365 1 John 3:18; John 13:35

366 1 Cor. 12; James 5:14–16

367 Prov. 27:17; Matt. 18:15–17; Gal. 6:1; C. S. Lewis also talks about how it takes a community to get to know an individual in his book *The Four Loves* (New York: Harcourt Brace Jovanovich, 1960), 61–62.

368 Eph. 4:11–16

369 James 5:14–16; Henry Cloud, and John Townsend, *Boundaries: When to Say Yes, How to Say No, to Take Control of Your Life* (Grand Rapids, MI: Zondervan, 1992), 63–65. May, *Addiction & Grace,* 172–174. Welch, "Chapter 12: Being Part of the Body." In *Addictions.*

370 e.g., Ps. 90:14

371 Luke 11:9–10

372 God doesn't call us to ignore our pain. We're to walk through it, but not to set up camp and refuse to deal with anything else (e.g., Eccles. 3:4; Ps. 30:5, 126:6; John 11:35). Nor are we to let our pain swallow up our view of truth.

373 Rev. 3:19–20

374 Hosea 2:13–15

Two Ships

I scrubbed my hands across my face, then steadied myself against the wall as the ship gently rocked. It was second nature; I'd learned to walk on sea legs. I opened my cabin door and sloshed my way above deck.

I walked over to the worn, wooden railing and took a deep breath of salty air. The sky around us remained clear, and the sea relatively calm. Joan sidled up beside me. She was a small woman, haggard from a lifetime of trouble. We were friends, as much as anyone could be friends on this benighted vessel.

"It's still there. Hasn't moved an inch. It isn't natural," she said in a low voice.

I stared at her. Of course it hadn't moved. No one had ever seen it move.

Someone else heard her. "Who cares? It'll never come. It's probably not even real."

I turned to identify the speaker. Folks congregated all over the deck, some beginning their breakfast, others ending a night of dissipation. They all seemed too wrapped up in their own lives to have spoken.

I turned back to stare at the inky blot on the horizon. I couldn't recall when I'd first realized it was there, but only recently had I begun to believe it was coming. I shivered. A ship killer for sure.

"Gives me the willies too," Joan said.

I grunted noncommittally. It didn't do to make your opinions too well known around here—one never knew who else was listening.

"I heard"—she bit her lip, then leaned closer, so close I could feel her breath on my cheek—"I heard the ship's broke and can't be repaired."

I covered my mouth lest someone lip-read. "Are you saying he's right?"

"Dunno. Never thought so before, but now . . . ."

"The water's up to the fourth step today."

She drew in her breath sharply.

"Target practice!" roared one of the sailors. We both jumped. He muscled his way up to the railing and pointed out to the ocean below. The usual crowd dropped what they were doing and jostled for a position. They stood there, weapons at the ready: some grim-faced, some with wide grins, all desperate for a distraction. Everyone else ignored the commotion and continued their activities.

Inwardly I cringed. The daily dilemma was upon me, and I was no nearer to knowing my own heart.

Across the water skimmed a gleaming row boat. I'd not seen many boats, other than the dilapidated lifeboats we kept on board. Everyone knew they were as watertight as sieves, so they'd been left to molder. Even our ship was old and weathered. Untold years of floundering amongst the filth of generations had left her dirty and rotting. The approaching boat, however, was everything I thought a boat should be: clean lines, trim, and shiny as the sea on a clear day; she was beautiful. The man rowing her strained at the oars, maneuvering her nearer and nearer. Was it my imagination or was the sea choppier today?

Every day he came. His ship was somewhere out there. Off and on someone would claim to have caught glimpses of it, or even to have been there.

The man came within hailing distance and anchored his boat. He secured the oars, then stood, perfectly balanced, perfectly at ease, despite the rocking waves. Today I stayed at the railing, anchored by his presence.

He cleared his throat and began. "The day of the Lord is at hand! The storm is coming." He gestured to the horizon. "God's wrath will soon be upon you."

"Did you boys hear that? Get ready! It's the end of the worrllld!" someone jeered.

Laughter broke out among those lining the rails. You'd think the joke would get old, but someone usually threw it out there . . . and people laughed every time.

"Your boat is damaged. You can't withstand the storm. Will you stay and perish?"

A whisper ran down the line. "On three."

"I'm here to rescue you." His eyes skewered me—so full of compassion and longing, yet piercing, as though he knew me and could see my soul. As though he were calling to me alone. "Come with me. Come to my ship and be safe."

My heart began to pound. More and more often his words seemed to drill into my soul. The same words every day. Once I could ignore them, but now they rang in my ears.

"One, two, THREE," the big sailor yelled.

Those at the railing fired their weapons and flung the missiles at hand—bottles, knives, rotten food, pieces of the ship. Only one's ingenuity limited acceptable projectiles.

I tore myself away and slipped out of the crowd. Hopefully, my behavior had gone unnoticed in the melee. I made my way back to my cabin. Without turning on a light, I crawled into bed and curled up in a ball.

I'd been at the railing often enough to know how it went. The barrage would continue as long as the man remained. The man would stay for those few who answered his call. About now a trickle of folks would be throwing themselves off the ship towards the boat. Somehow they always made it into the boat. All those missiles would fly right through the man, his boat, and anyone in the boat.

Most people thought he'd been born on the ship too. Some said he'd begun to give his crazy messages and been killed for it.

Some said he'd jumped overboard. Maybe he was a ghost, or a monster who took folks back to his lair and ate them.

Regardless, he looked human enough, but solid objects had no effect on him or anyone under his protection. I imagined the storm would be the same way. A frisson of fear went up my spine. The storm. Was there really a God? Couldn't the storm be just that—a natural storm? I shook my head. The storm had been around for longer than anyone could reckon. Every so often something would blow through, but that grandaddy of a hurricane never moved our way.

What if I jumped? Could I leave all I'd ever known? What if the man wasn't as trustworthy as he seemed? After all, I'd only recently begun to believe he spoke the truth. Before this year, I'd vacillated between ignoring him and using him for target practice. Maybe I was the crazy one. If there was a God and the man was His messenger, he deserved to be targeted. We'd all been left on this plagued ship to rot.

But you've chosen to stay. None of us have to stay.

The thought had come unbidden. I shut it down immediately. Time for a distraction. Time to fight the madness that was creeping into my soul. I vaulted out of my bunk and marched back up the flooded stairs. The man would be gone by now, and I could get back to living.

Later that night, Joan found me.

"Where'd you get to?"

I shrugged. "I had things to do. No time to waste on insanity."

She raised an eyebrow. "Maybe you're not interested then."

"Interested in what?"

"I found something."

I shifted. "What kind of something?"

She dragged me to a nearby corner. "I've seen how you look at him. You're thinking of jumping, aren't you?" she whispered.

"No! Why would I be thinking about jumping?" I looked at the wall behind her. "Only crazy people jump. Remember? No time for insanity?"

"Then I suppose you wouldn't want to hear more about him."

My eyes flew to her face. "Why? What did you find?"

"Not here. Come to my cabin during breakfast tomorrow. Bring a lantern."

I licked my lips, then nodded. I'd miss the man's appearance, but maybe if I could learn more about him, I'd be able to excise my fascination with him. At least that was the excuse I gave myself. I hurried off, eager to prove my feet were firmly planted on the deck.

I woke up early and lay there arguing with myself. What if someone saw us looking at whatever Joan had found? What if we were taken for crazy folk? What if I went crazy and jumped? Did it matter? I'd drive myself to the brink of insanity if I kept on this way.

I lowered myself out of the bunk. The floor was damp—mute testimony to the water seeping throughout. "I have to know the truth. Please let me find the truth," I begged. I wasn't sure who I was directing that to; maybe the universe in general. I secreted a lantern into my deck kit, then left, trying to look as though I hadn't a care in the world.

I tapped on Joan's door.

She was waiting, breathless. On her back, she wore a seaweed harvester's satchel. "Good, good. Did you bring the lantern?"

I nodded.

She pointed down the hall, towards the bowels of the ship. "We go this way."

With luck, most everyone would be asleep or at breakfast, and those few people we saw would take us for seaweed harvesters headed to the pens. After all, morning was hardly the time for illicit behavior. We chatted quietly about the day and the ship and the seaweed.

Finally, we reached the abandoned section. Few went in. Boards were rotten through and one was liable to get trapped—or worse—down here.

Joan stopped. "Step only where I've stepped. Got that?"

I gulped. "Yeah."

She walked forward and began to mutter under her breath. I heard things like, "Seventy-five, one over. Left?" The counting continued on and on.

Where was she taking me? A board creaked and bowed under my weight.

Joan whipped around. "Only where I've stepped!"

I slid forward, back to where her very feet had touched. "Are you—are you sure this is a good idea?"

A sheen of sweat covered her upper lip. "Be quiet. I need to concentrate."

We picked our way ever downward through a maze of deserted corridors, skirting open holes in the decking. In dry places, dust lay thick. In wet places, the mildew grew in profusion and footing was slick. The ship groaned with every lift of the waves. All else was eerily silent.

Sometime later Joan halted. "Let's rest for a minute. We're not far now, but this next bit is tricky." We huddled on the wet floor, our lanterns casting wavering shadows. Nearby I noticed a giant iron ring set in the floor. She dug a couple wrinkled sea fruits out of her satchel and handed me one. "Here."

I wolfed it down. Our trek combined with a missed breakfast had conspired to give me quite an appetite.

"Will you tell me now what you've found?"

"Swear you won't tell a soul, unless I give you permission."

I hesitated.

Her face hardened. "Swear, or I'll leave you here."

What choice did I have? I swore.

She searched my eyes, then nodded. "All right then. Best to see it yourself." She removed a rope from her satchel and tied one end to the iron ring. She handed me the rope. "Tie the middle around you."

I did so, and handed the rope back. She tied the other end 'round herself.

"Follow me."

"'Tricky" was an understatement. Jagged holes in the deck lay all around us. In places, water came in with the tide and rose up to our waists. Fortunately, there were old iron handholds along the halls. These we used to propel ourselves along in the sea.

More than once I considered suggesting we turn back. But every time, my longing for truth pulled me on.

At last Joan dragged us through an open door. Someone had rigged a sort of platform on top of the iron handholds. Joan clambered onto it, then helped me up. There was room to sit here but not space to stand, so I sat.

In front of us, someone had etched words and pictures into the ship itself. Somehow this wall had escaped decay, and the story remained perfectly clear. My eyes traveled the length of it. There, at the end—what was that? I started. The man's face looked out, depicted so clearly there was no mistaking it.

"It's him," I breathed.

Joan half-smiled. "That's what I think too."

"What is this place? How'd you find it?"

"My great-grandfather told me about it when I was a girl, back before he jumped. Said it had been here almost since the ship was built. Go on, read it."

I held the lantern up and scooted closer to the wall. Maybe at last I'd get the truth.

Being a chronicle of Joshua. In the first days, before even the sea, did God take the nothing and transform it into something. The sea He made with all her moods and glories. The sun to clothe her in light and the stars to sail our ship by. He filled the sea with plants and fruits for food and creatures great and small. Then He fashioned with His own hands a man and his wife and gave them this ship and sea charts to sail her by.[375]

Here the artist had included a carving of a large, graceful ship. She bore little resemblance to the broken down thing we lived on. I scooted closer, kneeling with my nose practically touching the wall and squinting. Could it really be our ship.

"See the name?" Joan broke in.

"Uh huh. *The Coeur.*" It was our ship all right.

And God traveled with His people. They sailed all around the world, being careful to stay in the currents God had put on their charts, for He had warned them death would follow if they sailed elsewhere. The sun always shone, and the sea was their friend during those endless days.

But one day, while the man and his wife were alone, a traveler arrived. A creature of the deep, he claimed to have seen wonders beyond compare—a treasure the likes of which no one could imagine. And so the man and his wife plowed their own path through the sea, one that was not on God's charts.[376]

Before long, the ship struck the mountains of the deep. Being ripped open, the ship could no longer travel. The man and his wife were trapped, away from the paths of the sea, away from God's presence. In that moment, the world itself broke, and a great storm appeared in the distance. The traveler vanished, leaving the man and his wife to their doom. But God did not leave His children there. Though they had wandered, He came to them. Full of sorrow, He told them He could no longer sail with them in the same way.[377] *In His love, He made a way out: Death would come to them and to their children, and the coming storm would destroy everything in its path, even the world itself.*[378] *He promised that He would return with a new ship to rescue them and their children. They had only to wait in hope for the ship and they would be saved.*

The man and his wife wept as they realized they could no longer sail with God. And they told their children stories of God and of the ship and world that used to be and of the ship that would come. Their children and grandchildren tried to restore the ship, but to no avail—they had not built it and could not repair it.[379]

Generations later a man named Joshua was born on the ship. He claimed to be God Himself,[380] *come to rescue His people.*[381] *Joshua walked the ship, healing some, but not fixing the ship. He claimed to be building a new ship—one that could withstand the storm. Over and over he spoke of the wrath that was to come and the one way of escape—through him.*[382]

Driven mad by his wild claims, his people did conspire to silence him. None could find a charge against him, for he had lived blamelessly.[383] *Yet on the appointed day, they bound him and whipped him with fishhooks. His flesh was torn until he was unrecognizable. Only then did they put him on the plank for all to see. They riddled him with bullets until his lifeless body fell into the sea and was swallowed by the deep. The people went away, satisfied his claims had been disproved. But then did Joshua rise from the depths and promise to rescue any who answered his call.*[384]

I leaned back on my heels. Was this my answer? Could this be the truth? I turned to Joan. "What do you think?"

Joan shook her head. "I don't know. It's not what I was taught, but there's something about it . . . ."

I nodded. "It almost makes sense, if you look at the world a certain way. The ship is here, and despite what everyone says, we aren't moving and it only seems to get more broken, not less.

"Then there's the man himself." I fingered the carving of his face. "His boat comes from somewhere. He comes from somewhere."

"What if he's the traveler in the story?"

I frowned. "I don't know." Joan had already guessed how the man called to me. Could I be honest with her? "He seems more trustworthy than that . . . as though there's no falsehood in him."

She nodded. "I feel it too."

"So why haven't you jumped?"

She hugged her knees. "I don't want to lose my life here. At least now, I can do what I want. What if this Joshua man is a tyrant?" She looked down at the platform. "Plus, I'm scared. When I see him, I feel like he can see all the bad stuff in me. It's enough to make anyone want to hide."

"Aren't you more scared of the storm?"

She glanced up at the ceiling, as though she could see through the sagging wood to the horizon.

"Maybe. Are you?"

I thought for a moment. "I don't know. Maybe."

A sudden wave sloshed up higher than the rest and drenched us. Joan held her lantern up, illuminating a rough scratch in the opposite wall. The rising water had almost reached it. "We'd best go. Once the water gets above there, we won't be able to make it back today."

The trip back was an icy nightmare. In places we held our breath and swam. If ever I'd doubted the ship's brokenness, seeing this section had convinced me. Near the edge of the abandoned section, Joan went into an old cabin and came out with two bags of seaweed. "Here. In case anyone sees us."

Shivering, I pulled the wet bag close. On our way back to our cabins, we dumped our seaweed in with the other harvesters'.

"See you tomorrow," Joan said.

I clasped her hand. "Thank you for showing me," I whispered.

Back in my cabin, I collapsed on the bunk. The night that followed was a feverish collection of half-dreams and tangled thoughts. The more I fought against the story, the more my soul proclaimed the truth there. I'd spent so much time trying to ignore the brokenness around me that it was hard to come to grips with the story. What if it were true? Maybe that's why people seemed miserable—this broken ship wasn't supposed to be our destiny.

I didn't have to stay. No one did.

I awoke the next morning, sandy-eyed. I massaged my aching temples. Another day and still no storm. Slowly, I made my way back up to the deck. Did I want to stay? Joan already stood at the railing. Was she as tormented as I?

"How'd you sleep?" I asked.

She looked up at me, red-rimmed eyes proclaiming her answer. "Do you think he'll come today?"

My eyes widened. I'd never considered that. In all the days I had ignored him, then fought him, and finally listened to him, I had never thought of a time limit. What if he didn't come? What if I didn't jump today and I couldn't ever jump again? What if today was the day the storm came?

"There! He's there!" she said, pointing to a dot in the distance.

Relief swept over me, quickly replaced with fear. He had come. He looked up at me and once again I felt that irresistible pull. My muscles bunched, as though my body prepared to jump, even against my will. I gripped the railing, knuckles white. Two ships. Two destinies. Which would I choose? Go or stay?

. . . if you confess with your mouth, "Jesus is Lord," and believe in your heart that God raised him from the dead, you will be saved.
~ Romans 10:9

375 See **Genesis 1–2**

376 See **Genesis 3**

377 **Isaiah 59:2:** But your iniquities have separated you from your God; your sins have hidden his face from you, so that he will not hear.

378 **Romans 3:23:** For all have sinned and fall short of the glory of God; **Romans 6:23:** For the wages of sin is death, but the gift of God is eternal life in Christ Jesus our Lord.; **Revelation 20:11–21:1:** Then I saw a great white throne and him who was seated on it. Earth and sky fled from his presence, and there was no place for them. And I saw the dead, great and small, standing before the throne, and books were opened. Another book was opened, which is the book of life. The dead were judged according to what they had done as recorded in the books. The sea gave up the dead that were in it, and death and Hades gave up the dead that were in them, and each person was judged according to what he had done. Then death and Hades were thrown into the lake of fire. The lake of fire is the second death. If anyone's name was not found written in the book of life, he was thrown into the lake of fire. Then I saw new heaven and a new earth, for the first heaven and the first earth had passed away, and there was no longer any sea.

379 **Isaiah 64:6:** All of us have become like one who is unclean, and all our righteous acts are like filthy rags; we all shrivel up like a leaf, and like the wind our sins sweep us away. **James 2:10:** For whoever keeps the whole law and yet stumbles at just one point is guilty of breaking all of it.

380 **John 8:57–59:** "You are not yet fifty years old," the Jews said to him, "and you have seen Abraham!" "I tell you the truth," Jesus answered, "before Abraham was born, I am!" At this, they picked up stones to stone him, but Jesus hid himself, slipping away from the temple grounds. **Exodus 3:14:** God said to Moses, "I AM WHO I AM. This is what you are to say to the Israelites: 'I AM has sent me to you.' "

381 **Matthew 1:21–23:** "She will give birth to a son, and you are to give him the name Jesus, because he will save his people from their sins." All this took place to fulfill what the Lord had said through the prophet: "The virgin will be with child and will give birth to a son, and they will call him Immanuel"—which means, "God with us." **John 3:14–19:** "Just as Moses lifted up the snake in the desert, so the Son of Man must be lifted up, that everyone who believes in Him may have eternal life. For God so loved the world that He gave His one and only Son, that whoever believes in Him shall not perish but have eternal life. For God did not send his Son into the world to condemn the world, but to save the world through him. Whoever believes in him is not condemned, but whoever does not believe stands condemned already because he has not believed in the name of God's one and only Son. This is the verdict: Light has come into the world, but men loved darkness instead of light because their deeds were evil."

382 E.g., **John 14:1–6:** "Do not let your hearts be troubled. Trust in God; trust also in me. In my Father's house are many rooms; if it were not so, I would have told you. I am going there to prepare a place for you. And if I go and prepare a place for you, I will come back and take you to be with me that you also may be where I am. You know the way to the place where I am going." Thomas said to him, "Lord, we don't know where you are going, so how can we know the way?" Jesus answered, "I am the way and the truth and the life. No one comes to the Father except through me."

Of the 1,870 verses Jesus spoke, 13% were about judgment and hell (John Blanchard, *What Ever Happened to Hell?* [Durham, England: Evangelical Press, 1993], 128).

383 **Matthew 26:59–60:** The chief priests and the whole Sanhedrin were looking for false evidence against Jesus so that they could put him to death. But they did not find any, though many false witnesses came forward. **John 18:38b:** With this [Pilate] went out again to the Jews and said, "I find no basis for a charge against him."

384 **Romans 5:8–11:** But God demonstrates his own love for us in this: While we were still sinners, Christ died for us. Since we have now been justified by his blood, how much more shall we be saved from God's wrath through him! For if, when we were God's enemies, we were reconciled to him through the death of his Son, how much more, having been reconciled, shall we be saved through his life! Not only is this so, but we also rejoice in God through our Lord Jesus Christ, through whom we have now received reconciliation. **Colossians 2:13–14:** When you were dead in your sins and in the uncircumcision of your sinful nature, God made you alive with Christ. He forgave us all our sins, having canceled the written code, with its regulations, that was against us and that stood opposed to us; he took it away, nailing it to the cross. **Ephesians 2:8–9:** For it is by grace you have been saved, through faith—and this not from yourselves, it is the gift of God—not by works, so that no one can boast. See Matthew 28:1–10.

ACKNOWLEDGMENTS

I planted the seed, Apollos watered it, but God made it grow. So neither he who plants nor he who waters is anything, but only God, who makes things grow. ~ 2 Corinthians 3:6–7

It would be ridiculous for me to take credit for this book. It is truly the fruit of more people than are named here—those who have built into my life and whom God has used to teach these lessons to me.

I have been so blessed to be a part of this process. So thanks first of all go to God, for allowing me to be involved!

Without the support of my husband, Evan, this endeavor would have been literally impossible. His influence is felt in every page, from the time he provided time for me to work on it, to the editing, verbal processing, indexing, typesetting, and constant encouragement. Babe, you are the greatest embodiment of God's grace in my life. I love being allies with you!

M & J, thank you so much for giving me time to work on this book. I'm so glad God put you in our family! You are a blessing!

Jennifer encouraged me as I fought these various wars in myself through the years. I know God used her to bring me along in more ways than I can express. You are such a gift, Jen!

My editors, Amanda Andrus, Ashley High, and Stacia McKeever, have been invaluable. Their work has made a huge difference in this book. Amanda, this book wouldn't be nearly as good without all your hours of work and encouragement (if it happened at all). I'm so glad God called you to this work, friend!

Kerry kept me from crossing my *i's* and dotting my *t's*. Thank you so much for helping this book to be readable!

My readers were also of more help than I can express. Thanks go to Allie, Angie, Jason, Marie, Mike, Stephanie, and

Virginia. Thank you so much for sharpening up my theology and expression, and for your encouragement!

Stephanie and Pete provided lots of extra time for work on this book—thank you! This would have taken at least another year without your help. ;)

Rebekah, thank you so much for all your consults on the cover! It turned out great!

Siblings, thank you for encouraging me to keep writing!

Beth Moore's Bible studies have also been invaluable in my growth process. The same is true of other Bible teachers who have encouraged me in my walk with God such as Dr. Rosalie de Rosset, Dr. David Finkbeiner, Dr. Jon Laansma, Chuck Missler, Pastor Mike Priest, and Dr. David Rim.

SCRIPTURE INDEX

Scripture Index

Made in the USA
Middletown, DE
19 December 2022